PRAISE

AUTHO͟ ͟ꓤꓕ ꓳК ROSS

Rektok Ross offers "readers genuinely diverse characters, each of whom continues to grow throughout the narrative... Brace for impact readers, [Ross] holds little back."

—*Kirkus Reviews*

Rektok Ross has "inborn talent for the kind of narrative driven storytelling that makes for a compulsive page turning read from cover to cover... Unreservedly recommended..."

—*Midwest Book Review*

"If you like action, suspense, and the horror real life can sometimes dish out, you can't go wrong... Rektok Ross delivers!"

—*Reader Views*

"[Ross] does a great job of making you care for [her] characters, keeps you guessing, and [gives] lots of chills."

—*Double the Books*

Rektok Ross is "an exciting addition to the YA scene."

—Evelyn Skye, *New York Times* best-selling author of *The Crown's Game*

PRAISE FOR SKI WEEKEND

*Winner of the WILLA Literary Awards, San Francisco Book Festival Awards, National Indie Excellence Awards, Next Generation Indie Book Awards, Independent Press Awards, Reader Views Literary Awards, CIBA Dante Rossetti Book Awards, Readers' Favorite Book Awards, American Fiction Awards, IAN Book of the Year Awards, and Firebird Awards!

*Named a Best Book of the Year by *Cosmopolitan, Entertainment Weekly, Yahoo!Life, Parade, Brit + Co., Book Riot, J-14, The Strand, She Reads,* and more!

"This is a suspenseful book that had me thoroughly hooked from page one... The emotional journey of *Ski Weekend* is relentless..."

—*Readers' Favorite*

"Rektok Ross delivers an absolute dynamic story packed with goofy teens, heart-stopping moments, romantic tension, and one adorable pup in this adrenaline-filled survival story."

—*BooknBrunch*

"Rektok Ross thrills readers with an electrifying winter tale that will have you wondering if that snow-filled adventure you've been planning is worth risking your life!"

—*Key Biscayne Magazine*

"A pacey thriller with moments of great tenderness—and spine-chilling horror."

—Lauren Kate, *New York Times* best-selling author of *Fallen*

"A nail-biter with some surprising moments. Recommended for high school and YA collections."

—*School Library Journal*

"Hand this to students who like thrillers and books about survival!"

—*Youth Services Book Review*

"Constantly twisting and emotionally relentless, *Ski Weekend* is a story of survival, friendship, and family... Alternately heartbreaking and hopeful—a chilling, thrilling read."

—Laurie Elizabeth Flynn, bestselling author of *The Girls Are All So Nice Here*

"This book will send so many chills up your spine, you'll feel like you're alongside the snowbound characters. The only time I don't recommend reading this book is right before bed. You won't be able to sleep, and you won't want to."

—Jeff Zentner, award-winning author of *Rayne & Delilah's Midnight Matinee*

"All the intensity and thrills of *The Hunger Games* packed into one car over a snowy weekend. Secrets, lies, strong characters, and twists will keep readers turning pages. If you've ever wondered how far you would go to survive, you need to read this book."

—Eileen Cook, author of *You Owe Me a Murder*

"Ripped from the headlines, *Ski Weekend* is so real you'll be shivering with the characters, fighting the elements, and asking yourself— what would you be willing to do to survive? Forget Netflix and chill. Binge this book."

—Sorboni Banerjee, Emmy Award–winning journalist and author of *Red as Blood*

"Ross weaves a stirring tale where each of her characters wrestle with choices that could result in life or death—some survive, and some don't."

—Paul Greci, award-winning author of *Surviving Bear Island* and *The Wild Lands*

"This pulse-pounding story of survival mirrors all the highs and lows of the hit reality TV show *Survivor*. In my case, I knew I could quit any time, but these kids aren't so lucky. Buckle up—this is one wild ride!"

—Corinne Kaplan, two-time *Survivor* and *Amazing Race* player and reality TV star

"Captivating and shocking! I loved it!"

—Elise Lee, owner at Away With Words Bookshop

SUMMER RENTAL

ALSO BY REKTOK ROSS

Ski Weekend

Summer Rental

*

**See all of Rektok Ross's books and find where to get them
on her website at:**

www.RektokRoss.com

*

NEVER MISS A RELEASE.

Get exclusive giveaways, review copies, and enter to win free gifts
and more by subscribing to Rektok Ross's newsletter:

www.RektokRoss.com

SUMMER RENTAL

REKTOK ROSS

Ic13 Books

Published by Ic13 Books

Wilmington, Delaware, USA, 19808

www.Ic13Books.com

Ic13 Books name and the Ic13 Books logo are trademarks of Ic13 Books or its affiliates.

Published 2023

Printed in the United States of America

Print ISBN: 978-0-9882568-2-8

E-ISBN: 978-0-9882568-3-5

Library of Congress Control Number: 2023935087

Cover design by Dane Low and team

Interior design by Leila Pullen

For those who dream big and never never give up.

Revenge is a dish best served cold.

—French Proverb

CHAPTER 1

DAY 1: Thursday—Three days before July Fourth

I t isn't supposed to rain in paradise.

At least, that's what the sign said when we turned off the highway and onto the rickety, two-lane bridge moments ago. It was painted a bright tropical yellow and read, *"Palm Key Island: it's always sunny here!"* Naturally, the "i" was dotted with an orange.

As I watch the rain fall from my cramped middle seat in the back of the SUV—the absolute worst spot in the car, of course—I tell myself it's just one of those quick summer showers we get in Florida. It won't last long. They never do. But when we pull up to the driveway of our rental home for the weekend and the rain still hasn't stopped, I start to worry.

We all hop out of the car and I eye the dark, ominous clouds with growing concern. The five of us hold jackets and sweatshirts over our heads and rush to grab luggage from the cargo area of Cam and Val's brand-new Range Rover. It's just one of the lavish gifts the twins received from their parents at graduation a few weeks ago.

"Just a little rain, everybody," Cam says next to me, overly cheery as usual. She runs a hand through her dark sleek bob, pushing glossy hair off her face and behind pearl-studded ears. "It'll clear up any minute."

"You sure?" I ask, dodging raindrops.

"Yes, Riley. I'm sure," she says, laughing as she elbows me

lightly in the ribs. She surveys the rental house with a pleased expression on her pretty face. "Look! It's perfect—just like I said it'd be!"

Other than the pesky drizzle, I have to admit she's right. It looks way better than I expected. For starters, the two-story house is much larger in person than it was in the photos. Elegant and charming, it even has a big wraparound veranda and two dreamy, towering columns that make it seem like something off the cover of a romance novel. A row of palm trees on either side of us catches the late afternoon breeze, green leafy fronds gently blowing back and forth. The unmistakable salty scent of the ocean wafts in my direction.

When Cam first told me about the summer rental, I'd been suspicious. We were still dressed in our orange and blue Bishop Lake Preparatory High School graduation gowns when she pulled out the rental agreement from her shiny white Gucci tote. Another graduation gift. Val got one too, although hers was fire-engine red, her "signature" color.

Right away, I thought the posting was fishy. No way a house directly on the sand in ritzy Palm Key Island was only a few hundred bucks during the busy July Fourth holiday weekend. Something had to be wrong. My money was on a broken air conditioner, or maybe a gross, putrid smell like rotten eggs the owners couldn't get rid of. Not that I could be picky. The only reason we were getting a rental in the first place was because I couldn't afford a room at the fancy hotel where everyone else from school was staying. Somehow, Cam convinced her snobby twin sister Val and our other two best friends, Blake and Nia, to join us.

"I can't wait to see the inside!" Cam races toward the house, rolling her designer luggage behind her. Her initials "CGR"—for Camila Gisele Ramirez—are custom-painted in pale pink along the trim.

Her twin sister sprints after her. Val's colorful, vibrant dress billows behind her and catches the wind. Full and plush lips, painted her usual bold shade of red, are set in a pout as her stiletto Louboutins click along the pavement. Val bought the shoes yesterday even though she already has dozens, just like them, in her closet back home. What Valentina Lorraine Ramirez wants, she gets.

"I get first dibs!" Val yells as Cam opens the lockbox hanging on the front doorknob.

The rest of us watch from a safe distance by the car as the twins fight over the key. Val attempts to claim the biggest room in the house, even though she did none of the work to book our trip.

"What a brat," Nia mutters next to me, rolling her eyes. Nia has the most gorgeous eyes. Fox-shaped and the color of liquid onyx with lashes so long and thick you'd think they were extensions like Val has, but Nia's just lucky to be naturally stunning.

"Typical Val," Blake says. "Fifty bucks says Cam caves and gives her the master. She's such a pushover."

"Cam's just a people pleaser," I say, defensive of my best friend, even if I sort of agree. We all know Cam lets her twin get away with murder. "Besides, I'm sure all the rooms are nice."

"Whatever." Blake grabs her surfboard and throws it over one tan, muscular shoulder. Beautiful, beachy blonde hair bounces down her shapely backside. "Let's just unpack and change. I wanna hit the beach."

Nia gives me her suitcase to bring inside and pulls her iPhone out of her pocket to film her arrival for her social media followers. She smiles and waves at her "Nia-maniacs," as she likes to call them, her toothy grin even brighter than usual against her flawless dark skin. Nia just landed a brand deal with a toothpaste whitener, and they gave her a year's supply of product.

Just like Cam predicted, the rain stops, and the sun appears as Blake helps me unload the car. We go fast, hoping to have time to lay out before the sun goes down. The six-hour drive from Bishop Lake took far longer than expected.

First, Val made us late by insisting on bringing two enormous suitcases, even though we didn't have room. Cam's begging didn't work; it wasn't until Blake threatened to throw Val's suitcases into the lake in front of the twins' house that Val recanted. Blake could do it, too. She was our state champion in both shot put and discus throw and has a full ride to Stanford in the fall.

Then, after waiting for Val to repack—and listening to her complain the whole time—we missed not one, but two, of the highway turnoffs. Combining that with Nia's demands we make multiple bathroom stops on account of the new flat-tummy tea she was drinking for an Instagram collab, it's a miracle we made it before nightfall.

"Jesus, Cam. What'd you put in here—*bricks?*" I ask, entering the foyer like a pack mule with Cam's massive nylon duffle slung over my shoulder and dragging Nia's bulging suitcase and my roller bag behind me. I drop Cam's bag down and wince, rubbing at my aching muscles.

"Sorry." She grins. "I didn't know what we'd need, so I packed everything. Beach towels. Sunscreen. Paddle ball," she says and then gestures around the place. "So what do you think? Cute, right?"

"Totally." I suppress a groan. Only my friends would call this place "cute."

The rental is huge. The apartment my mom and I share back home could fit in the foyer alone. The dark wooden floors are freshly mopped, and the rich cream walls, though bare, are crisp and bright, as if newly painted. Cool air blows from the vents above my head, so I know my fears of a broken air conditioner were unfounded. Best of all, no bad smells. If anything, it smells strongly of bleach, as if recently cleaned and scrubbed from top to bottom.

I take a few steps down the hall to find a formal dining

room. Past that, the hallway opens up to reveal a gorgeous spiral staircase and spacious living room amply furnished with two overstuffed leather couches and matching recliners. On the other end of the house is a kitchen that butts up against floor-to-ceiling glass patio doors. A big deck and screened-in pool is out back. I can even see the beach from here.

Blake rushes into the living room and stands in front of the enormous fifty-five-inch flat screen TV. She grabs an iPad off one of the couches and starts pushing buttons until Lady Gaga comes on, and upbeat dance music plays from the wireless speakers overhead. Blake grins over at us and turns the volume up super high, singing along and shaking her booty to the beat.

Val inches toward the stairs. "So, I'm just gonna head up and unpack and—"

"I already told you," Cam says. "You can't take the master bedroom, Val. We're drawing numbers."

A strangled whine erupts from Val. "And I told you, *Camila*. I need the biggest room for all my clothes and makeup."

"It's fine with me," I say to make things easy for Cam. She's always caught in the middle, trying to appease Val's over-inflated sense of entitlement while not pissing off the rest of our friends.

"Me too. I don't even wear makeup," Nia says, coming up behind me. If I didn't know better, I might believe she's being sincere. She really doesn't need makeup. "Besides," she adds with a mean little smirk, "you're gonna need all the help you can get with that nasty little breakout on your chin."

Val pulls down her oversized designer sunglasses. "Very funny," she says, curling her freshly painted nails into a fist. "Keep it up and you're gonna need help for a black eye."

Val and Nia don't exactly get along. Cam told me they used to be tight, but that all changed last year. Before then, the wide consensus was that Valentina Ramirez was by far the most beautiful girl at school. That all changed, seemingly overnight, after Nia's braces came off and her boobs grew in. Now they're rivals. I guess it also doesn't help that Nia just started dating Val's latest ex-boyfriend, Tyler Singh.

"Great, so we all agree Val can have the master," I say in my peppiest voice, trying to diffuse the tension. "Put me anywhere. I'm just happy to be here."

Blake frowns at me and I know what she's thinking—that I'm a pushover, too, just like Cam.

She's not wrong.

"I still can't believe your mom wouldn't give you enough money for the hotel," Val says. "The Seasider looked so lux, and the spa has those special hydro-facials from Sweden, and—"

"Val," Cam warns.

Val shrugs. "I mean, I guess this is fine, too."

"I'm really sorry. She's the worst," I say, shoving my hands into the pockets of my cut-off jean shorts and doing my best to ignore the winces of guilt. I don't like lying, but it's necessary. I've worked too hard building up a certain image for myself, and I'm not going to jeopardize that now. I know people say real friends should like you for the "real you," but those people don't hang out in the same circles I do.

My friends would never understand the truth. Their families are all *rich* rich. Nia's dad is a former professional basketball player, and Blake's parents own a real estate business, building homes all around the state. And the Ramirez family, well, they're one of the wealthiest families in the South. The twins' grandparents started the largest American-Spanish language television network in the country.

I used to be like them. My dad was a well-respected financial adviser in Miami. We had it all. The six-thousand square foot house. Luxury cars. Ski trips to Aspen in the winter and beach trips to Saint-Tropez in summer. Everything was perfect until Dad's firm got caught embezzling client funds. He went to prison, Mom filed for divorce, and we changed our last names and moved to central Florida. The only thing we had left was Dad's old 'Benz and enough money for a shitty, low-income housing apartment to start over.

I was lucky to get into Bishop Prep for senior year. My academic scholarship paid for school, but I had to get an after-school job for everything else. Working at the Mouse Trap, a cheesy restaurant near Disney, gave me money to help Mom with bills and just enough left over to afford the right clothes and makeup so I could fit in. If it wasn't for Mr. Ramirez's black Am Ex helping with my share of the already cheap rental, there's no way I'd even be on this trip.

"I'll take this room," Blake says and plops her surfboard in front of the downstairs bedroom closest to the pool. I know from the pictures it has an insane ocean view. Blake might not go head-to-head with the twins, but she's not going to take scraps, either.

"I'll take whatever's left. I don't plan on sleeping here, anyway." Nia digs into her suitcase and pulls out a skimpy neon green bikini. "I'm gonna freshen up and meet the guys."

"Guys?" Val asks, her voice tight. "What guys?"

Nia struts toward the guest bathroom and closes the door without answering.

"That little *puta*!" Val turns to the rest of us, angry red blotches forming on her tanned, over-contoured cheeks. "She's talking about Ty, isn't she?"

"Relax," Cam says. "It'll be fine."

"But I told you. I don't want to see that asshole!" Val hisses.

"What's the big deal?" Blake asks. "I thought you dumped Ty. And Nia likes him."

"Nia likes to piss me off—that's what Nia likes," Val grumbles. "She's been like this ever since second grade. Remember when I won the Miss Orange Blossom Pageant instead of her? She always wants what I have. It's pathetic." A flash of panic flickers across her face and she turns, grabbing me by the elbow. "You don't think Ty really likes her, do you? I mean, she's not even that pretty."

"Oh no." I hold my hands up and back away. "I'm not getting in the middle of this."

"Ugh, you're so spineless, Riley," Val says and turns hopefully to Blake.

"You're joking, right?" Blake asks. "Nia's smoking hot." She starts changing out of her tracksuit right there in the hallway and puts on a sexy one-piece that runs so high up her backside it might as well be a thong. Blake has an amazing body from sports. She's not afraid to show it off, either. To boys. To girls. She doesn't discriminate.

"Oh, never mind." Val makes a dismissive face at her. "You'd screw anyone."

"Forget Ty, would you?" Blake proceeds to throw sunscreen, towels, and a football into her beach bag. "This place is gonna be crawling with hotties. You don't bring sand to the beach."

Val seems to consider this for a moment, licking at her bottom lip thoughtfully.

"You know what? You're absolutely right," she says. "And at least if that dirtball is here, that means Seb's coming." She lets out a dreamy moan. "He's sooooo sexy."

My chest flutters at his name. Sebastian Ramos is easily the best-looking guy in school: dark green eyes that turn colors with his mood, six-one inches of muscled, ripped body that just won't quit, and a Colombian accent so hot he could melt ice. The boy is charisma incarnate.

Unfortunately, he's off limits. Val's been in love with him for years.

"Hate to break it to you, babe, but that's never gonna happen," Blake says.

Val crosses her arms over her chest. "You don't know that."

"Yeah, I do. You've been trying to get back with Seb ever since he dumped your ass in ninth grade," Blake says. "If it was gonna happen, it would've happened by now."

"That's not—"

"It's okay," Blake says, cutting Val off with a knowing grin. "He doesn't like me either, and trust me, I've tried many, many times. Such a shame. I bet he's a great kisser. And other things." Cam and I giggle as Blake pretends to hump her surfboard. "Sadly, Seb's a sucker for those nice, quiet, do-gooder types. Like our little Ri Ri over here…"

"Oh no. Seb and I are just friends," I say, my cheeks heating. Sebastian doesn't like me like that. He's made that painfully obvious, which is probably a good thing. Val would lose her mind if Sebastian and I ever got together.

We'd been close all year, it's true. Sitting next to each other in class and studying in the library. I went to as many of his soccer games as I could. Sebastian was the star of our school's team with a full ride to Princeton. Of course, I had a huge crush on him—like everyone else in school.

There was a time I thought he might have feelings for me too, right after he kissed me at Nia's graduation party, but the next day he acted like nothing happened. He's avoided me ever since. I had no idea he was coming this weekend. I wonder if—

"Forget Sebastian Ramos." Cam gives me a sympathetic look. She's the only one I told about the kiss. "I've got someone way better and—good news—he just texted he's here."

"Who?" I ask, my chest tightening. I'm pretty sure I know the answer, and I'm not nearly as excited as she is. "Jonathan?"

"Yes!" she shrieks.

Cam has been trying to set me up with Jonathan Chang all year, always trying to get us together every time he's home from college on break. He's a year older than us and cute enough, but... I don't know. He's so awkward. Always getting too close and trying to touch me. Always staring at me for too long or when he thinks I don't see. He's never crossed the line or anything, it's just... Something about him creeps me out a bit.

The girls used to be tight with his younger sister, Jordyn. She died last summer. I never met her, though, of course, I knew of her. Everyone knew the 10-Squad. They were the most beautiful girls in town—the rich bitches that ruled Bishop Prep. The Ramirez twins, Blake Sampson, Nia Williams, and Jordyn Chang. People called them the 10-Squad because they were all tens. Tens in looks. Tens in wealth. Tens in status. After Jordyn died, the nickname fell away, but there's never been any doubt who ran the halls at school.

"Lucky you, Ri Ri." Val sneers. "Jonny boy's a real catch —if you like your boyfriends slightly unhinged."

"Don't be a jerk," Blake says. "Jon's a great guy. I'm glad he's here. It'll be good for him to get away—you know, with it being July 4th." An uncharacteristically sad look passes over her face, and I remember hearing that Jordyn died over the holiday weekend last year.

"I'm just being honest." Val gets to the top of the stairs and hangs over the railing, looking down on us. "We all know Jon's got a few screws loose. He did go to the loony bin."

"It was a mental health clinic," Blake corrects.

"Besides, he's fine now," Cam says. "That was months ago."

"Just to be safe, we should probably find the nearest nut house and make sure they've got an opening." Val giggles and disappears inside the master bedroom.

"Don't listen to her." Cam gives me an encouraging smile. "You two will hit it off."

"Can't we have fun this weekend—just us girls?" I ask.

"Hell no," Blake says. "I didn't drive all this way to sit around braiding each other's hair and have pillow fights. I'm getting laid." She looks me up and down with a slow, measuring glance. "And you should, too. You're way too cute to be single, Ri Ri."

It's not that I'm anti-dating. I've just got other things on my mind. Like for one, I still have no idea how I'm going to pay for college in the fall. I'd been holding out hope until a few weeks ago when I'd gotten the bad news no scholarship was coming. Soon everyone will head off to their fancy universities and, despite having one of the highest GPAs in school, I'll probably be at the community college down the street.

"The bed in here is huge!" Val pops out of the master, her lipstick and blush already touched up. "Hey Ri Ri, wanna room with me?"

"She's taken," Cam says, throwing an arm around my shoulder.

I smile back gratefully. From personal experience, I know Val is a terrible roommate. She's a total slob who leaves mounds of clothes everywhere and expects me to pick up after her like her housekeeper does back home.

Cam grabs her bags, and I follow her to the wraparound staircase. As we get to the base of the stairs, there's a loud clicking noise and the floor shudders below us like the sound of something turning on. I take another step closer and notice, with a little shock, that the staircase continues down to another level.

"Looks like a basement," Blake says, coming up behind me and gazing over my shoulder.

"In Florida?" I ask.

"It's expensive, but my parents have them in some spec homes. You can reinforce them with concrete," Blake says and heads down to check it out. She gets to the door and reaches for the knob, twisting it. "That's weird. It's locked."

The sounds below us deepen and then vibrate.

It's just a coincidence, I tell myself, my mind going instantly to the bad dreams I've been having recently. They started right after graduation. Crazy, vivid nightmares of someone with an axe chasing me down into a basement filled with the bodies of all my dead friends. It freaked me out so bad, I'd Googled it. Apparently, dreams about being chased are super common. It means you're stressed out and avoiding something important, which I guess I am.

A loud knock sounds at the front door, and Nia bursts out of the bathroom. She races across the hall, her dark box braids piled on top of her head. She looks amazing, like she just stepped off the cover of the *Sports Illustrated Swimsuit* edition.

At the same time, Val prances out of the master bedroom in the hottest scarlet red bikini she owns. Her jaw locks on the back of Nia's head, eyes sparking. I know it's about to go down. Valentina doesn't give up anything, especially a guy, without a fight.

A war is coming.

I just hope we all make it out of this weekend alive.

CHAPTER 2

Cam and I change into our swimsuits and head to the beach to meet the others. As we walk down the busy access path running along the edge of our rental house, I wipe sweat from my eyes. The hot Florida sun beats down on us in full force now. Other than a few little puddles that are already almost evaporated, you'd never know it was pouring earlier.

Along the way, we pass dozens of beachgoers about our age. Some cute, shirtless guys with big smiles and dark tans high-five us and ask for our numbers. Cam ignores them and rushes me forward.

When we get to the sand, the gang is already posted up in the center of the beach. Nia sits in Tyler's lap, giggling and preening while Tyler, an attractive Indian guy with cognac-colored eyes and the best head of hair I've ever seen, massages her shoulders. The two of them make a striking couple. Next to them is an oversized, packed cooler. One of the reasons Palm Key is so popular is the "blind eye" drinking policy. The Bishop Prep seniors who came here last year told us the police don't bother you, as long as you aren't obvious about it.

Sure enough, a few of Tyler's basketball teammates laugh and chug from what looks like an Evian bottle—but I'm certain is filled with vodka instead—while tossing Blake's football back and forth. She's the only girl playing but is better than all of them. She throws the ball so hard that one of Tyler's good friends, Mason Larper, misses it. It nails him in the shoulder and he curses, yelping like a little girl, and threatens to quit. Mason's a bit of a douche.

Further down the beach is Val, sunning herself as far away as possible from them. She holds court between a group of admiring guys I don't recognize with smooth, tanned muscles and preppy swim trunks, the kind with whales and pink palm trees.

It figures.

We've been here for less than thirty minutes, and Val already has a fan club.

"Ri Ri! Cammy!" Blake spots us and shakes the football in our direction. "Get your sexy asses over here and come play."

I hesitate, chewing on my lower lip. I hate sports. The last thing I want to do is pass a ball with cannon-arm Blake and the starting lineup of our basketball team. With my luck, I'll probably break something. Someone with any self-respect and a backbone would politely decline, but I never say no to my friends. I've learned my friendship with the 10-Squad works best that way.

"Maybe later," Cam says for us, so I don't have to. "Jon's here," she whispers in my ear and points toward the shoreline. "Let's go sit with him."

I follow her finger to where Jonathan lies on a striped towel, reading a thick paperback. He's wearing a goofy bucket hat and white zinc is smeared over his nose. The pale skin on his chest is already starting to burn and freckle. On the other side of him is Sebastian.

A ripple of excitement rushes through me. I haven't seen Sebastian in person since our secret kiss weeks ago. Now here he is, looking like some toned, bronzed god that's wandered off Mount Olympus for a beach day.

"Maybe we should hang with Blake?" I mumble, over-come by a sudden bout of self-consciousness. I pat at my hair, certain it's already a mess of frizz from the salt and humidity.

"But you hate football?" She cocks her head, confused. "And Jon's waiting for you."

I look back at Sebastian. No way do I want to run up and say hi to him first after he's avoided me for weeks. That would be pathetic, right?

"Can't we chill for a bit? Just us?" I take a few steps toward Blake and the rest of our friends. "Girl's weekend, remember?"

"Oh, for the love of God." She groans. "Please don't tell me you're still hung up on Sebastian Ramos and that stupid kiss."

"I'm not—"

"How many times do we have to go over this?" She shoots me an impatient look. "Seb's a player and, sorry to say it, obviously not into you. Time to move on, babe."

I'm momentarily stunned by the ruthless bite in her tone. Cam is so sweet—most of the time—I forget how casually cruel she can be when it suits her.

"Damn, Cammy," I say. "Tell me what you really think."

"It's called tough love, sweetie," she says, putting an arm around my shoulders and squeezing. "Trust me, you need it." She grabs hold of my elbow and I sigh, letting her lead me toward the guys. It's not like I have anywhere else to go.

"Hey Cammy! Riley!" Jonathan jumps up from his beach towel as we approach. "I'm so pumped you're here," he says, giving Cam a hug before pulling me into a sweaty embrace. I pretend to enjoy it so Cam won't give me shit later.

Ewww. I think he just smelled my hair.

As I carefully extricate myself from Jonathan, I glance over to find Sebastian watching me with an amused smile on his handsome face. He stretches his arms overhead and stands up slowly from his beach towel. I catch a view of the most insanely toned, tanned abs I've ever seen as he walks over to greet us.

"Hey March, good to see you," he says in his deep, sexy Colombian accent.

"Yeah, you too," I say, trying to sound cool even though I practically melt at the cute way he always calls me by my last name. He's so close I can smell some heavenly combination of sweet vanilla, coconut, and something manly.

Cam moistens her lips. "Nice to see you out of hiding, Seb."

"Yeah, things have been insane with soccer," he says. "This is the first weekend I've had off in weeks."

"What took you guys so long?" Jonathan asks us. "We've been here for hours. Seb drove like a maniac."

"New car. You know how it is." Sebastian's gorgeous green eyes light up with a twinkle of mischief and everyone laughs. I join in, even though I don't know how it is. I don't have my own car anymore. I have to share with Mom.

"It was mostly Val's fault," Cam says. "We had some packing issues."

Sebastian snorts. "Why am I not surprised?"

"Well, I'm glad you made it. You look amazing," Jonathan says, his eyes fixated on my chest. His intense stare causes gooseflesh to raise on my bare arms. This is not the kind of look guys usually give when checking me out. I know those looks. Jonathan's looks are different, like he's sizing up a juicy steak he'd like for dinner.

Actually, it's like he's sizing up the entire cow he wants to kill for that steak dinner.

The guys drop back down to the sand to get some more sun before it sets for the day. Cam finds a place on the edge of Sebastian's towel while Jonathan enthusiastically dusts his off to make room for me.

"Here—come sit," he says, patting at the empty spot beside him.

"You sure we aren't bothering you?" I eye the book in his

hand, doing my best to ignore the uncomfortable feeling as I take in the title. *Helter Skelter.*

I remember learning in English class that it's about the Manson family murders. Creepy true crime books are not my thing. I've never understood why people like them, especially someone like Jonathan, who's already experienced such a horrific tragedy in real life after losing his sister.

"Oh this?" He extends the book to me, smiling sweetly. "I just finished. You wanna borrow? Cammy said you like to read. It's great—has all the gory details."

"Uh…" I hesitate.

"She'd love to." Cam elbows me sharply in the ribs and takes the book from him. She pushes it into my hands. "That's so nice of you to offer, Jon. Isn't it so nice, Riley?"

"Um, yeah. So nice," I repeat, fighting back waves of unease as I awkwardly hold the book. "Thanks."

This is why I have such mixed feelings about the guy. On one hand, he's thoughtful and considerate. He's always doing nice things like offering me stuff, going out of his way to talk to me at parties and bringing me drinks, but I don't know… something about him weirds me out.

"Want some lotion? You're starting to burn." He picks up a bottle of sunscreen and squeezes a huge white blob into his hands. *"It puts the lotion on its skin, or else it gets the hose again,"* he mimics in a deep voice, cackling as he reaches for my shoulders.

"What do you mean?" I ask, dodging his hands. "What hose?"

"It's Buffalo Bill," he says.

"Huh?"

"You know—the serial killer in *Silence of the Lambs*?" He blinks at me, looking shocked. "Only one of the best horror movies ever made? Based on the bestselling book?"

Sebastian offers me a bemused smile. "Sorry. He doesn't get out too often."

"C'mon, Riley. Turn around. Let me get your back," Jonathan says and reaches for me again with the damn sunscreen in his hand.

"Shoot! I just remembered I, um, have to ask Val something." I stammer, keeping my tone as polite as possible even though my skin is crawling now. "We'll be right back," I say to the guys with forced cheer and tug at Cam's hand, dragging her away. As much as I want to hang out with Sebastian, I'd rather find him when he's by himself.

"What're you doing?" Cam angry-whispers to me after we're a few feet away. "Jon is really into you."

"I tried, I swear, but I am *not* letting Buffalo Bill over there touch any part of my body with his lotion, okay?" I shiver. "Ugh. Gross."

"Alright, alright. I get it," she says. "So Jon's a little awkward, but he means well. You just need to give him a chance."

I shrug noncommittally to avoid an argument and sneak a peek backward to see if Sebastian is watching us. I snuck into Mom's closet yesterday and swiped her cutest designer swimsuit from back when we had money. She's going to be pissed when she finds out, but it was worth it. The hot pink really sets off my long chestnut brown hair and aquamarine eyes.

I know I look good but, sadly, not only is Sebastian not watching me, his attention is now on someone new. A gorgeous redhead with great legs sits at the edge of his towel, giggling and flipping her hair.

Oh well. Maybe it's for the best.

The fewer complications this weekend, the better, and Sebastian Ramos is definitely a complication.

We walk over to Val's chair and she introduces us to Rhett, the cute guy sitting next to her. He's big and burly with long shaggy brown hair. It turns out he's renting the house next door to ours with some of his frat brothers from the University of Tennessee.

"Nice to meet, y'all," he says in a warm Southern drawl, extending an arm the size of my calves to shake hands. "So you're the ones who rented 21 Seashell Lane? Y'all must be brave." A large grin overtakes his features. "I wanted to book it myself and save us some cash, but the others were too chickenshit about the murders."

"Stop messing around," Val says, playfully jabbing his shoulder. "I told you, there's nothing wrong with the house." She slides her sunglasses down to squint at Cam. "Except for the lack of an on-site spa and room service."

Cam rolls her eyes, laughing.

"Murders?" I squint, certain I heard him wrong. "What murders?"

"Forget about it," Val says. "It's just some stupid story Rhett was telling me earlier. Some silly urban legend the locals use to mess around with tourists."

"Whoo-wee!" Someone cat calls behind us. I turn to see a pair of gorgeous cornflower blue eyes and a perfect smile with teeth so straight it's as if they've been drawn in. "If all the honeys in Florida are as pretty as y'all, I'm transferrin' schools next fall."

Rhett chuckles at his friend. "Relax, Luke. You're gonna scare them off."

Everyone laughs as Cam and I make ourselves comfortable on the edge of Val's chair. I'm used to this sort of attention, especially when I'm with the twins. They share the same sexy Latina traits—brown doe-shaped eyes, killer curves other women pay for, and glorious thick hair, though Cam keeps hers short and slick while Val's is long, curly, and filled with body.

If you ask me, Cam is more conventionally pretty, but in an understated, natural way. If you look closely, you can see Val has tiny acne scars on her chin and her nose is bigger and wider than Cam's, but Val is a whiz with makeup and knows how to conceal her flaws. She's also into fashion and picks tight, body-hugging fabrics to appear as sexy as possible. Cam leans more conservative, preferring preppy staples like her mom's pearls and Lilly Pulitzer gingham dresses.

Rhett holds up a water bottle filled with some brown liquid that smells like whiskey and passes it around. Val takes a shot first before handing it to her sister. Cam turns up her nose at the cheap alcohol. I grab the bottle next. Though I'm not a huge whiskey fan myself, my alcohol budget is limited and beggars can't be choosers. I take a few sips, trying not to gag from the heavy metallic taste burning down my throat, and then give the rest to Luke.

Warm sweat sticks to the back of my neck as I tilt my head back toward the shoreline. As if they have a mind of their own, my eyes find Sebastian. *Damn.* He's still chatting up the pretty redhead.

I feel my heart break a little. He can't be into her so soon, can he? They've known each other for—what?—five minutes?

He catches me staring and I freeze. My face reddens as he smiles and waves back politely. Or is the wave inviting? I can never tell with him.

Maybe I should say something this weekend and clear the air between us? This is the last chance I'll get before everyone leaves for college in a few weeks. If nothing else, even if he tells me the kiss was a mistake—which I'm pretty sure is the case—we can at least go back to being friends. Friends is better than nothing with a guy like Sebastian.

"Do you have my cell?" Val asks, looking hopefully at Cam and me. "I lost it again."

I grin. "Shocker."

Val is always losing things. I guess there isn't a real incentive to be responsible when Daddy can buy you whatever you want.

"You left it on the kitchen counter," Cam says and pulls out Val's phone from the massive mom tote she brought.

"You're the best sister ever."

"I know." Cam smiles, handing Val the phone and pulling out suntan lotion next. It's SPF 50, the highest they sell at the stores. "Now put this on."

"No way." Val sticks out her tongue. "I wanna be super tan."

"The UV index is a seven. You could get sun poisoning," Cam says, her forehead furrowing with concern. "Or cancer."

Val gives her sister a look. "You know we're Latina, right?"

"Yep, and the rate of melanoma has risen twenty percent among Latinos in the past twenty years," Cam says.

"Lighten up, would you? We're eighteen. We're too young for anything bad to happen." Val turns back to the guys with a flirty look in her eyes. "So what's the hot spot for tonight?"

"Beach Club, for sure," Rhett says. "You in?"

"You know it," Val says and gives him a sexy wink.

Cam's lips press together. "But it's our first night here," she says softly to Val. "I thought we could go to dinner at that nice place Mom and Dad recommended right on the water. They said it's their favorite."

"Awww, forget food. You gotta party with us." Luke turns his dazzling white smile on Cam. "With all this storm talk, we gotta make the most of tonight. No telling what's gonna happen tomorrow."

I turn my face toward the cloudless, sunny sky. I vaguely remember hearing about some tropical depression in the Bahamas the other day, but I thought it'd already turned. Now all the rain from earlier makes sense. I knew it wasn't a typical summer shower.

I'm a little surprised none of our parents have texted us about it yet, but I doubt they've heard. These things move so fast. We get tropical storms every summer in Florida. They appear quickly and tend to disappear even quicker, usually without so much as a fallen leaf.

"Yeah, right." Val scoffs. "Big storms never make it this far. They always turn up the coast."

"All the same, half our house is already packing up and fixin' to head home in the mornin'," Rhett says.

"What's the matter?" Val gives him a teasing grin. "You big Tennessee boys afraid of a little rain?"

"Not afraid," he says. "Just respectful of good ol' Mother Nature."

I stir uneasily in Val's beach chair. It's not that I'm worried about the weather either, but if everyone's talking about leaving the island tomorrow, we should probably take it a little more seriously.

"Maybe we should call our parents?" I ask my friends. "What if they want us to come home?"

"To Orlando? And miss the Fourth?" Val's eyes almost pop out of her head. "Absolutely not."

I turn to Cam. She's always the more reasonable twin. Maybe she'll—

"Don't be an idiot, Riley," Cam says, raising a hand to shush me. "We're not going anywhere."

I sigh and look away. It occurs to me, not for the first time, that sometimes my friends are huge assholes to me.

On the other side of the beach, Nia lets out a high-pitched giggle and leans in to give Tyler an exaggerated kiss, somehow managing to videotape their make-out session at the same time. I'm sure it'll wind up on her Instagram later. Val watches on with a fiery, hostile glare.

"What we're gonna do is have fun tonight, just like we planned," she says, a tiny vein in her forehead pulsing. "Screw Mother Nature."

CHAPTER 3

A few hours later, Blake, Val, and I are crammed into a smelly bathroom stall, taking shots from the little silver canteen Blake snuck inside the Beach Club. Val is the only one of us with a fake ID. One of her many older ex-boyfriends got it for her as a gift. It's awful, though, and doesn't work half the time. That's why the three of us are forced to hide out in the bathroom, drinking from contraband like a bunch of criminals, in order to keep our buzz going.

Blake wipes away the excess alcohol that drips down her chin, giggling, as I take one last gulp of the vodka and pass the rest to Val. After Val finishes it off, Blake takes the canteen and shoves it back down into the bottom of her oversized hobo fringed bag. Val unlocks the stall door and pushes us through the crowd of sweaty girls in skimpy dresses and flip flops until we're all the way at the sinks.

"I can't believe Cammy isn't drinking tonight," Val says with an annoyed sigh, turning on the faucet. "What a baby, huh?"

"Be nice," I say. "She's just bummed you didn't want to go out to dinner with her."

"Well, what did she expect? It was a stupid idea," she says. "No one wants to go to some fancy sit down meal for three hours. We're eighteen—not eighty." She snorts. "I swear, she's such a bore sometimes."

I scoot in closer to her and check my reflection in the dirty mirror. *Ugh.* I look like a drowned rat. I'm used to heat from living in Florida my entire life, but the humidity on this island is ridiculous. The makeup Val did for me earlier has already melted off my face.

"Oopsies," she says, looking over as I wipe away the black glob of runny eyeliner and mascara gathered underneath my eyes with a paper towel. "Guess I should've used waterproof on you too."

I can't help but notice her makeup is still picture perfect.

"Here—reapply." She pulls out her signature red lipstick, *Vixen*, and her diamond tennis bracelet sparkles under the fluorescent lights. I'd be terrified to bring something that expensive on a beach vacation, but Val never leaves home without it. It has so many diamonds it could probably put me through college.

"I told you to stop using that crap." Blake yanks the lipstick out of Val's hand and shoots it across the room like it's a basketball. It lands straight in the center of the trash can, clear on the other side of the bathroom.

"Hey!" Val says. "That was new."

"Next time buy cruelty-free. Only barbarians still buy makeup that tests on animals." Blake fishes around in her bag and pulls out a lipstick. "Here—try this," she says, handing the tube to Val. "It's vegan."

Val puts it on and smiles, admiring herself in the mirror. She gives a little spin and pulls down the top of her sexy red dress even more to show off her ample cleavage. I watch her preen, biting the inside of my cheek to keep from saying anything I shouldn't. I'm still annoyed she made me change my outfit earlier.

I blew an entire month's paycheck on a dress I found online that would've been perfect for tonight. My friends all have endless clothes budgets so it's hard to keep up, but I found something amazing right as it went on sale. I was so excited to wear it out our very first night clubbing, but Val took one look at me and threw a fit. She was already wearing red.

Knowing better than to argue with Val, I put on my second cutest outfit, a white jumpsuit I grabbed from Mom's closet when she wasn't looking. But then Nia saw me and freaked out because she was also wearing a jumpsuit. Only one of us can wear a jumpsuit on the same night. That's how I wound up in my cut-off jean shorts, one of Cam's super preppy tops, and my only pair of heels that don't match at all.

"By the way, you look adorable, Ri Ri," Val says. Her lips twitch as she tries not to laugh.

"Don't be an asshole." Blake tucks her silky long blonde hair behind her ears to show off her earrings. She has an insane collection of hoops and studs for her multiple piercings. "You should've let her wear that damn dress. She looked great."

"Red is *my* color. Everyone knows that," Val says. "Besides, she looks fine."

"Yeah, right," Blake says. "She looks like Daisy Duke."

"Oh, geez. Thanks a lot." I frown at myself in the mirror.

Blake is right. I look ridiculous.

"If it helps, you're a super hot Daisy Duke," Blake says with a grin as I tug my shorts down. They're giving me a major wedgie.

"Enough about Riley. Did you all see how good Seb looks?" Val pulls the bottom of her dress higher to show off her tanned, toned legs. "I'd sell my soul for another shot with him."

Blake laughs. "If you had a soul."

"I'm serious. I think tonight might be the night."

"Oh, c'mon, Val," Blake says. "You've been throwing yourself at Seb for years, trying to win him back. Besides, Ty's his best friend. There's, like, bro code and shit." Blake bends down to adjust her sandal straps to show off her new tattoo of

Freya, the Viking goddess of war. It takes up almost her entire ankle.

"You don't get it." Val smiles knowingly. "Guys like Seb think they can have anyone they want. You gotta make them jealous. Brings out their inner caveman."

"I don't think Seb is like that," I say, tying my damp hair up in a ponytail and fanning at my face to cool down.

Sebastian has always seemed to operate differently from the other guys in school. For one thing, he doesn't jump from one girl to the next like his friends do. Even though he's by far the hottest guy in our class and girls are always trying to get with him, I've never seen him randomly hook up. Besides Val in ninth grade, I've only ever heard of him dating two other girls at school. Missy Baker, our class president, and Jessica Yerman, who's a year below us and in the band. Jessica is always helping throw community concerts in the park. Though pretty, neither of them is part of the cool crowd like my friends and I are.

"All guys are like that. Watch and learn, ladies." Val throws us a wink and heads for the door.

Blake rolls her eyes and grabs my hand. She pulls me close behind her as we follow Val into the crowded, sweaty night-club. Pulsing electronica dance music pounds as we make a beeline for the dance floor. I spot Cam sitting with Jonathan at a table in a dark corner of the club, talking, a pitcher of water sitting between them.

Cam looks bored. Jonathan sees us right away and stands, waving us over. I cringe as I take in his outfit—khaki shorts and a blood-splattered graphic tee that says *Slasher Movies and Chill* with a picture of Freddy Krueger and his infamous fingernail-knife glove. Why is this guy so obsessed with serial killers?

"Let's go say hi," Blake says and starts for their table.

I pull on her hand. "Please don't make me."

"You sure? Jon's a sweet guy once you get to know him."

"Uh huh. I bet that's what they said about Ted Bundy too."

She lets me lead her away, though I'm sure this is not the end of my friends' matchmaking endeavors for the weekend. I risk a backward glance in time to see Jonathan sneak some pills out of his pocket and chug them down with his drink when he thinks no one is watching. Cam, distracted and texting on her phone, doesn't notice. Hopefully, it's just Advil or something and not serious drugs, but with all the rumors about Jonathan, who knows? Nothing would surprise me where he's concerned.

We get to the dance floor where our friends are the center of attention, like usual. Nia looks like an African goddess in her white jumpsuit and gold wrap-around sandals, laughing as she grinds against Tyler. Mason dances next to them, wearing a pink pocket square—*barf*—and a white blazer covered with Gucci logos. It's a ridiculous outfit under normal circumstances, but even more so in this sweltering heat. I snort as he gets too close to a petite girl on crutches who looks like she's had too much to drink. She's the perfect victim for Mason. Even if she figures out what an ass he is, she won't be able to get away.

Sebastian is there too, looking cool as ever. He casually drinks his beer while Val spins and twirls nearby to catch his attention. His crisp linen shirt is just tight enough to show the hint of abs and arm muscles I saw earlier on the beach, his fresh tan setting off the emerald green of his eyes.

Damn. Val was right.

He looks amazing.

"She's shameless," Nia says as Blake and I walk up. Her plump bottom lip curls upward in disgust as Val puts on a show for Sebastian. Val's an amazing dancer. She and Nia were both co-captains of the cheer and dance squad. "And she looks like a skank in that dress."

I blink. "But you told her you loved it earlier?"

Nia smiles viciously. "Did I?"

"I think she looks hot," Tyler says, slurring his words.

Nia's smile disappears. "Maybe you should go dance with *her* then," she says and gives him a hard shove.

Tyler stumbles, spilling his beer all over the floor. I almost feel bad for the guy. Tyler's never been all that bright to begin with, and the alcohol isn't doing him any favors. He was just being honest, I suppose, but honesty can be a mistake with our friends. Sometimes lies are better.

My eyes drift back to Sebastian. I can't help but smile as I watch him dancing by himself, oblivious to Val circling around him like a shark. He's either ignoring her on purpose or he's just adorably clueless.

I inch closer to him, the vodka from the bathroom kicking in and giving me extra courage. Sure enough, he looks over and gives me an irresistibly devastating grin that sends my pulse racing. Almost tentatively, his hand extends in my direction, and he takes a step toward me.

A dizzying current jolts my insides. He's coming over.

This is it! This is actually happening!

But the next instant, a girl appears out of nowhere. She dances right up to him, trapping him in place. I notice with disappointment that it's the redhead from earlier on the beach.

Val stares at the girl with a clenched jaw. I'm not the only one annoyed by the newcomer. Val waits until Sebastian's back is turned, and then she shoves the redhead so hard the girl almost crashes into the edge of the stage where the DJ plays. The girl seems dazed for a moment, as if unsure what just happened, but then she shakes herself off and prances right back up to Sebastian. Val flexes a fist behind her back, preparing for more.

I glance around, expecting to see Cam heading our way to intervene like she always does when her sister goes off the rails, but she's nowhere to be seen. Her purse lies on the table where Jonathan now sits alone, laughing to himself as he watches something funny on his cell phone.

Well, that's just great. Cam must be in the bathroom or something.

I groan and head for Val myself. Playing babysitter is not how I saw this night going down, but I'm the only other person besides Cam that Val will possibly listen to when she's like this.

"Let's get you some water," I say, and sling an arm around her sweaty shoulder. "You need to cool off."

"Go away, Ri Ri. I'm fiiine," she slurs. "Go pester someone else."

For a moment, I wish I could. Val can be a real bitch sometimes. She deserves to embarrass herself. It might do her some good. The only problem is Cam. I can't do that to her. She'd be so upset if I let Val make a fool of herself.

I reach for her again, more forcefully. "But I need your help," I say and add a little whine to my voice. "I saw a cute guy at the bar, and you know how bad I am at flirting." I blink my eyes and make myself look as pathetic as possible. I don't have to try hard. My friends all know I'm a terrible flirt.

"Well, why didn't you say so in the first place?" Val grabs me by the elbow and leads me toward the bar. If there's one thing Val likes even more than hooking up with guys, it's helping her friends hook up with guys. "Tell me more. How cute are we talking? Scale of one to ten?"

I have her full attention now.

"Oh, um—"

"Wait, hold on." She reaches up and pulls my long brown hair out of its messy ponytail. With expert precision, she unknots the sticky strands and smooths them down. "There, that's better."

"Hey, give that back," I say, reaching for my hair tie. "It's a sauna in here."

"No way. Ponytails don't get laid." She throws it across the room and shoves me forward. "Ohhh! Is that him? The hottie over there?"

I follow her pointed finger to find a ridiculously good looking Black guy. He's got spiky brown hair cropped close to his scalp and the most beautiful eyes I've ever seen. Big and wide, they're a blueish gray color so striking I wonder if he's a model. We're not too far from Miami Beach, the modeling capital of the South, so it's possible. He sits alone, peeling off the label of his beer. The scruff on his chin makes him appear a few years older than us, but I don't think it's by much.

"Damn, Ri Ri. Good eye." She marches me straight up to the guy and taps him on the shoulder with a sexy grin. "Hey handsome, wanna buy us some drinks?"

The stranger looks up and grins, regarding us with amusement. "Love to," he says and lifts his wrist, showing off a neon yellow band that reads *Over 21*. "Got one of these?"

"Oh shoot." Val flashes her most charming smile. "Ours fell off in the bathroom."

He laughs and raises his hand, flagging down the female bartender. "Hey Roxy," he calls out to her. "Two of your finest waters, please."

"Make that three." Blake comes up behind us. She pants in my ear, out of breath from all the dancing. "Hi, I'm Blake," she says, reaching out to shake his hand.

"Grant," he says and turns to me. "And you are?" His eyes lock on mine, and my insides melt, flattered by his attention.

"She's Riley," Val says for me. "And she thinks you're hot. You interested?"

"Val!" Heat rushes through my body. "I'm sorry," I mutter to him, worried I might die right there on the spot from embarrassment. "Ignore her. She's drunk."

His mouth quirks with humor. "So where're you girls from?"

"Bishop Lake," Val says.

He lifts a brow. "Fancy."

"What about you?" Val asks.

"I live here."

The bartender gives Grant a familiar, warm look as she arrives with our drinks. I study her, wondering how she knows him. Is he a regular? Do they hook up? She's very pretty, in a gothic-beachy-witch kind of way. Her outfit is all black, and she wears a beaded choker made up of dark-colored seashells. Her hair is bright cherry red, a color that Mother Nature doesn't make.

"Hey there," Blake says to the bartender in a flirty tone as she reaches for her water. "What's your name?"

"Roxy." The neon bar lights catch the silver nose piercing in her left nostril.

"Hi, Roxy. I'm Blake."

"Well, Blake. My shift's over in an hour—come find me." Roxy gives Blake a big wink before walking away to tend to other customers.

A loud cheer erupts on the dance floor as the DJ mixes in a popular new EDM song. Val squeals and pushes away her water, jumping out of her seat. I try to stop her, but I'm too late. She's already racing back to the dance floor, tripping and banging into a group of older women along the way.

"I'll make sure she's okay," Blake says, getting to her feet. She puts a hand on my shoulder, leans in close, and whispers. "You stay here and have fun."

After my friends are gone, I drink my water and sneak little looks at Grant, not sure what to do next. I'm so bad at this stuff. Should I talk more? Do I ask him to dance?

A moment later, he pushes his empty bottle to the edge of the bar. "Afraid I gotta get going," he says, standing. "Early shift in the morning."

"Oh, okay," I say, disappointed. I sort of thought he was into me, and we might hang more, but he hasn't even asked for my number. "It was nice meeting you."

"You too." He pauses, his brows drawing together. "Be

careful getting home, okay? This island's pretty safe, but you never know."

The way he says it almost sounds like a warning. It catches me off guard. Everyone told us Palm Key Island is super safe. But before I can ask him what he means, he's already gone.

I finish my water and think back to the conversation on the beach with the Tennessee guys earlier. What if Rhett was telling us the truth? What if something bad really did happen in our rental house?

My fingers hover over my cell phone as I contemplate Googling our address, but then I shake my head and put the phone away. We're already here, and I'm too broke to stay anywhere else at this point. If I'm stuck in the rental house either way, I'd rather not know anything bad about the place. Ignorance is bliss, right?

Glancing over at the dance floor, I search for my friends. Everyone is gone but Nia. She stands alone, chatting with one of the Tennessee guys—Luke, the one with the perfect smile. I hope it's just a coincidence and that Val and Tyler are both in the bathroom or on the outside patio for a smoke, because if they're somewhere hooking up, there's going to be hell to pay in the morning.

Sighing, I push my empty water away and get up. I have no idea where everyone else went off to and, of course, no one responds to my texts. It would piss me off if it wasn't so damn typical. My friends are always getting drunk and forgetting about me.

With nothing else to do, I call myself an Uber on the account the twins let everyone use and wait outside for it to arrive. Even though I'm only a few feet away from the front door of the packed nightclub, it's unnaturally quiet and empty on the streets. I can't help but feel as if I'm all alone. Vulnerable. Split from the pack.

A tingly sensation lifts the hairs at the back of my neck as I get this eerie sense of being watched. My eyes dart around, looking for something—or someone—that seems out of place.

There!

Over in the corner by the garbage cans is a shadow. It's huge. As big as a person. Slowly, it detaches from the wall and starts to move. Is it my imagination or is it heading straight for me?

Tires squeal behind me and I jump at the sudden sound, heart racing, but it's just my Uber. I sprint to my ride and slam the door shut behind me, sinking into the seat with relief. I know I'm being ridiculous. It was probably just a stray cat or some poor homeless person, nothing to get so worked up over. I'm such a chickenshit. This is why I don't read those horror books of Jonathan's or watch scary movies. I can scare myself plenty enough without more stimulation, thank you very much.

Ten minutes later, the driver drops me off at the rental house just as the night begins to deteriorate and the rain starts to fall.

CHAPTER 4

I expect to see at least some of my friends already back at the rental house, partying it up, since leaving a club without telling me isn't exactly outside the realm of possibilities with this crew. Instead, only silence greets me as I approach the front door. The place looks completely empty.

That's strange. When I left Beach House, it seemed like Nia was the only one still there. So where is everyone else?

I bend down to grab the extra key Cam hid under one of the fake pink flamingos on the front porch only to realize, to my dismay, that I don't need it. The front door is already unlocked and cracked open a few inches.

With an annoyed sigh, I push the door all the way open and step inside. Even though I repeatedly told Val—the last one to leave—to lock the door, she must have forgotten. She's truly the least responsible person ever. Then again, I guess you don't learn a lot about responsibility when you live in an enormous mansion in a guarded, gated community and your parents hire people to do everything for you.

I flick on the lights by the door and glance around the foyer, debating for a moment whether I should catch another Uber back to the club. Nothing seems out of place, but I'm not exactly thrilled to be alone in a house that's been left open for half the night. I hover close to the door, listening for any telltale signs that someone is already here, just waiting around to murder a bunch of idiot girls who made it far too easy by leaving their front door wide open. Fortunately, it's almost eerily quiet. The only thing I hear is my own stilted breathing.

Surely, if someone was here, they would have made themselves known by now, right?

I stifle a yawn before taking another tentative step further inside, locking the door behind me. My legs are heavy and wooden. It's been a long day, and I've had a lot to drink. All I want to do is get into bed and sleep. At this point, I'm more tired than I am scared. Besides, it's already after midnight. My friends will be home soon.

The floorboards of the old house creak and groan as I come to a decision and proceed to walk up the stairs and to the bedroom I share with Cam. After taking off my makeup and changing into pajamas, I shoot off a few text messages to let my friends know I'm home safe—if anyone has even noticed I've left, which I doubt. I get into the king bed and scoot all the way over to the edge, leaving plenty of room for Cam. She already claimed the side furthest from the window because it has plugs for her phone and iPad. Her pink silk pillow cover, eye mask, and matching cashmere throw are already in her spot.

As I watch the rain fall harder and faster outside the window, my spirits start to sink. I'm used to Florida weather, but this feels different. Our rain showers are usually quick and furious. I can't even recall how many times the skies have opened up out of nowhere and drowned me for a good five to ten minutes before clearing again to a cloudless sunny blue for the rest of the day. But this rain just keeps going, on and on, with no signs of stopping.

I groan and pull the covers over my head. It hasn't even been twenty-four hours and this weekend already seems like a bust. Potential major storm on the way. Upcoming battle between Val and Nia over stupid Can't-Keep-It-In-His-Pants-Tyler-Singh. Plus, it appears Sebastian still has zero interest in me. This trip was a mistake.

We probably should've gone back home, but I think I know why my friends really want to stay here and it isn't just for the partying. No one said it out loud, but I'm certain a big part of the reason we came to Palm Key Island this weekend is because of their dead friend Jordyn. My friends want to be somewhere far away during the first anniversary of Jordyn's suicide. Perhaps they think it'll be easier to cope with the loss and pain if they aren't back home. Or maybe they don't want to think about it at all because it hurts too much. They don't talk to me about Jordyn, so I don't know for sure what their logic is. I don't blame them for wanting to avoid things, either; I just don't think distance will help. Death isn't something you can escape by driving away in your brand-new Range Rover for a few days.

I'd never met Jordyn Chang myself, but I had seen her. Once. It was late last spring when Mom drove me to Bishop Prep so I could drop off my admissions paperwork. That was right after the divorce and our move from Miami. Mom was convinced that Bishop Prep was the answer to all our prayers. Now that we were broke, I needed college scholarship money, and Bishop Prep's stellar reputation of top grades and test scores was my best hope of going to a top college.

I had snuck through the hallways that day worried someone would see me holding the Bishop Prep financial aid application. I was terrified I'd be flagged as the token poor kid who needed charity to go to school. After dropping my papers off at the front office, I rushed to the girl's restroom, needing to pee from all the nerves. I'd just flushed the toilet when the 10-Squad entered. Of course, they weren't my best friends back then. They were just a group of impossibly beautiful girls I could see through the gaps in my bathroom stall.

"Please Val, you can't show anyone," Jordyn had cried out, her voice laced with desperation. "My parents will kill me!"

"If you were so worried about your parents, why'd you do it in the first place?" Val asked. Not exactly mean, more like she was curious. Water started to run as she turned on the faucet. "Really, Jordyn. I don't know what you were thinking. Going at it under the bleachers like that, where anyone could see?"

"It was just a kiss," Jordyn said. "We thought everyone was gone from practice. It was just that one time."

"You sure?" Val giggled. 'Cause it looked pretty steamy from what I could see."

"Leave her alone, okay?" Blake joined Val at the sink. She ran a brush through her long blonde hair while I watched, huddled in the stall, enraptured by these perfect girls. They were larger than life—like movie stars.

Jordyn pivoted around to face Blake. "I told you this would happen!" she said, loud and accusing. "I warned you someone might see!"

"Don't yell at me," Blake said. "I didn't make you do anything you didn't want to."

"Ugh. Why is everyone being so dramatic?" Nia asked as she exited the stall next to mine. "My manager says being gay is totally in these days. Everyone's coming out."

"My parents don't care about what's *in*, Nia. They're, like, completely insane." Jordyn's voice cracked. "If they see that video, they're gonna murder me."

"That reminds me," Val said as Cam approached the sink to wash her hands. "You're the only one who hasn't seen the video, Cammy. Aren't you dying to watch?"

Val rustled through her backpack and pulled out her cell phone from the side pocket. With a giggle, she tossed it over to her sister. Jordyn tried to grab the phone mid-air but was too slow. Cam hit play, and the sounds of lips smacking and tongues touching echoed throughout the bathroom.

"Please. Just delete it," Jordyn moaned, slumping against the wall. "I'm not gay. The kiss meant nothing; I swear. It'll never, ever happen again."

I heard a quick intake of breath as Blake rushed for the

exit, her sneakers making loud stomping sounds as she flew past the group. The door slammed with a loud, shaky thud behind her.

"Geez. What's her problem?" Nia asked.

"She's probably on her period," Val said, and they all giggled except for Jordyn.

Even though I didn't know Jordyn, I couldn't help but feel awful listening to these girls—her *friends*—laugh even harder as Jordyn's sobs grew louder. These girls were ruthless. Meaner than any of the girls back at my old school in Miami. These were the kind of girls I would be going to school with in a few weeks?

I fidgeted in the stall, waiting for them to leave.

"Jordyn, sweetie," Cam said after she'd finished watching the entire video. "We're your best friends. We don't care if you're gay. We love you no matter what." She paused, handing the phone back to her sister. "But you shouldn't lie. You should tell your parents. Get it all out in the open."

"No! You don't understand. If they find out, my life will be over. I'M DEAD!" Jordyn wailed. "Please, don't tell anyone. I'll do anything."

"Anything?" Val asked, a mischievous look on her face. "You swear?"

"Val…" Cam warned.

"Oh, relax, Cammy." I could hear the smile in Val's voice as she started for the door. "I won't show the video to anyone, okay? I just need a little help with my schoolwork." She glanced back at Jordyn. "Perhaps all my homework for the rest of the semester?"

"Sure. Whatever you want," Jordyn said, blowing her nose as she trailed after Val, exiting the bathroom.

"Good grief! What a baby," Nia said, grinning at Cam as the two of them finished up at the sink.

"Little Ms. Perfect kind of deserves it though, right?"

Cam's voice dissolved into laughter as they headed for the door. "A little blackmail will knock her down a few pegs."

After they were gone, I'd snuck out of the stall to wash my hands. I thought I was safe, but Val returned seconds later to grab a lipstick she'd left behind at the sink. It must have been my face, but right away she somehow knew I'd witnessed the entire thing. She made me promise not to tell anyone what I'd heard about the video on her phone or the blackmail.

A few weeks later, Jordyn Chang was dead.

The sounds of waves crashing outside the window bring me back to the present. I shake the memories away. I don't like to dwell on the past and what happened after. How when Valentina Ramirez singled me out the first week of senior year to eat lunch with her at the popular kids' table, I knew she wasn't doing it to be nice. How I made friends with the 10-Squad so fast, not because we had a lot in common or they thought I was nice or funny or smart or any of the other reasons people decide to be friends, but because Val wanted to buy my silence and everyone else always did what Val said.

A sharp, clicking noise below makes me jolt upright.

What the hell is that?

I shiver in the bed and pull the covers up to my chin, listening, trying to figure out where the sound is coming from. Other than the odd clicking underneath my bedroom, things are far quieter than I would have expected on the busy island. The once-packed, rowdy beaches outside our patio deck are empty now. Even the neighboring houses lining the street are silent. Everyone must still be out downtown, partying at the bars and nightclubs. I didn't expect to feel so isolated back at the house.

The noise below me grows louder, more insistent. It sounds almost like something—or someone—is trapped below, trying to get out.

Or trying to get *in*.

My pulse starts to race as I remember the weird sounds

coming from the basement earlier during our arrival. Why was the basement door locked? Was there something down there the owners didn't want us to find? Could that be what I'm hearing now?

Oh God.

Why did I think it was a good idea to come home alone to a strange house?

What if—

I straighten in bed and shake the creepy feelings away, forcing myself to stop this terrifying train of thought. I'm going to give myself a heart attack if I keep going like this. What I need to do is relax. Be logical. It's nothing nefarious; probably just bad water pipes.

Back when we had money, before Dad screwed up all our lives, we used to go on ski trips in the mountains to fancy places like Aspen and Mount Sierra in California. Sometimes when it was very cold, the plumbing pipes would rattle within the walls of the ski cabins we rented. That's what this sounds like now. It must be a plumbing issue.

I wipe sweaty palms against my pajamas and start my iPhone playlist to drown out the sounds. Taylor Swift begins singing "girl power" pop rock anthems, and I turn back to the window and watch rain fall to the beat, willing myself to calm down.

Are you guys heading home soon? I send in the group text.

When no one responds right away, I follow with another text.

Hello?

The minutes tick by and still no one texts back, though this is not unusual. When my friends are drunk and having a good time, they tend to have one-track minds. They're fun, yes, but not the most thoughtful people on the planet.

A flash of bright light catches my attention outside the window. At first, I assume it's lightning, but then no thunder follows. When it happens again, it takes a moment for my brain to realize it's the beam of a flashlight. Someone is on the beach below me.

How odd.

Why in the world would someone be out this late? And in the rain, no less?

I push my nose against the glass, peering closer to get a better look. It's dark, so I have to squint hard to see anything from my vantage point on the second floor. I'm just able to make out a shadowy figure hovering along the side of the house. They stand as still as a statue, wearing dark pants and a yellow rain slicker with the hood pulled all the way up. They could be male or female. I can't see a face from here. Average height. Average weight.

Something about the hooded raincoat makes me think about the reoccurring bad dreams I've been having recently, and a flash of memory comes back to me. The guy with the axe in my nightmares, the one trying to kill me and all my friends in a damp, dark basement—he wears a hooded jacket, too...

It's only a neighbor, I tell myself, ignoring the goosebumps crawling up my arms. Nothing to be worried about. Just someone cutting across the beach, or maybe one of the Tennessee guys from next door got locked out of their house and is trying to go around the back to get in. It isn't some crazy stalker who followed me back from the club and wants to kill me, and it's definitely not some imaginary axe murderer from my dreams—right?

My cell phone screeches so loudly next to me I let out a terrified scream.

Shit! I forgot I was holding the damn thing.

I smile with relief as soon as I see the screen. Finally, a text back from Cam.

On way. C U soon.

My eyes flicker back to the window, but the figure has disappeared. Already, I feel better as I stare out into the empty darkness. Whoever they were, they're long gone, and my friends will be home any minute.

P.S. Val is M.I.A. Think she's with Ty. Nia FREAKING OUT!!!

This text is just to me, obviously. I chuckle at the head-exploding emojis Cam sends to punctuate it and type back a few choice emojis of my own.

A text arrives from Nia next: *Put more beer in fridge. NOW.*

I try to ignore the flicker of annoyance at her bossy tone. My friends are always assuming I have nothing better to do than cater to their every whim. What if I was already asleep or busy doing something important?

For just a moment, I smile to myself and imagine having a little fun. What I should really do is text Nia back and tell her I'm already in bed and she can put beer in the fridge her own damn self. If I said no to my friends, even just one time, they'd lose their minds.

But of course, I don't do that.

Like the spineless, good little minion I am, I head downstairs to do as ordered. The old wooden floor creaks and groans under the pressure of my bare feet, and another flicker of yellow catches my eye as I grab the warm beer on the kitchen counter. I turn to get a closer look and my heart almost leaps out of my chest. Just past the sliding glass patio doors is the person in the raincoat. They stand on the pool deck, only a few feet away.

Panic settles over me like a smattering of fresh rain droplets.

Should I run?

Hide?

My feet are frozen in place. I can't stop staring out the glass doors, mesmerized.

What in the… what are they doing?

I blink, disbelieving, and rub at my eyes. No way I'm really seeing this. It looks like the person in the raincoat—whoever it is—is dragging something long and limp across our patio pool deck. Something with arms and legs that looks alarmingly like—

I gasp.

They're dragging a person!

All the warmth drains from my body. I let out a scream so loud and shrill, the hooded figure startles and drops whatever they're carrying to the ground with a loud thump. They turn slowly in my direction, noticing me for the first time. I realize screaming like that and calling attention to myself is the absolute stupidest thing ever, but I don't have time to dwell on my mistake.

Adrenaline shoots through my body and without stopping to think any further, I bolt toward the front door. My pulse pounds like a rocket ship in my chest as I run. Footsteps sound behind me like someone is chasing me. I can't tell if the stranger has somehow gotten inside the house or if I'm simply imagining things, and I don't dare look back to find out. My sweaty hands shake with fear as I fumble with the knob on the door. The simple act of unlocking it takes far longer than it should. I start to panic, praying I can escape before it's too late.

Suddenly, the front door pushes open from the other side and the sound of laughter pours into the house. My friends have returned home, just in time.

CHAPTER 5

DAY 2: Friday—Two days before July 4th

"I still can't believe what happened," I say to my friends as we sit poolside the next day. Cam, Blake, Nia, and I decided to grab lunch on the outside patio deck at the Seasider Inn, one of the two posh hotels on Palm Key Island. It's early afternoon, but I'm still just as freaked out about everything as I was last night. *"I was almost killed!"*

Okay, maybe I'm being a tad dramatic.

Not killed, exactly, but it's hard to imagine some trespasser disguised in an oversized yellow rain slicker, lurking on our patio late at night—with a dead body in tow—had good intentions for me.

"Not this again." Blake yawns as she applies sunscreen to her freckled shoulders and chest and adjusts her newest Stanford baseball cap. This one is black with gold writing that says *Track Star*. "We've been over all this. There was no one on the patio. You were just wasted."

"You seriously think I was so drunk I—what?—imagined everything?" I stare at Blake across the restaurant table. She must be kidding.

"Relax, Ri Ri. No one's saying that." Cam pats at my head like I'm a little kid. "We just think you, uh, misread the situation. It was dark. Late at night. You were tired." She unbuttons the pink, frilly sweater she wears over her bathing suit as a cabana boy comes over and takes down the umbrella above our table now that the rain has stopped.

"I didn't misread anything," I say. "There was someone outside. I *saw* them."

Nia sighs, looking bored. "I told you—that was Rhett running over to get alcohol for the afterparty."

"Unless he was dragging a body behind him, I highly doubt it," I grumble.

"Okay, so maybe it was Val coming home?" Blake asks. "She probably dropped something on the ground and was picking it up. Like a jacket?"

"For the millionth time, I know what I saw!" I say, not exactly yelling but pretty damn close to it. "It wasn't a dream, or a drunk hallucination, or Val's jacket, for God's sake. There was someone on our patio, and they were going to hurt me."

"Geez. Take it down a notch, okay? My head is killing me." Nia looks at me crossly, kneading at her temples. She pulls her wide-brim straw hat and big dark sunglasses lower until they cover most of her face.

"Let's get a drink," Cam says to me and waves at the waiter. "It'll chill you out."

I cross my arms over my chest and sink into the chair, looking away. I guess they mean well, but their dismissiveness pisses me off. Plus, I'm still upset about how they all behaved last night. I thought for sure they'd insist on calling the police or at least our parents after I told them what I saw, but they talked me out of it. They just wanted to keep drinking.

Across from us on the deck, the pool party is getting started. It was raining all morning, but now the sun is starting to peek out above the aquamarine ocean visible just past the edges of the hotel's back gate. The DJ turns up the beat, blasting the kind of loud tropical house music they play at beach club parties and on rowdy cruise ships. Partygoers in tiny bikinis and colorful swim trunks sway in the shallow end of the pool and inside cabanas that line the deck. A few people get up on the table next to us and start to dance.

Val is going to be so bummed she's missing this. She lives for a good party. It's her own fault, though. She didn't respond to any of the group text messages this morning or to our knocks on her locked door before we left. We could hear her phone ringing in the master bedroom when we called, so we know she made it home safely. The question is if she made it home alone... or with Tyler. No one saw them after Beach Club.

"Okay, fine." I straighten my chin. "Even if you aren't worried about the person on our patio, what about all the creepy noises? It sounded like someone was right underneath my bedroom last night."

Cam squints at me. "I bet it was the air conditioner."

"It didn't sound like that," I say. "It sounded like someone trying to get in."

"Probably some poor animal that got trapped under the house." Blake leans back in her seat and flexes her arms over-head, cracking her fingers at the knuckles. "I bet it's a mouse or something. My parents sometimes get rodents at their rentals, too."

"I'll get hold of the owner when we get back," Cam says. "They can call the exterminator."

"You can't do that!" Blake stiffens in her seat, looking aghast. "They'll lay out traps and poison."

"So?" Cam shrugs. "Isn't that the point?"

"It's totally inhumane. They'll die!" Blake says.

"Good." Nia's lip curls. "Mice are nasty."

"It sounded a lot bigger than mice," I say.

"Oh really?" Cam's mouth starts to twitch. "Maybe we should have the owners call Ghostbusters instead?"

They all burst into laughter.

I feel a little stab of hurt. "That's not funny."

"Sorry," Cam says, but she's laughing so hard she can barely get the word out.

I stare at my sandals, my eyes beginning to prick with tears. Why are they making this all into one big joke? Don't real friends listen to and support each other?

Even though I try my best, a tiny sniffle escapes. I feel stupid for getting so upset over their silly teasing, but I don't like being made fun of. Of course, my overreaction only makes them laugh more.

"Chill out, would you?" Nia rolls her eyes, snickering. "You're being a real buzzkill."

They're still laughing at me when the waiter comes over. He's attractive with a big, friendly smile and a smattering of freckles across his nose. Long, floppy brown hair peeks out from the sides of his carnation pink Seasider Inn visor. He looks like he's already graduated college, just a few years older than us.

"What can I get you ladies?" he asks and lowers the red service flag on Cam's chair.

Blake pulls down her mirrored aviator sunglasses and eyes him up and down. "Everything looks so good, Cody," she says, licking her lips as she eyes his name tag, her flirt mode activated. "What do you suggest?"

The waiter makes a bunch of recommendations. I only order a small basket of fries, even though I'm starving. It's by far the cheapest thing on the overpriced menu. My friends, of course, order whatever they want. Expensive hangover food like wagyu beef sliders and gourmet goat cheese pizza and avocado toast. My stomach grumbles as he writes it all down. Hopefully, they'll feel bad enough for being such assholes, they'll let me eat their leftovers. Only Nia abstains, ordering just a plain green salad—no dressing.

"And to drink?" he asks.

"I'll have a mimosa," Nia says, tapping her long neon

yellow nails against the edge of the table. "Hold the champagne—too many calories. I gotta post bikini pics today."

Blake stifles a snort.

"Uh, but that's just orange juice?" he asks, rubbing at the scruff on his chin.

Nia blinks. "Yep."

"Okay." He shrugs. "One OJ coming up." He turns to the rest of us. "What can I get everyone else?"

Without Val and her fake ID, we're forced to order drinks that are easy to spike under the table with Blake's trusty canteen. Virgin daiquiris. Virgin Bloody Marys. That sort of thing. Our waiter gives us a funny look as we order, but he says nothing. He clearly knows what's up, but he's young and being cool about it. It doesn't hurt that Cam flashes her daddy's credit card in his face and tells him to "charge it all and keep it coming for a big tip."

"Thanks, Cody," I say with a grateful smile as he leaves to fill our order.

Cam tilts her head back toward the sky. She lets out a happy sigh as the midday sun beats down deliciously on us, and a light breeze ruffles our hair. "I can't believe Val is missing this to sleep in," she says.

Nia's lips flatten. "All I know is, she better be sleeping *alone* —and not with *my* boyfriend."

"Ty will pop up any minute," I say. "Don't worry."

"I'm not worried!"

Blake grins wickedly in Nia's direction. "Maybe you should be."

After our food arrives and we start eating, familiar voices waft down from above. I glance up to see the guys stumbling down the hotel stairs, jostling one another as they head down to the pool area. Right away, my eyes are drawn to Sebastian, like a magnet, and a thrill runs through me.

He's at the front of the pack, wearing a preppy white collared shirt over swim trunks. His baseball cap is turned backward, showing off the collector's edition Orlando Magic logo patch on back, and dark designer sunglasses cover half his face. Jonathan and Mason flank his sides, similarly dressed in rich-boy beach attire, except Jonathan has swapped out the standard polo shirt for another horror movie tee—this one says *Camp Crystal Lake Counselor*. Mason, always extra, has accessorized with a loud Louis Vuitton logo hat and matching scarf.

Cam raises a hand and waves them over to our table. The boys grumble back something that barely amounts to English and shuffle toward us. Seeing them hurting from all the alcohol last night makes me thankful to have Cam's family's signature hangover remedies. As soon as we got up this morning, she had me chugging coconut water, Tylenol, and the "Ramirez Special"—a miracle mixed drink with Clamato tomato juice her mother learned to make growing up in South America.

Mason plops down next to Nia. I look up at Sebastian and smile, hoping he'll take the empty seat beside me, but he just hovers nearby and stares out at the ocean. Jonathan takes the spot instead, moving so close our legs are almost touching. Without asking, he grabs one of my fries and drops it into his mouth.

"Morning, Riley," he says, giving me a sweet smile as he chews on my meager lunch. "You look really pretty today." He plops a new book down in front of me. "Finished another one, if you wanna borrow?"

I wrinkle my nose at the cover. *In Cold Blood* by Truman Capote was one of the "free read" options in my AP English class last semester. According to the syllabus, it was about the 1950 bloody murders of an entire family in a small-town farming community in Kansas. I know it's a classic, but seriously? Hard pass.

I start to dismiss his offer but then feel bad for being so judgy. At least Jonathan reads, which is more than I can say for a lot of guys our age. Plus, maybe his fascination with all this creepy macabre stuff is just the way he deals with the horrible things he's been through. From what I've heard, his life has been pretty rough.

Everyone knows he went to some rehab clinic in Northern Florida last year right after his sister committed suicide. Sebastian tried to cover for his friend by telling people Jonathan was away at baseball camp, but no one believed him. After that, Jonathan's parents got divorced and his dad remarried and moved away. The man has a whole new life in Atlanta with a baby on the way, and Jonathan never sees him. Then Jonathan's mother's alcoholism got worse. She was recently diagnosed with liver disease. The guy has been through a lot. Who am I to say what books he should be reading?

"Sure, thanks," I say with a friendly smile and reach for the book.

To make up for my inner bitchiness, I offer him the rest of my French fry basket, even though they're delicious, and I'm still hungry.

"Damn, look at those swells." Sebastian stares longingly at the crashing surf a few yards away. The waves must be at least eight feet high. "Storm's really bringing 'em in," he says with a wistful sigh before finally taking a seat next to Mason.

"Where's this damn waiter? I'd give my left nut for some red meat," Mason says, eyeing Cam's burger. He snaps his fingers in the air and looks put out that no one is serving him yet, even though he's only been sitting down for a few minutes. "Can you add foie gras on your burger? Like the Club does?"

Even though I'm not a member, I know he's talking about the Bishop Lake Country Club. It's the super exclusive country club back home that everyone's families are members of.

Well, everyone but mine.

"Gross." Blake gags, pressing a fist against her mouth. "Do

you know how they make foie gras? They torture those poor ducks."

"Duh. That's why it tastes so good," he says, smacking at his lips. "Fear is delicious."

My innards curl as he reaches across and grabs Nia's orange juice. He chugs the rest of it down in one gulp without so much as a thank you and then takes a bunch of drags from his vape pen. Blake coughs dramatically, clearing Mason's smoke away with her hand.

"You're such a douchebag," she says to him.

"And you're wrong." Jonathan looks at Mason, an odd expression on his face. "Fear actually makes meat less tender. It's better if your prey is relaxed when you kill it." He pauses. "For taste reasons, I mean."

Mason rolls his eyes. "Okay, you psycho."

Our waiter returns then to take the guys' orders and passes out a red flyer with a bolded title that reads: Tourism Advisory #3. The words HURRICANE HELENA catch my eye as I scan the page. There's a color-coded map of the island with areas marked as an evacuation path and a list of instructions on how to prepare for a storm and where to take shelter.

"Make sure you read it," he warns as he fills up our water glasses. "If the storm keeps tracking this way, we'll go on lockdown soon."

Nia tilts her head toward the clear sky in confusion. "Lockdown? But it's not even raining."

"Maybe not right now, but the storm's already been upgraded to a Category 1," he says, clearing the empty plates from our table. "If it doesn't turn, the island will shut down. Hotel is already talking about closing tomorrow."

Sebastian stiffens. "But we're staying here all weekend. Where're we supposed to go if that happens?"

"You can stay with us," Cam offers with a warm smile. "We have plenty of room."

"Hell yeah!" Blake rubs her hands together, her face lighting up with excitement. "We'll have ourselves a little hurricane party."

As our waiter leaves again to attend to his other tables, Sebastian turns to Nia with an impatient look on his face. "Is Ty on his way or what?" he asks, drumming his fingers on the table. "We're supposed to go surfing."

"Isn't he upstairs with you?" Nia asks.

"Nope." Sebastian shakes his head. "We thought he was at your place."

Nia fidgets in her chair, an anxious expression across her face. "We got in a fight last night. He hasn't been answering any of my texts."

"But didn't he go to your house?" Jonathan's brow lifts in surprise. "I thought I saw him leave Beach Club with Val."

There's a long, terrible pause.

"You saw him leave with *who?*" Nia's eyes blaze.

"Shit, Jon." Mason groans. "Way to go."

Jonathan realizes his mistake a little too late and tries to backpedal, but no one believes him when he says he was probably just confused. I wish my earlier suspicions about Val and Tyler had been wrong. This is sure going to put a damper on the rest of our trip.

Not that I'm surprised. Val works fast when she wants something, and I doubt Tyler put up much of a fight. Tyler's man-whore reputation is well known around school. Even if he is with Nia now, it's hard to pass up a night with Valentina Ramirez when she sets her sights on you. I just wish they hadn't decided to screw around during our summer vacation.

Tyler should've worked harder to keep it in his pants, and selfish Val should know better, too. It's not about sex. I couldn't care less how many guys Val hooks up with. Women should be free to do whatever they want with their bodies, but messing around with your friend's boyfriend isn't cool. This might be the last time we're all going to be together like this, and those two idiots are ruining it for everyone.

"That's it! I'm going to kill her!" Nia stands and shoves her chair into the table so hard our glasses and plates shake.

"Calm down, okay?" Cam rushes over to Nia's side of the table. "Take a breath," she says, gently attempting to push Nia back down into her seat. "Let's be reasonable."

"You're absolutely right," Nia says. "I'm going to kill *him* first. He's the cheating bastard." Her nostrils flare as an angry blush of red spreads across her cheeks. "Then I'll kill her."

"To be fair, we don't know that anything—"

"Don't you dare." Nia whips around and glares at Sebastian. "Do not cover for that asshole."

"I'm not." Sebastian holds his hands up. "I just don't think we should make assumptions until we know for sure what's going on."

"If Ty and Val went home together, it wasn't to play patty cake," I say.

I know Sebastian is only trying to protect his friend, which is a loyal and honorable thing to do, but he can't really think this behavior is acceptable. Guys shouldn't ghost the girls they kiss—like how Sebastian did to me—and they definitely shouldn't cheat on their girlfriends.

Across from me, Nia sucks in air. She blinks away angry tears, and I feel like a jerk. I can't imagine being in Nia's position, finding out in front of everyone that your shitty boyfriend is running around on you with one of your best friends.

"Er—sorry," I say.

"Why are you apologizing?" she asks. "You didn't screw my boyfriend too, did you?"

"C'mon, you can't blame the guy, can you?" Mason asks, taking in another long, drawn-out puff from his vape pen. "No one with a dick would turn down Valentina Ramirez."

Nia whips around, baring her blinding white teeth in his direction. "You wanna be my third victim?"

"Hey, why're you getting mad at me?" He grins. "I'd screw you, too."

Blake takes a slow sip of her spiked drink and stretches her toned arms overhead, staring up to bask in the warm rays. She sighs blissfully. "Can you all fight about this later?" she asks. "I'm trying to enjoy the sun while it lasts."

"You're joking, right?" Nia asks. "You don't really expect me to sit here and—what—*tan?*—while Val is off banging my boyfriend?"

Blake shrugs, unbothered, and reaches for more tortilla chips. "I mean, it *is* turning out to be a magnificent day. And if they did bang, the damage has already been done. They can't exactly unbang, now can they?" She dips another chip into the guacamole and salsa bowls, saturating it with big fat dollops of each topping. "Besides, this might be our last good beach day," she adds, happily munching away. "And I, for one, am not letting Val ruin it."

"You know what? Screw all of you." Nia huffs and throws her Dior canvas tote over one shoulder. "You can all choke on your damn guac and chips, for all I care!"

The guys all shift in their seats, looking uncomfortable, as Nia stomps away and heads up the stairs to the hotel lobby.

"Damn… I would not want to be Ty right now," Mason says, snickering.

I look around the table, unsure what to do. "Should I go after her?"

"No—let her go." Blake smiles over at me, lazily. "Stay here. You need a tan, trust me."

It's not that I want to leave the hotel. I'd much rather hang by the pool with everyone and tan all day, too. I don't want to go chasing after Nia, but she's our friend and she's upset. I know I'd want someone to go check on me if things were reversed. Plus, I feel bad about the stupid comment I made.

I wave the waiter over and gather up my things, while Cam signs the bill to pay for our lunch. As Cam and I get up to leave, I glance back at Blake one more time with a meaningful look. She rolls her eyes and jumps up from her chair, throwing her towel and tanning oil into her backpack.

"Ugh, fine! I'm coming. Because this is exactly how I want to spend my summer vacation—dealing with Val and her shit," she says, her voice thick with sarcasm.

"Good luck." Mason starts to laugh. "You're gonna need it."

"I don't know what you're giggling about," Sebastian says, scooting his chair out from under the table. "We're going with them."

"Wait—what?" Mason sputters, looking crestfallen. "I thought we were gonna surf?"

"Seb's right," Jonathan says. "If something happened, Ty's gonna need our help dealing with *her*." He jabs a finger in the direction where Nia ran off to.

On the way out of the restaurant, I grab the hurricane flyer off the table and drop it into the bottom of my beach bag. I make a mental note to take a better look and read all the details later today. It's going to have to wait until after I deal with the current mess. Right now, I have my hands full.

One storm at a time.

CHAPTER 6

By the time we get Cam's Range Rover from the Seasider Inn valet and drive back to our rental house, Nia is already upstairs and having a total meltdown. She's still in her string bikini, banging on Val's bedroom door with one hand. In the other hand, she grips her cell phone to her chest. I can hear Tyler's voicemail answering message echoing over and over on the speaker.

"I know you're in there!" Nia yells at the locked door of the master bedroom. "Tyler Andrew Singh—you better open up this damn door!"

"Hey, take it easy," Sebastian says, putting his hands on her slender shoulders and pulling her away from the bedroom. He coaxes her down to the floor and takes a seat next to her.

Next to me, Cam sets off the *Find My iPhone* alert on Val's phone. The high-pitched alarm sounds from inside the locked bedroom. Nia's eyes dart back to the bedroom door, and she dials her boyfriend again, punching numbers angrily into her phone.

"How can he do this to me?" she asks, sniffling. "Doesn't he know I'm almost at 100,000 followers? I can get any guy I want!"

"Val?" I sidestep past Nia and Sebastian and reach for the door handle. "C'mon. Let us in," I say, turning the knob back and forth. It doesn't budge, even after I give it a few hard knocks and a kick for good measure.

What a bunch of jerks. I can't believe they're ignoring all of us when we're here right outside the bedroom.

Nia cries louder and rips my beach towel from my hands, blowing snot into it and then discarding it on the ground. Unsure of what else to do, I sit down next to her and pat at her back. I feel bad for her, sure, but what did she expect? This is Tyler Singh. He's always been like this, even when he was with Val. He's good looking, yeah, but a total player.

Besides, it's not like they were going to keep dating in college. She's moving to Los Angeles to become a full-time Instagram influencer, and Tyler's going to Florida Southern to play Division II basketball. Her reaction is a bit over the top for a guy she's only been dating two weeks—but that's typical of Nia. She loves attention.

Blake traipses up the stairs, her arms full of longneck bottles of beer from the fridge. She goes to hand them out, but everyone except Mason refuses. We're all too annoyed to drink. The two of them sink to the floor together and clink their bottles, cheering each other.

"Does anyone else think this is a little weird?" Jonathan asks, his eyes narrowing as he stares at the bedroom door. "This doesn't seem like Ty. I can see him ignoring Nia—no offense," he says, giving her an apologetic look, "but I don't think he'd ghost the rest of us."

"Yeah, well, it's not like we're dealing with the most considerate people in the world," I say.

"Maybe we should go downstairs and watch TV or something while we wait?" Cam asks. "They've gotta come out sometime, right?"

"Not necessarily..." Jonathan's voice trails off, and he gives the bedroom door another suspicious sidelong glance.

"What do you mean?" Cam asks.

"Well, not if they're dead."

"Dead?" I repeat, a fluttering of unease in my chest. Why

does Jonathan always say the weirdest shit? "Why would you say that?"

"I'm just stating one obvious reason why they wouldn't come out of the bedroom," he says. "I mean, I don't think they *are* dead. I'm saying they don't have to come out if they are."

Mason snorts into his beer. "No one is dead, you doofus," he says and swipes one of the true crime books from the front pocket of Jonathan's backpack. He shakes it in front of Jonathan's face. "I told you. This crap rots your brain."

Sebastian walks over to the bedroom door and peers at it. He studies the keyhole above the doorknob, as if trying to figure something out in his head. "Do you guys have a master key?" he asks, looking back at us.

"We only got a key to the front door," Cam says.

"Well, did you try to use it to open this door?" he asks. "Maybe it works for both?"

Cam pulls out the key from her khaki-colored chino shorts and hands it to Sebastian who slides it into the doorknob. It opens right away. Nia pushes me aside and jumps up from the floor, charging for the door. The others follow behind her, but I hang back in the doorway and scan the room from there.

There are piles of Val's fancy designer clothes strewn all over the bedroom floor and on the huge canopy bed. Most of them still have the tags on. Enough makeup to fill an entire Sephora store has been dumped onto the white carpet on the other side of the room where Val propped up a travel-sized lighted mirror to create a makeshift vanity area. Her curling iron is still plugged into the outlet nearby. Her cell phone sits next to the iron, still in the charger. It all looks pretty normal, except no sign of Val or Tyler.

Nia bends down to check underneath the bed and lifts the covers as if Tyler and Val might be hiding under them. She's no longer crying, but she doesn't seem happy about the situation either. We all know just because Val and Tyler aren't in here doesn't mean they aren't together somewhere else.

"I don't get it," she says, shaking her head. "Where are they?"

I turn to Jonathan. "Are you sure you saw them leave together last night?"

"Positive."

"This doesn't make sense," Cam says, strolling over to Val's cell phone on the ground. She picks it up off the charger. "Why would she leave her cell phone?"

"And you're absolutely certain they didn't come back to your hotel room?" I ask the guys, raising a brow. I don't want to outright accuse them of lying, but it's the most logical explanation. "Because if you're covering for Ty, now's the time to come clean."

Jonathan hesitates. "I mean, I'm not a hundred percent," he says. "But I think I would've seen them come in. I slept on the couch."

"I don't know why everyone keeps assuming they're together," Sebastian says, folding his arms over his chest. "Maybe they both hooked up with different people, and that's where they are?"

Somehow, he says this with a straight face even though it's beyond obvious Val and Tyler ran off together. I have to admire his loyalty in continuing to stick up for his slimeball friend.

"I don't like this," Cam says, clutching her sister's phone to her chest. "I'm worried about her."

"Oh come on, this is Val we're talking about. She's always disappearing like this." Blake pops the cap off her second beer and starts chugging.

"Blake's got a point," I say. "Remember Miami?"

Last winter break, the Ramirez family invited the five of us to Miami Beach for the weekend. We flew on their parent's private jet and stayed for free on the family yacht, *The Pich-*

incha, named after the northern Ecuadorian region where the twins' grandparents were born. On New Year's Eve, we went to their aunt's party on Star Island. Val never made it back to the yacht.

The twins' parents were so trashed they didn't even notice. Cam and I found her the next day at some nightclub all the way up in Ft. Lauderdale, forty minutes away, after tracking her cell phone. She'd befriended one of the club promoters she met at her aunt's house and stayed up all night, partying with him all over South Florida.

"And don't forget spring break," Blake says.

"Yeah, that's right." I nod along, thinking about the trip to Cabo that Nia's mom took us on a few months ago with her new boyfriend. "Val shacked up with that guy with the sailboat all week. We barely saw her."

"But what if something's wrong this time?" Cam asks softly. She gives me an imploring look. "You did say someone sketchy was on the patio—"

"She's fine," I say and walk over, giving Cam a half hug. She seems so worried, I almost regret making such a big deal earlier about the lurker in the yellow raincoat. It probably was just a neighbor. I'm sure it has nothing to do with Val and Tyler.

"Let's not waste any more of a perfectly good afternoon, okay?" Blake asks and sits down at Val's makeup area. She bends over to pick up one of Val's fancy powder compacts and dusts her freckled button nose in the lighted mirror. "We all know Val will turn up when she wants to and not a second sooner."

"Besides, nothing bad ever happens on Palm Key. This place is safer than Disneyland," Sebastian says.

"Although for the record, bad things do happen in Disneyland," Jonathan says.

"Jon—" Sebastian warns.

"What?" Jonathan asks. "It's true. People die there all the

time. They keep it secret. I heard about it on a podcast. The park removes people from the premises before the local authorities can declare them dead, so hundreds of people have actually died there and—"

"That's it." Cam shoves her sister's cell phone into the back pocket of her shorts and heads for the door. "I'm going to the police."

Mason turns to Jonathan with a little smirk. "Nice job."

"This is so stupid," Blake mumbles. "There's no need to freak out. It hasn't even been a day."

Even if I agree with Blake, if it will make Cam feel better, there's no harm in going to the station with her. Besides, I'm sure the police will tell Cam the same thing we've already said to her. That she doesn't need to worry about her sister and this island is safe. That Val will turn up sooner or later—most likely with a new boyfriend in tow.

We all follow Cam down the stairs. She looks all spun up as she grabs her car keys off the side table in the entranceway, and marches toward the front door. Sebastian reaches for my arm.

"Do you want us to go with you?" he asks me.

"Awww man. Do we have to?" Mason asks in a whiny voice. "Can't we go to the bar and wait there? We can get a drink and some ass." His lips curl into a pervy leer. "Just like Ty's doing right now."

Sebastian elbows Mason in the ribs.

"Knock it off," he says and turns back to give me an apologetic look. "Sorry."

"That's okay." I smile. "Don't worry about us. Go have fun."

He almost looks disappointed, though I'm not sure why. Going to the police station is not the way anyone in their right mind would want to spend their vacation. If I could go to the bar with them instead, I would, but Cam needs me. I'm not going to make her go to the police alone.

Nia peels off and heads to her bedroom downstairs, claiming she needs to post videos and wants to take a lavender detox bath to clear away the "negative energy." I don't blame her for wanting to be alone. Even if Val isn't off somewhere with Tyler and is hopefully with a different guy, Nia's boyfriend is still missing and ignoring her. Chances are, that's not a good thing during a party weekend like this. Not for a guy like Tyler with a reputation.

It's not until I buckle up in the passenger seat of Cam's SUV and we drive away, that I remember the hurricane flyer from lunch.

Shit.

I'd planned to read through it and discuss it with the guys before they left, but I forgot with all the other drama going on. I reach into my beach bag and confirm the crumpled paper is still there. As soon as we figure out this whole Val and Tyler situation, I'll deal with that crisis next. If we're lucky, the storm will already be turning around by then and ruining someone else's Fourth of July.

As we head into the center of town, I'm surprised to see how empty the two-lane road is. Just yesterday, it was jampacked with cars driving bumper-to-bumper. It took us forever to get downtown last night even though it was only a few miles from our rental house. It's crazy to think people have already started leaving town when this storm is still miles offshore with plenty of time to turn around.

My eyes widen as we pass by buildings already covered with metal storm shutters or plywood. "Closed" signs hang from their doors. Further down the road, the marina is almost empty. The few people that are there are bustling about and securing their boats. Ropes are wrapped with protective covers. Windows, doors, and hatches sealed off.

I can't believe what I'm seeing. Surely, this is all a tad premature?

Finally, we get to Main Street right around dusk and park.

The island, one of the southernmost spots in the U.S., is famous for its magical sunsets. Most weekends, throngs of people crowd the sidewalks to claim a spot to watch the sky transform into a gorgeous blend of orange, yellows, and pinks. Today, it's just us and a handful of tourists. The sun is hidden away by thick dark clouds crowding the horizon. Drops of rain fall from the sky and dampen my hair, frizzing it, as we walk to the police station. I wish we had thought to bring along umbrellas.

It's strange to see downtown so quiet on a Friday evening. Last night, the streets had been filled with people flitting in and out of dive bars and shops selling souvenir T-shirts with slogans like *"Florida, Where You Never Have to Shovel Sunshine"* and personalized Florida state keychains. Val had pissed off one of the local owners, too, laughing and making fun of the hand-made jewelry in the window. According to Val, if it wasn't Cartier or Tiffany, it wasn't worth wearing.

When we arrive at the police station moments later, we march straight up to the front desk. The uniformed officer on duty behind the counter plexiglass stands and greets us. When his gorgeous eyes meet mine, I'm not sure who is more shocked.

"Riley?" he asks, his lips curving into a surprised but pleased smile. Blazoned across his well-muscled chest is a name tag that reads: *Officer Grant Topper.*

CHAPTER 7

I approach the plexiglass of the police station counter, my stomach fluttering something fierce. Even under the harsh fluorescent lighting, Grant is as good looking as I remember from the bar last night, especially in his uniform.

"Grant! What are you doing here?" I ask.

He points to the badge on his chest and laughs. "I sort of work here."

Duh.

"Oh, right." I blush. "It's just… I didn't know you were a cop. You look kind of young."

He doesn't look old enough to be the only police officer manning the desk. Maybe the rest of them—the more experienced ones—are out on active duty?

I take another look around the station. Besides Grant, the place is almost empty. The only other officer I see is a woman so old she could be his grandmother. She sits behind him, way in the back and far from the intake window, pecking away at a desktop computer.

"Yeah, I get that a lot," he says good-naturedly. "I'm twenty-three. Just got out of the Academy."

"Hey!" Blake snaps her fingers, recognizing him then. "You're that hot guy from last night."

"Guilty as charged," he says with an easy nod before turning back to me. "So, what can I help you ladies with?"

"Oh, I'm sure we can think of a few things, eh, *Officer.*"

Blake lets out a flirty giggle and jabs me in the ribcage. "Isn't that right, Ri Ri?"

"Knock it off. This is serious," Cam says. She steps in front of Blake and pushes us out of the way. "It's my sister, Officer Topper. She's missing."

Grant's friendly smile disappears. He straightens in his chair on the other side of the glass and pulls out an iPad. His fingers hover over the keypad, ready to take notes. He's all business now. "Start at the beginning," he says. "Who's missing?"

"My sister," Cam repeats. "Her name is Valentina Lorraine Ramirez."

"And our friend Tyler Singh," I say.

"Oh." His face relaxes as he takes his notes. "So they're together?"

"Yeah, you could say that," Blake says and snickers to herself.

Cam frowns at her. "We don't know that."

"Uh yeah, we sorta do," Blake says.

Grant looks back and forth between Blake and Cam as if he's unsure who he's supposed to listen to. He jots down a few more notes on the iPad and then clears his throat, continuing on with his questions. "And how old are they? Valentina and Tyler?" he asks.

"Eighteen," Cam says.

He glances up and stops typing. "So they're both of legal age?"

Cam nods.

"And when's the last time you saw them? Place and time would be helpful."

"Last night at the Beach Club," Cam says. "I remember seeing Val there at least until around eleven. She was on the dance floor. Tyler was with her, or maybe he was with Nia, I'm not sure." Her brow scrunches up. "They were definitely together at some point, though. Maybe around midnight? That's when I got tired and wanted to leave. I went to look for Val, but she was—" Cam stops. She stares at Grant, her eyes narrowing. "Hey—why aren't you taking all of this down? You stopped taking notes."

"I think I've got everything I need," he says.

"Alright, so then what are you going to do?" she asks. "Does a patrol team go out and find her? Do you send out an APB? An Amber Alert?"

His lips twitch. "You realize July Fourth weekend is our busiest time of the year, right? We've got thousands of people from all over the country here, partying it up, passing out everywhere. Last night alone, we had three stomach pumps at the Urgent Care," he says. "Your friends are adults. They haven't even been missing for twenty-four hours. Has it occurred to you they're probably just hung over and sleeping it off somewhere?"

"Told you," Blake says to Cam with a knowing look. "Now can we please go back to partying and stop wasting this nice officer's time?"

"But she left her phone at home, Officer Topper." Cam holds out Val's cell phone and presses it against the glass so Grant can see the screen. "And Ty isn't answering his phone, either. It just keeps ringing."

"In fairness, Val forgets her phone a lot," I say to Grant with a little shrug.

Cam gives me a look like I've committed the ultimate betrayal, even though all I did was tell the truth.

I mouth back "sorry" even though I'm not. I think it's important to share all the facts with the police. Grant should know it's not all that unusual that Val doesn't have her cell phone on her. It doesn't mean something bad has happened.

"Has Valentina ever done this before?" Grant asks. "Does she go off with guys without telling you?"

Blake snorts. "Only every trip we've ever gone on."

Now it's Blake's turn to be rewarded with Cam's nasty looks.

"I don't know why that matters," Cam says, turning back to Grant. "If you're implying that just because my sister likes to have a little fun, we shouldn't take this seriously—"

"Whoa. Slow down." Grant holds his hands up, his eyes widening. "It's nothing like that. I'm just trying to ascertain all the facts. Habits of the missing person in question are important, like if they often disappear—for whatever reasons," he says. "Does your sister have any life-threatening medical conditions?"

"Only that she can be a real pain in the ass," Blake whispers this time, so only I can hear her. I bite my lip, trying hard not to laugh. I don't want to piss Cam off more.

"No, nothing like that," Cam says.

"And have you told your parents she's missing?" Grant asks.

Cam's soft brown eyes go big. "No—why? Do I need to?"

Her fingers fly to her necklace, and she twists around the string of oversized pink pearls. The twins' parents are on one of their jet-set, high luxury vacation trips. If Cam can even get hold of them in Barcelona, which could be a problem, her mom will be furious to hear about Val's disappearance. She'll blame Cam, like usual, for failing to keep track of her irresponsible twin.

"I don't need parental consent if they're eighteen, but your parents will most likely find out if I file a missing person's report." He leans in closer, his pretty gray eyes narrowing as he studies Cam. "But if you're really worried, why wouldn't you tell them?" He pauses. "Are you sure you're telling me everything? If drugs or something illegal are involved here, I need to know right now."

Cam gasps. "Oh, no. It's nothing like that, Officer. It's just that they're out of the country. I don't want to bother them if

Val's, like, partied too hard and passed out somewhere," she says. "So should we file something or not?"

Grant nods his understanding and closes his iPad. He pushes it away and leans back into his leather seat, folding and unfolding his hands a few times before steepling them under his chin. His dark brow wrinkles with concentration.

"Okay, here's the deal," he says. "Technically, we can file a missing person's report any time, and if you want the station's help, you'll have to make a formal report. We aren't supposed to expend police resources without one." He leans in closer to the plexiglass. "But I gotta tell you, it's hard to get much attention when the missing person isn't under eighteen, or elderly, or some other life-threatening issue. We're a small force, and we're almost always understaffed—especially now during a holiday weekend and with this hurricane on the way." He gestures around the empty station. "As you can see, it's pretty bare bones."

"It sounds like we should wait then?" I catch Cam's eye. "No reason to panic your parents when there's not much good it'll do."

"Totally," Blake says, nodding along. "I'm sure those two idiots are together somewhere having the time of their lives. They probably drank too much, and now they're scared to deal with the consequences. Ty knows Nia's gonna kill him."

Cam sucks in a deep breath, as if considering all this. She looks back over at Grant, her face filled with uncertainty. She doesn't appear convinced.

"Are you sure we shouldn't do anything?" she asks.

He straightens in his seat. "Listen, if you're really worried something bad has happened to your sister, like, if you saw her with a suspicious person or you think she might've been drugged, then we should file a report right away. The first few hours can be critical," he says. "But if this is typical behavior for her, I'd try to find her on your own first. Go check out whatever bars are still open. Go by the beaches. Pool parties. My guess is they turn up in one of those places."

"Yeah, okay," Cam says, nodding. Her face starts to relax. "That's a good idea."

"I'm sure your friends are fine," he says with a big, comforting smile. "But if you can't find them, come back here and we'll file that report."

"Thanks, Officer. We'll do that," she says.

Grant picks up his iPad again. "Most everything is already shutting down because of the storm. That's a good thing. It'll help flush them out for you," he says and types a few last notes on the matter. "But you can always call the station, okay? I'm happy to help with anything you need." He looks up and gives us a little wink. "That's what I'm here for."

"You got it," Blake says, batting her lashes at him. "We'll keep you in mind for all of our *needs*, Officer." She elbows me in the ribs again. "Right, Riley?"

I groan and turn red.

That Blake. She's incorrigible.

As soon as we're out of the police station and walking back to our car, Blake fans at her face and pretends to swoon. "Damn. What a hottie," she says. "And he couldn't take his pretty little eyes off you, Ri Ri."

"You mean the cop?" Cam frowns. "He's way too old for her."

"*Old?*" Blake stops in her tracks. "It's a couple years. That's nothing. Remember that cute banker from South Beach that I hooked up with on New Year's? He was turning thirty."

"But this guy is a police officer. He's an authority figure," Cam says. "It's totally different."

Blake's mouth curves into an impish grin. "Yeah, makes it even sexier."

I laugh at her. "You're shameless."

Back inside Cam's SUV, we agree to hit the Beach Club first. The plan is to ask around and see if anyone saw something last night. Blake texts her new crush, Roxy the bartender, who tells us to come by. It sounds like the bar will only be open a few more hours. Even though it's Friday night, her boss plans to close early because of the hurricane.

When we arrive ten minutes later, the place is busier than expected. Unlike the empty streets downtown and the deserted roads earlier, it doesn't seem like the threat of an impending storm has affected the party-hard crowd yet. We have to wade through packs of people, chugging drinks in colorful hurricane bowls and yardsticks, getting in one last big bender before the storm.

It takes a bit, but we eventually find the manager at the back of the club. He's a nice guy who answers all our questions, but he doesn't remember anything helpful. Neither do the bouncers or the door guy that he introduces us to.

Just when it seems like our trip to Beach Club was a total waste of time, we get some good news—well, sort of—from Nia in the group chat. It turns out she's finally heard from Tyler. He texted her that his cell phone battery had died overnight. He wanted her to know he was sorry, but he was with Val now. They'd gotten back together and were hanging out on the island at one of the hotels, waiting for things to blow over.

"What a scumbag," Blake says as Cam and I let out sighs of relief.

"I'm just glad they're okay," Cam says.

I grin. "Well, at least until Nia gets her hands on them."

"I told you it'd be fine, didn't I?" Blake says. "Now, can we enjoy ourselves? So far, all we've done is chase after stupid Val. I'm so over it. This was supposed to be a fun weekend to get away from, well, you know…" She swallows hard and looks down, but not before I can see the sadness fill her eyes. I can tell she's thinking about their friend Jordyn.

"You're not the only one who misses her, you know," Cam says. "Jordyn was my friend, too."

Blake's head jerks up. "Well, you sure don't act like it. You never talk about her."

I'm taken aback by the fury searing in Blake's eyes. Blake rarely loses her cool.

"That's because talking about our dead best friend is a major downer," Cam snaps.

Blake opens her mouth to say something back to Cam but then abruptly closes it. The emotion melts right off her face, her sudden flash of anger gone as fast as it came on.

"Fine, whatever. Let's do shots." She shoots us one of her typical happy-go-lucky smiles, party-girl Blake returning just as her crush, Roxy, shows up to hook us up with a prime table in the center of the action. Roxy gives us a stack of *Over 21* arm bands and a round of beers and purple hooter shots "on the house." As a thank you, Blake gives the pretty bartender a slow, passionate kiss.

Right as I'm about to take my shot, I get that creepy feeling again from last night when I was waiting for my Uber outside the club. It's almost as if I can physically sense someone watching me. I turn sharply, my eyes searching the club, expecting to see someone looking at me. A few drunk guys in the corner are staring at our table, checking us out, but that's not it. This feels way different from guys on the prowl and hoping to score. I keep scanning the room until...

There!

A dark figure slinks into the corner, right near the bathroom, catching my eye. He's dressed in an oversized yellow raincoat with the hood up, and he's staring right at me. I blink a few times in the dimly lit club to clear my vision, but it's too dark and I'm too far away to see a face.

My stomach lurches as I remember the intruder from last night. Could it be the same person from the patio? Did he follow me here?

"Riley!" Blake's hand is on my shoulder. She waves the

purple hooter in my face. "What're you doing? Take your shot already."

"Don't you see him?" I point toward the bathroom with a shaky hand. "He's there—staring at me. The guy from the patio."

Cam turns around in her seat. "Where?" she asks, craning her neck. "I don't see anyone?"

"He's right there! By the bathroom!"

Blake gives me a strange look. "Uh, there's no one there, babe."

I blink. The hallway is empty now.

I don't understand. Where did he go?

"What did you see?" Cam stands up and glances around the club, still searching. "What did he look like?"

"I don't know," I say. "I couldn't see his face, but he was in that yellow slicker again. It was definitely him."

Blake groans. "It's hurricane season. In Florida. Look around, Riley," she says and gestures around the crowded club and dance floor. "There must be dozens of people out in rain-coats tonight."

"Yeah, but—"

The words catch in my throat as the man in the raincoat reappears. He's now just a few feet from our table. My pulse thumps in my chest as he takes another step closer. And then another. He's coming right for us!

His hand reaches into his jacket pocket. I open my mouth to scream for help, certain he's about to pull out a gun, or a knife, or some other deadly weapon and then—

"Jonny?" Blake starts to smile. "What took you so long?"

It takes a moment for the cold, paralyzing fear to clear and for reality to take over and catch up to my racing heart. I can't believe how badly my imagination ran away with this one. There's no psycho killer in the club about to murder us at our table. It's just Jonathan dressed in a stupid, oversized yellow raincoat. He's the guy in the bathroom hallway who was watching me moments ago.

"What're you doing here?" I ask, annoyed at him even though it's not his fault I freaked out. I feel like a total idiot.

"I invited him, duh," Blake says, standing up to give him a hug and passing out more shots.

Jonathan takes the seat next to me and pulls off his damp yellow raincoat, hanging it across the back of his chair. He gives me a shy little smile and hands me a book from inside the pocket of his coat. It wasn't a weapon he was reaching for after all; it's a copy of *Silence of the Lambs* he picked up for me today at the local island bookstore.

Great.

Now I really feel stupid.

Blake lifts her beer high in the air toward us. "Now that we're all here," she says, "it's time to finally have some fun!"

CHAPTER 8

DAY 3: Saturday—One day before July Fourth

The sound of waves crashing against the shore with a deafening roar wakes me early the next morning. I sit up in bed, wiping the sleep from my eyes, and turn to look outside the bedroom windows. The rain is coming down in buckets now, leaving mean, angry streaks against the glass. Heavy clouds loom overhead and have turned the sky a shade of gray so deep and dark it's almost black. All along the beach, a furious wind whips up the sand. The side yard below me is already flooding.

My stomach sinks as I pull the comforter up to my chest and shiver at the sight. It appears the storm has not turned around like we'd all hoped. In fact, it seems to be getting worse.

The front doorbell begins to ring shrilly downstairs. I wince, putting a hand to my ears and letting out a loud grown. Damn Blake and all the shots she made me take last night. My head pounds like an entire drum line is playing inside it.

I grab a bottle of water from the nightstand and pound it, trying to quench my dry mouth. My cell phone shows it's only eight a.m., but already I have a bunch of missed texts from Jonathan.

Morning Riley. U up?
Hotel closing. Says we gotta leave NOW!
We're coming over!!!

And then there's a text from Mason in the group chat: *Hurricane Party starts now, BITCHES.*

Little pieces of the night start flooding back. I vaguely remember Blake telling Jonathan that the boys should come over today to the rental house if the storm got worse. Sometime in the night we texted with our anxious parents, promising to leave the island in the morning to get them off our backs. We were so drunk, we weren't worried about it ourselves, though. Then I recall dancing like crazy on the dance floor and on top of tables until the owner kicked us out at midnight to put up plywood on the club's windows.

The boys begin to pound on the front door. I put a pillow over my head and wait for Blake or Nia to answer the door since they're in the downstairs bedrooms, but the knocking just continues, getting even louder.

Next to my head, my cell phone chirps. It's another text from Jonathan:

Wendy, I'm home… Let us in!

He follows the message with an axe emoji and a row of blood spurts. I have no idea who "Wendy" is but, knowing Jonathan, I'm guessing it's another stupid horror movie reference.

With a reluctant groan, I pull the sheets off my body and stumble out of my warm, cozy bed. I shake Cam awake first before heading into the bathroom to make myself look halfway presentable. Let the guys knock. They can wait a few more minutes. No chance I'm letting Sebastian see me with bed-head and smeared makeup from last night because I was too wasted to wash my face.

After a quick triage session in the bathroom, I throw on my favorite cornflower blue Columbia University hoodie over my pajamas and jog downstairs. I let out a little gasp when I open the front door. Our driveway is so flooded it's turned into a shallow lake. The pavement is covered in at least a foot of murky water in some places, with debris and twigs floating along the surface. Rain makes loud plopping sounds as it falls from the sky and hits the standing water.

On our doorstep, Sebastian stands next to Jonathan and Mason. The three of them huddle together, shivering, under the house's covered front awning. Their beach clothes and flip-flops are soaked through from the rain and wet luggage is at their feet. Behind them, Sebastian's shiny black Mercedes sports car sits parked in the drive. The tires are already partially submerged.

"Took you long enough." Sebastian's eyes crinkle adorably as he greets me with a smile.

"Sorry. You woke me up," I say and step aside to let them in.

The three of them head for the kitchen. Sebastian's mouth twitches playfully as he goes by and shakes out his spiky hair in my direction, trying to get me wet. I laugh and dodge the droplets as they smatter across the wood floor instead.

"I'll get you guys some towels," I say.

"That'd be great," Jonathan says and wipes the rain from his face with the bottom of his *Murderinos Do It Best* tee, revealing seriously toned, though sunburned, abs.

I will say this for the guy—he may be a weirdo, but he's not hard on the eyes.

The linen closet down the hall is packed with brand new fluffy white towels, price tags still attached to the corners. I reach inside and grab a few, bringing them back to the guys.

"What happened at the hotel?" I ask and pass towels out.

"Mandatory evacuation," Jonathan says. "Police came by this morning. They're making all the hotel guests leave."

"Total shit show," Mason grumbles, helping himself to one of Blake's energy drinks in the fridge, without even asking.

"We can still crash with you though, right? Like you said last night?" Jonathan looks at me hopefully. "Until we figure out what to do?"

I sneak a little glance at Sebastian's handsome face as he

towels off his body. A thrill of excitement rushes through me at the thought of him staying here in the same house as me. What if they have to stay the night? Will he ask to sleep in my room?

"Yeah, sure," I say and shrug coolly, as if I couldn't care less. "I guess that'd be fine."

My head won't stop throbbing, so I walk over to the coffee maker and fill the carafe with cold water. I smile as I open the cabinet above my head and spot Cam's expensive coffee. Thank goodness she brought it with her. The beans make the most delicious coffee. Her mom imports the stuff from South America to make "cafezinho," a traditional coffee drink made with sugar—or "rapadura" as Mrs. Ramirez calls it.

I grind the beans and drop them into the coffee maker. Almost instantly, a heavenly smell fills the kitchen. My stomach rumbles with anticipation.

"Can't you make that any faster?" Mason yells. "I'm dying over here."

I try not to roll my eyes. Heaven forbid Mason has to wait more than five seconds for anything.

"Good morning, everybody," Cam calls out, bouncing down the stairs with a big smile.

Seeing her makes me self-conscious about my own appearance. Her sleek bob is swept back with a sparkly new headband, and she's wearing a preppy, pleated white tennis dress that I know is designer. It hugs her curves perfectly. True, she had a lot longer to get ready than I did, but I can't help but feel envious of how put together she looks.

"Wait—where's Val and Ty?" she asks, pausing in the kitchen doorway. She turns to the guys. "Aren't they with you?"

"I texted Ty to meet us here," Sebastian says. "I'm sure they're on the way."

Cam takes a seat at the island between Sebastian and Jonathan. I grab a few mugs from the kitchen cabinet and begin pouring the coffee for everyone. Naturally, Mason snatches his cup first before anyone else can get to theirs.

"I bet they're halfway back to Bishop Lake by now," he says.

"What do you mean?" Cam asks.

Mason snickers. "Just that I really don't see them joining our little party after how they screwed over Nia."

"Oh yeah?" Jonathan asks, lifting a brow. "In what car? Seb drove us here."

"It's called Uber, duh," Mason says.

"You think they Ubered all the way *back to Orlando*?" I ask, trying to calculate in my head what that would even cost. An entire month's salary working at the Mouse Trap, for sure. Maybe more. "Isn't that, uh, expensive?"

"Nah." Mason shrugs. "Just a few hundo?"

No one else bats an eye at his nonchalant answer while I struggle to control my face. It's insane how much money everyone else around me has. Sometimes I forget that paying hundreds of dollars for things on a whim—like a last-minute car ride home—isn't an obstacle for any of them. Only me.

"Hm. I don't think ride shares are running in this weather," Jonathan says.

"Okay, so? What's your point?" Mason asks. "Then they flew home."

Jonathan picks up his cell phone and gazes at the screen, searching for something. "I don't think so. I thought I saw on Twitter that they already shut down the airport—"

"Will you two stop?" Sebastian asks, the corners of his mouth twisting with exasperation. "I already told you—Ty won't leave without me. We're waiting 'til he shows."

The downstairs bedroom door creaks open and Blake slinks out. Her hair could use a good brushing and her black eyeliner from last night is all smudged, but none of the guys are looking at her face. Her skimpy pink satin slip dress is paper thin and shows off her toned, muscular body to perfection. All my friends are in shape but none like Blake. The girl doesn't have an ounce of fat anywhere.

"What're you boys doing here so early? Can't get enough of us?" She gives the guys a sexy little grin.

"They got kicked out of their hotel," I explain.

"Oh, scandalous. What'd you do?" she asks in mock-shock, giggling. She flounces around the kitchen, making herself a fruit smoothie, not even bothering to cover up.

"Don't you want to maybe go put on a robe?" Cam asks her with a critical squint.

"Nope," Blake says.

"We didn't get kicked out. We were evacuated," Jonathan clarifies. "'Cause of the storm."

Blake's face drops. "Ah, well, that's not nearly as exciting."

"Refill!" Mason snaps his fingers and shoves his empty mug in my face like I'm his personal barista. "And more sugar this time, Hun. I like my coffee like I like my women—extra sweet," he adds with an obnoxious little wink.

I try not to vomit.

Oh Dear Lord. I think—*ugh*—Mason Larper is flirting with me.

"Get it yourself, man," Sebastian says, pushing the mug back at Mason and jabbing a finger over to the coffee maker. "She's not your servant."

I smile back gratefully at him.

"So we all hanging today or what?" Blake asks. "'Cause if so, I wanna invite Roxy over to hurricane party with us. She was cool last night, right?"

"She was great!" Jonathan grins.

"Yeah, super nice," I agree and nod along even though I don't remember a whole lot about Roxy. Heck, I don't remember much of anything after the third purple hooter shot Blake forced down my throat.

Cam shrugs. "She was alright, I guess."

"Awesome! I'm gonna go call her right now."

Blake skips back into her room with her fresh smoothie in hand, and I smile as her door slams shut. It's nice to see her this excited. I haven't seen Blake crush on anyone this hard in a while. Her conquests, while vast, are notoriously short-lived and mostly superficial.

Now that I think about it, I don't know that I've ever seen her date anyone—girl or guy—for longer than a few weeks. She's got an endless stream of suitors and hooks up often, but she never seems to let them get close. At the Homecoming Dance last fall, I watched her dump her date right in the middle of the dance floor, leaving the poor girl bawling her eyes out while Blake then proceeded to go home with someone else's date.

I once asked Cam about it. Blake and I get along pretty well, but she isn't into talking about feelings. Not with me, at least. Not with any of the girls, either, from what I can tell. According to Cam, Jordyn was the one Blake confided in.

Cam told me Blake's "relationship issues" stem from stuff with her parents. Apparently, they're too busy for Blake and her sister Blair, always juggling multiple million-dollar construction projects and traveling out of town. They're never home, and when they are, they're pretty much checked out. Having parents like that would suck.

We may be poor, but at least Mom is around, and I know how much she loves me. Even with Dad, as much as I hate what he did to our family, I know he cares. He's always sending me these heartfelt letters, asking me to come visit and doing everything he can to make amends.

After everyone finishes up their coffee in the kitchen, we split up for the rest of the morning. Cam grabs Nia from her bedroom and they head upstairs to get in a workout on Cam's pilates app before we lose power. Mason and Jonathan decide to take a nap on the living room couches since they had to wake up so early to check out. Mason grabs both the blankets and all the throw pillows to use while Jonathan yawns and uses his backpack to prop himself up.

That just leaves me and Sebastian.

"Wanna watch some TV?" He looks over at me and smiles, almost shyly.

My heart flutters.

Be cool, Riley. Don't act like a weirdo.

"Sure." I shrug while doing my best not to completely freak out. "Not much else to do in this weather anyway, right?"

He puts the news on as we sit down next to each other on the living room floor. The newscaster is a handsome older lady with blue hair and bright coral lipstick, wearing a top covered in palm trees. As she talks about the latest headlines, I sneak furtive little glances his way. He doesn't even notice. His eyes are glued to the TV.

I wonder if he's only hanging with me now because no one else is available. Is he just bored? Or does this mean he likes spending time with me, after all? Ever since that kiss graduation night, things have been so confusing. I can't tell what he's thinking anymore.

It wasn't always like this with us. Things used to be great.

I still remember our first real conversation, something more than a passing hello in the hallways at school. It was around Halloween last fall. The teacher paired us up as lab partners in our physics class. Sebastian suggested we meet at a local coffee house after his soccer practice to work on our assignment.

Before then, I only knew what Val and Cam had told me about Sebastian. Apparently, Val and Sebastian had been hot and heavy throughout most of ninth grade. Inseparable. They were the perfect couple, even being crowned the prince and princess of the homecoming dance until Sebastian dumped her. Val said he was the best guy she'd ever dated; Cam said he was nothing but trouble. Knowing how adored he was at

school by all the girls and the guys too, I expected Cam to be
correct. I was sure he'd be conceited and sort of a jerk. How
could he not?

Those first few moments at the coffee shop were stiff and
awkward. I didn't know how to act around a guy like him, and
as a result, I'm sure he thought I had a stick up my ass. Then
everything changed when the waiter—an elderly woman who
told us it was her first day on the job—accidentally gave me a
strawberry scone instead of the blueberry one I'd ordered.

I loathe strawberries. It turns out Sebastian hates them,
too. We bonded over how gross they are—the absolute worst
berry ever—even though everyone else in the world seems to
love them. But now I was stuck. I couldn't eat the scone, but I
didn't want the waitress to know she screwed up and feel bad
on her first day at work. She should've been somewhere
surrounded by adorable grandkids, not forced to work her
twilight years in some crappy coffee shop. I'll never forget
watching him smile that beautiful smile of his as he picked out
all the strawberry pieces in my scone so I didn't have to eat
them, but also so the waitress wouldn't get in trouble. After
that, I was a smitten kitten.

Even after our physics assignment was over, Sebastian
would go out of his way to hang out with me. In class. At
lunch. Even at parties. He would find all sorts of reasons to
spend time with me, like insisting on being my study partner
for all our midterm and final exams. Cam warned me not to
overthink it. She said it meant nothing other than Sebastian
thought I was smart and nonthreatening. Plus, Val would be
pissed if something happened between the two of us. Even if
they hadn't dated in years, he was off limits as the one guy
who had broken her heart.

I know Cam was just looking out for me. She didn't want
me to get hurt. But I couldn't stop myself from liking Sebastian. I had it bad. That's why I'd been so happy on graduation
night when he'd kissed me and told me he'd been crushing on

me all year, too. I still don't understand what happened afterward and why he ignored me in the days that followed. Maybe now that we're talking again, I can find out.

If I have the nerve to ask him, that is.

Sebastian turns the volume up as the blue-haired newscaster starts talking about the storm. My alarm grows as we listen to the latest report. Hurricane Helena is now a Category 2 hurricane with maximum sustained winds of up to one hundred and ten miles per hour. An animated video plays on the screen and demonstrates what a Category 2 hurricane is capable of. Storm surge. Extreme winds. Flash floods. Even tornadoes. The hurricane is predicted to make landfall early tomorrow morning. Scrolling along the bottom of the screen, in bold red font, is a warning. The Overwater Highway—the bridge that connects Palm Key Island to the rest of Florida and the only way out of town—will close at midnight. Anyone who doesn't leave by then will be trapped until after the storm passes.

A fist of anxiety curls deep inside my chest.

"Well, that doesn't sound great," I say. "Are we sure it's a good idea to stay here?"

"That's just how the news is," he says and flips to a soccer match. "They always like to make things sound worse than they are. Good for the ratings, you know?" He shrugs. "Besides, we can leave as soon as Ty and Val get here. We've got hours before they close the bridge."

I nod, relaxing. "Yeah, good point."

He sounds so confident about things, I already feel better.

"It's nice of you to stick around and wait for your friend," I say. "I bet you wish you were spending July Fourth anywhere but here." I glance toward the sliding glass doors and make a sad face at all the rain.

"It's not so bad. You're here." His gaze meets mine and my heart turns over in response, a dizzying current racing through me. "Besides, Ty's my best friend. I'm not condoning what he did, but he always has my back and I've got his. I'm not going to leave him stranded."

From the look on Sebastian's face, it's clear how much he cares about Tyler. It's nice to see how a real friendship is supposed to work. I know my own friends would never stick around and wait for me if I was the one who'd disappeared instead of Val. Take our first night here. My friends weren't even willing to leave the club early for me.

The truth of it is, other than Cam, I'm not sure how much my friends truly care about me. Oh, I know they like me just fine, but I'm not sure how much deeper it goes than that. I'm pretty enough to be seen with, and I'm easygoing, and I do whatever they ask me to. We go to all the best parties together and have a lot of fun, but I'm not blind to things. It's not as if I don't realize that, most of the time, my friends use me as an accessory or a prop. I'm someone to do things with or someone to do things for them.

I'd never admit it to anyone but, if I'm being honest, I know that I use them, too. I like being popular. It's nice to be admired. It feels good to fit in. When Val took me under her wing that first week of school and saved me from having to eat lunch all alone, I was ecstatic. I was so terrified I wouldn't make any friends coming into Bishop Prep my senior year. I was worried people would find out I was on scholarship, and I'd be shunned. Instead, because of Val, I was hanging out with the "It" girls at school on the very first week.

If it later turned out that our friendships weren't super deep, and we didn't stay up at slumber parties to talk about all our hopes and dreams and maybe—with the exception of Cam—my friends weren't even all that nice, so what? They were cool. They made me someone important. That was what mattered, right?

Plus, this kind of friendship was a double-edged sword. It allowed them to keep their distance, but I got to keep my distance, too. We didn't have the type of heart-to-hearts that could be dangerous, where I might feel like I had to tell them the truth about my family's secrets. I was able to hide it all from my friends, and they didn't even notice I was doing it.

The soccer game ends then and Sebastian turns off the TV. He shifts on the floor of the living room and peers over at me. Something intense flares in his green eyes as they meet mine.

"Can I ask you something?" he asks. His voice is low, just loud enough to be heard over Mason and Jonathan's heavy snoring and the rain falling outside on the patio. "It's important."

CHAPTER 9

I'm caught off-guard by Sebastian's sudden line of questioning. One minute ago, he was enjoying his soccer game on ESPN. Now, seemingly out of nowhere, he looks very serious as he stares at me. I have no idea what he wants to talk about. What "important" thing could he have to discuss with me?

My pulse quickens. Could this be about our kiss?

"Uh, sure," I say, my fingers tensing in my lap. "You can ask me anything you want."

"Do your friends ever talk about Jordyn? You know—Jon's sister?"

I blink, confused. I sort of thought talking about Jordyn Chang was off limits with this group.

"That's random. Why do you ask?"

"It's just... I'm sure you know she died last July Fourth. I've been thinking a lot about her recently." He glances down for a moment and swallows hard before continuing. "I always thought it was strange how your friends acted after. They never talked about her. It's like they wanted to forget her or something. I guess I was wondering if there was a reason. Like, did something bad happen between them before she died?"

I think carefully before choosing my words.

"No one's ever said anything to me."

That's true enough. I may have witnessed a few things in the bathroom last spring, but I've never understood the specifics of what I heard, and my friends have certainly never brought it up to me. Not even Val, who is the only one who knew I was there the entire time, eavesdropping.

Of course, I've never asked any of them for more details, either.

"See, Jon's always thought there was more to it," Sebastian says. "Turns out Jordyn left a suicide note. She said she had no friends, and everyone was against her. Jon thinks the girls were bullying Jordyn. He thinks that's why she killed herself."

"No way." I shake my head. "I never heard anything about a note. I heard she was depressed."

If there had been more going on with my friends and Jordyn, I would have heard about it. There would be signs. You couldn't be responsible for someone's death and then just go back to normal, acting like everything was alright. You don't attend homecoming, and prom, and parties, having fun and cutting loose, if you know you caused someone to slash their wrists in a bathtub. My friends aren't the nicest people on earth, but there's no way they're capable of something like that.

Okay, sure, I've caught them all doing some shady things before. Like the time Val snuck off with my prom date to go have sex in his BMW. Or when Nia was filming videos all night and forgot to do her English homework and stole my paper instead. I had to beg our teacher for an extension to write a new one. That was the only class at Bishop Prep I got a B- in, all because of Nia.

Blake and Cam weren't as bad, though I'd caught them doing other things like telling little lies. That didn't bother me much, though. Girls always lie to each other. Little lies, like saying an outfit looks good, even when it doesn't, and big lies, like saying we're happy even when we're really not. None of that is the same as bullying a friend into killing themselves and then covering it up, though. That's sociopathic.

"Sorry. I don't mean to pry," he says. "It's just that Jordyn

was so nice. Sweet." He smiles softly at me. "Like you, actually. I really liked her."

A question I hadn't thought of before occurs to me.

"Did you two date?"

"Jordyn and me?" His eyes widen as if I've said something
crazy. "No. Of course not. I wasn't her type."

"You're everyone's type," I say.

It takes a minute for my brain to catch up with my mouth.
Oh shit, I can't believe I said that out loud.

"Except yours, huh?" he teases.

I sit there and blush like an idiot until his eyes meet mine
and then he inches in even closer. I feel a shock, like I've been
zapped by a bolt of lightning. The air between us changes. It
becomes charged. Electric.

"You know, I keep trying, but I can't quite seem to figure
you out, March. What's your deal?" he asks.

"What do you mean?"

"I was just wondering why I never heard from you after
graduation… Did I freak you out or something at Nia's party?
Is that why you ignored me—or do you just ignore all the guys
that kiss you?" He looks over with an almost shy, nervous smile
ruffling his mouth. I've never seen Sebastian Ramos look
nervous about anything.

"What are you talking about? *You're* the one who ignored
me."

"That's not how I remember it."

I study him for a stunned moment. Is he screwing
with me?

He has to be.

We both know he's the one who didn't return my texts or
calls, not that I want to point that out. I'm still embarrassed
about how desperate I acted afterward. Cam told me not to
contact him after our kiss, that I'd seem pathetic and clingy,
and she was right. I did.

I wonder if him pretending like this now is his way of

letting me off the hook nicely. If he really wanted to fix things with us, wouldn't he be apologizing for ignoring me rather than acting like it never happened?

"Like you should be talking." I smile back, deciding to deflect. If he wants to play dumb, so can I. "What's your deal? The only girls I've ever seen you with are Jessica and Missy."

"Yeah, I'm not exactly the best at relationships." Red blotches creep along his neck. "I have a hard time juggling. My life can be... complicated."

"Too complicated to *date*?" I smirk.

"Kinda?" He sighs deeply. "I've got two-a-days at soccer to get ready for Princeton," he explains. "After that, I'm running around helping my little brothers and sisters with summer school and camp because Dad is always too busy. Then if I'm lucky, I pass out before midnight, just to wake up and do it all over again." My heart squeezes as he glances down and blinks hard, pushing back some strong emotion.

"I'm sorry. That's a lot."

I remember how he told me about his mother passing away years ago from cancer. Sebastian is the oldest of four siblings and close to all of them. He's the one who takes care of everything his younger siblings needed. He even helps coach his little sister's soccer team on the weekends.

"It's okay," he says. "Not your fault."

I reach for his hand and squeeze. "Things will get better when you're in college."

"Yeah, you're right." His thumb rubs against the softness of my palm, sending shivers through me. "Sorry, I wasn't planning to bore you with my melodramatic life story today." He grins a bit sheepishly. "It's just that you've always been so easy to talk to. My friends don't understand, but I feel like you get me."

For a moment, his vulnerability makes me want to be honest with him, too. It would be nice to share my family problems and let someone else in. To be the real "me" for once. Except… How well do I really know Sebastian? This is the first deep moment we've had in weeks and the last time I opened up to him, when we kissed, he disappeared.

Can I trust him?

Can we really trust anybody with our deepest, darkest secrets?

A sharp knock at the front door interrupts our conversation, and Sebastian and I both jump up to answer.

On the front porch stands Officer Grant Topper. Clad in his full police attire, he cuts an intimidating figure. He's a much bigger guy than I realized, tall and well built, comprising far more muscle and height than I'd thought. Then again, I guess both times I've seen him, he's been sitting down. Now that he's standing, I see he's well over six feet tall.

"Something we can help you with, Officer?" Sebastian blinks, a confused expression on his face.

I give Grant a friendly wave and turn to Sebastian. "This is Grant," I explain. "He's the police officer we spoke with yesterday at the station."

"Actually, it's Officer Topper when I'm in uniform, Riley." Grant gives me a little wink. "Mind if I come in?" He doesn't wait for an answer, just wipes his wet boots on the welcome mat and strolls straight inside like he owns the place.

"Is someone here? Is that Roxy?" Blake asks, popping out of her bedroom door. Her blonde hair has been straightened, and she's changed into leggings and a sporty crop top that shows off her abs.

"Oh, hey there," she says, wiggling her fingers at Grant when she spots him in the foyer. She sidles up next to me and giggles in my ear. "*Ooh*, looks like Officer Hottie makes house calls."

I blush. Thankfully, no one else hears.

Grant turns to me. "So how're things going?" he asks. "I hope you've heard from your friends?"

"Yeah, Tyler texted last night. They're on their way over now," I say.

"That's great news." A kind smile breaks out across his handsome face. He reaches out and gives my shoulder a squeeze. "I was worried about you."

Sebastian's lips press into a thin line. His gaze fixates on Grant's hand, still touching me, and I can feel the annoyance rise off his skin like heat.

He moves to stand in front of me, blocking me from Grant. "That's real nice, Officer," he says, "but how did you know where Riley is staying? Did you look her up in some police database or something? Because that seems sort of sus to me, and not at all like a proper use of government resources."

I suck in a breath. "Oh my God, Sebastian!" I elbow him in the ribs and turn to Grant, knowing my face is beet red. "I'm so sorry. I can't believe he just said that."

Grant, to his credit, keeps smiling. "That's okay," he says and meets Sebastian's skeptical stare head on with a measured one of his own. "Chief's got me going door to door, making sure people are evacuating before we barricade the Overwater Highway."

He doesn't look mad at Sebastian's ridiculous questions, but I notice he takes a few steps away from me, distancing himself. He continues to watch Sebastian carefully, sizing him up to determine whether he's some kind of threat or going to cause trouble. While Grant is taller and bigger, Sebastian is no slouch either. Years of playing championship soccer have made him lean and strong in all the right places.

Grant is the first to break whatever weird staring contest those two have going on, and his gaze travels past Sebastian, toward the living room. His eyes widen as he takes in our other friends lounging around the house in their various forms of disarray. Mason and Jonathan wave from the couches, still half asleep, as Cam and Nia jog down the stairs to get waters from the kitchen. They're still dressed in their workout clothes, sweating buckets and laughing as they plop down on the couches next to the guys.

"You *are* leaving, right?" Grant asks, his forehead wrinkling with worry as he turns back to me.

"Of course," I say. "I mean, if our friends show up soon, that is." I shuffle my feet back and forth. "Otherwise, I guess we'll make the best of things and ride out the storm here."

"I don't think that's such a good idea." He undoes a few buttons of his collar and loosens the tie of his uniform. "This storm's coming in fast. Once we close the highway, there'll be no way off the island until after it passes."

Sebastian shrugs. "Yeah, but you don't know it's hitting for sure, do you? No one ever does with these things." He picks a piece of lint off his cargo shorts. "You know how many times I've gone to bed hearing a storm's gonna hit, only to wake up the next day and... nothing."

Blake nods along. "Remember Hurricane Martha?" She snorts. "That was barely a sprinkle."

Everyone laughs except for Grant.

"This isn't a joke," he says. His hands go deep into his pockets as he glances around the house, making stern eye contact with each one of us. "You need to understand how dangerous this is. If you decide to stay, you won't be able to leave until after the storm passes. Even then, we have no way of knowing how bad things will get or when the highway will open again. You could be stuck here for days." His tone grows more urgent. "Weeks even."

Sebastian yawns. "Not worried."

"Well, you should be," Grant says. "You'll have to be prepared to be self-sufficient. Electricity and water won't work. And no restaurants or grocery stores." He smirks in Sebastian's direction. "No fancy UberEATS or Door Dash delivery, either, like I'm sure you rich kids like to use."

Mason sits up in the couch. "Wait—you're saying we'll have to cook our own food?"

"Not to mention, statistics show most people are actually killed in the aftermath of a storm—especially during cleanup," Grant continues. "And you'll get no help if anything goes wrong. The police and fire departments will be too busy helping the people who really need it." He gives Sebastian a long, pointed glare. "Not the young, healthy, entitled ones too stubborn to leave when they had the chance."

"We'll be fine," Sebastian says.

"You sure about this?" Jonathan tilts his head back, peering at Sebastian. "I mean, if the police are making house calls, telling us to leave, maybe we should listen?" He turns to Grant. "Is the evacuation mandatory, Officer?"

"Technically, we're supposed to tell everyone to leave town for their own safety, but I can't actually force you to leave," Grant says. "We're not arresting people and throwing them in jail, if that's what you're asking."

"So we can stay?" Sebastian prods. "That's what you're saying, right?"

"I would advise against it."

Nia bites at her lip. "I'm with Jon. Maybe we should—"

"No." Sebastian shakes his head. "Not without Ty."

Cam clutches at her water bottle. "And I'm not leaving Val."

Grant lets out a long, tortured sigh. I can tell we aren't the only people he's talked to today that have refused to leave. He must be tired of convincing people to be safe and smart. I'm sure it's exhausting, but Floridians are stubborn folks, especially about the weather. We like to do things our way, and we always think we're right.

To be fair, it comes from years of experience and getting burned. The first time you hear about a storm, you do all the right things. Even though it takes time and money, you prepare and evacuate. But then nothing happens. You do it again a few more times each summer until you grow skeptical and tired of wasting all that energy for nothing. They call it storm fatigue. You start to think you're invincible.

"What if you at least go to the mainland and wait for your friends there?" Grant suggests. "I'll be here. I can be on the lookout for them."

I smile at him. Good looking and thoughtful. A rare combination.

A huge part of me wants to say yes to his kind offer. It does seem like the right call to get off this damn island, but I know better than to contradict Cam. She would kill me if I left her. I don't want to upset Sebastian either, not when he's finally talking to me again. For whatever reason, it seems like Grant has gotten under his skin. I want Sebastian to know I'm on his side.

Besides, it's still early. We have plenty of time to leave before the highway will close.

"That's nice of you, Grant—uh, I mean Officer Topper," I say. "But I think we're gonna stay put for now and see how it goes."

"Okay, fine." He lowers his head in disappointment. "If I can't convince you to leave, at least make sure you have enough food and water for two weeks. Go now, before the grocery stores close," he warns and surveys the house, taking in the layout. "And get some plywood for those windows." He points over to the sliding glass doors by the patio deck. "Gas up your cars, too. And charge your phones before you go to bed."

"Oh, come on. You really think all that's necessary, Officer?" Blake huffs, crossing her arms over her chest. "Storms this far south always turn at the last minute."

"This one isn't turning." He gives us a long, meaningful stare. "Just make sure you're prepared."

There's a long, brittle moment of silence.

Sebastian clears his throat. "Alright, you heard the man,"

he says and pulls his car keys out of his pocket, jingling them at Jonathan and Mason. "Let's go."

He marches toward the front door, pausing to check the hall closet and finding some umbrellas to grab for the drive. Jonathan jumps up from the couch and jogs after him, but Mason—the lazy ass—doesn't move a muscle.

"Mason?" Sebastian glances back down the hall. "You coming?"

"Ugh, fine." Mason reluctantly peels himself off the couch. "But we better be stopping for fireworks for tomorrow."

Cam texts the guys a list of things to pick up from the store, so it's on their phones and they won't forget. A minute later and they're outside the house, the loud rumbling of Sebastian's sleek sports car engine sounding in the driveway as they pull away.

Grant follows. His heavy boots stomp along the wooden floor as he heads to the front door. He reaches for the knob, stepping one foot through the doorway before hesitating and turning back to me.

"I'll try to check up on you later," he says and twists the doorknob so it locks. "Make sure you keep your doors and windows locked during the storm, okay? It'll prevent things from blowing open and causing damage." He pauses and then adds, "Actually, in this house, best to keep 'em locked all the time."

I tilt my head. What an odd thing to say.

"What do you mean?" I ask.

He shakes his head, his mouth spreading into a thin-lipped smile. "Never mind. Just a silly urban legend," he says. "Don't worry. Nothing to be scared about, but it's always good to take precautions. You know how to find me if you need anything, right?"

I grin. "Yeah, your number's 911?"

He chuckles and dashes back into the pouring rain,

pausing for a moment to give me one last little wave. The blue and red police lights atop his car flash against the darkening sky as he drives away to warn the next house about the dangerous storm coming.

His offer is nice, but I can't imagine actually calling him for help. I've seen bad storms before, especially growing up in Miami and living through hurricane season every summer. Three years ago, everyone was saying Hurricane Martha was going to be a catastrophic Category 5 hurricane. Mom had a panic attack and made us evacuate, driving hours to Atlanta. When it hit, it was barely a tropical depression. There were some leaves in the pool outside and a few fallen branches on the street. That's it.

I don't see why this storm should be any different.

CHAPTER 10

T he boys return a few hours later with arms full of grocery bags and some plywood, hammers, and nails. They shake off their soaked umbrellas, leaving them dripping in the entryway, and drop supplies onto the kitchen counter. Cam, Blake, and I pause the soapy TV show we're bingeing on Netflix to help them unpack. Nia is still busy in her bedroom, frantically posting photos to her Instagram feed, terrified the power might go out any second. Just as we get to the kitchen, the doorbell rings again.

Blake grins and runs to the door to let Roxy in. She helps her out of her raincoat, revealing an oversized black *Metallica* tee cut low enough to show off a row of raven tattoos above clearly enhanced cleavage. Her fluorescent red hair is pulled back into a ponytail, showing off long dangling angel wing earrings, and she wears purple lipstick so dark it's almost black. The color might look weird on other women, but she pulls it off.

Blake wraps her freckled arm possessively around Roxy's curvy waist as she introduces her around to the guys like a prize she just won. I make an effort and give Roxy a big hug, but Cam isn't any friendlier today than she was last night. She looks the bartender up and down with a slow, measured stare, her eyes going straight to Roxy's flashy chest tattoos and staying there. She wrinkles her nose with disapproval. Body art and tattoos are definitely not Cam's thing.

Right before Track and Field Regionals, Blake got her

own ankle tattoo of the warrior goddess Freya for "extra moti-vation." Blake told us she chose Freya because she was a badass Norse deity of battle, and also because Freya was known for being a "party girl" that knew how to use beauty and sex as weapons to get what she wanted—not unlike Blake herself.

When Cam first saw Blake's new tattoo, she threw a fit, saying Blake was ruining her body and making a huge mistake. It was all very dramatic. Cam refused to talk to Blake for an entire week afterward in protest. Cam is a master in the art of guilt trips and sulking.

"Whoa, so this is the place, huh?" Roxy surveys the rental house with a wide-eyed stare, looking a little spooked as she squeezes excess rainwater from her hair. "I have to say, it looks nicer than I expected." Her expression makes me think about those pesky little murder rumors again. She doesn't elaborate further though, and I don't want to ask. She reaches into her black leather shorts and pulls out a pack of Marlboro Lights. "Mind if I smoke?"

"I'd rather you didn't," Cam says rather sharply, but then Blake catches her eye, frowning. "You don't mind, do you, sweetie?" she adds with one of her charming smiles.

"Uh, I guess not?"

Roxy tucks the cigarettes away, back into her shorts. A flash of metal catches the light when she speaks, and I realize she has a tongue ring, too. I didn't notice it before. Blake must be in heaven.

Everyone helps to unload the shopping haul onto the kitchen counter. We stack the purchases in rows so we can see what we've got. Supplies like flashlights, batteries, lighters, and candles. Two cases of light beer. A handle of vodka and one of tequila. Hamburgers and hotdogs, but no buns. Instead, the guys bought a few loaves of nasty rye bread—the kind of bread always on the shelves, no matter how busy the store is, because no one ever wants it. Ketchup. Mustard. Cheese.

Marshmallows, chocolate bars, and graham crackers for s'mores. A dozen cans of chicken noodle soup and tuna fish. Three jars of peanut butter and some jelly. Chips and some stuff to make dips with. Four gallon-sized jugs of water.

"That's it?" Cam frowns at the kitchen counter. "That cop said we need two weeks' worth of food. This won't last us more than a few days."

Sebastian gives her a sidelong glance. "We're lucky we got this. The store was almost empty."

"Yeah, Seb had to fight off a soccer mom for the tequila," Mason says. "This crazy lady tried to grab it right out of our shopping cart. I swear she was gonna bash our heads in with her margarita mix." Mason lets out a loud guffaw and elbows Sebastian in the side. "But then Seb worked the ol' charm on her. Next thing you know, she's offering him the tequila, her margarita mix, *and* her panties."

Cam's lips pucker. "That's gross."

"And totally untrue," Sebastian says but then his mouth quirks with amusement. "It was just her number."

"Hell, yeah it was! MILFs are the best." Mason cackles. "Let's invite her over to par-tay."

"I didn't take it, you idiot," Sebastian says, and I feel a quick rush of relief even though I shouldn't care whose phone number Sebastian gets.

"If you didn't take it, then you're the idiot," Mason says. "Soccer moms give the best head."

"You really are disgusting," Cam says to him.

While Cam and Mason make ugly faces at each other, I grab some water jugs and help Sebastian fit them all in the fridge. His hand brushes against mine as he grabs one of the jugs from me, sending little tingles up my arm.

"I don't think we have enough," I say. The bottled waters we brought from home are almost gone. Even with the four new gallons, it's not much for all of us. "Should we get more?"

"I don't think you heard us." He frowns down at me. "We

drove around the whole island. This is all that was left."

"It's like *The Town That Dreaded Sundown* out there," Jonathan says, coming up behind me to place the hamburger and hot dog meat onto the bottom shelf of the fridge. "Everyone's all panicked. Everything's boarded up."

I swallow hard. "Seriously? It's that bad?"

"We can fill the bathtubs and sinks with water," Roxy says. "That's what we did when the last storm almost hit a few years ago."

"Tap water?" Mason looks at her, cringing. "No thanks. I'm strictly an Evian guy."

Blake grabs an empty red plastic cup off the kitchen table and winds up her throwing arm, aiming in his direction. "I swear, one more douchebag comment…"

"Oh relax, Captain America." Mason grins, wide and annoyingly. "I'm just saying, there's no need to drink from the faucet, like a poor person, when there's plenty of palatable drinking water in places without hurricanes—like, say, South Beach. And I hear they have insane July Fourth pool parties. If we leave now, we can get there in plenty of time."

"Give it up already, man." Sebastian groans. "I already told you. We're not leaving without Ty."

"But—"

"No one's making you stay," Cam says. "Feel free to Uber yourself out of here anytime. Trust me, we won't miss you."

"Bitch," he mumbles, and the slick Cheshire grin drops from his face as he stomps back to the couch. He finds a football game on TV and turns the volume up until the screeching of the referee's whistle and booming cheers from the fans echoes throughout the house.

I scowl at his backside. He truly is an ass.

At least one good thing about everyone going their own way next year is that after this weekend, I'll never have to see Mason Larper again.

Good riddance.

Now that we have all our supplies—or at least whatever supplies we're able to get—there's still a lot of preparation work to do before nightfall. Nia finally emerges from her bedroom, and Cam splits us all up into groups to make things fair. Sebastian, Jonathan, and Blake are assigned to cover windows around the house with plywood to protect them from flying debris if the storm hits. The rest of us will help make dinner while we still have power. Only Mason refuses to participate. He's too busy drinking beer and sulking on the couch.

None of us tasked with cooking are what you'd call experts in the kitchen. The twins have a live-in private chef, so Cam never learned much about the art form of cooking. The others have an endless delivery budget or parents that like to eat out at fancy restaurants, so they're not much help, either. Since I'm the only one who seems to know how to use the stove top, Cam assigns me the main course—hamburgers. Basically, this means I get to do all the work while Cam hovers over, watching and ordering me around.

As I flip patties, I think about how lucky we are that Grant showed up when he did. Before that, we'd assumed all we had to do was make it through the storm itself. None of us had given any thought to what Grant said about being prepared to last days afterward or how dangerous the aftermath might be. Having a plan for being stranded was a real concern if we didn't want to wind up starving to death. That had almost happened to my cousin Gavin and his friends in California a few months ago.

Their story had been all over the news. During a high school ski trip, a group of seniors and their dog had accidentally gone the wrong way down an old logging road that was closed for the winter. They plowed straight into a snow barrier and were trapped for a week during a terrible blizzard. When they were eventually found, all their food was gone. They were lucky to be rescued in time.

Well… those that lived were lucky.

Gavin said not all his friends made it, and everyone agreed if they'd been trapped much longer without food, they'd all be dead.

I've never much liked the snow. Give me the sun and beach any day of the week. The mountains scare me. It's the type of place where Mother Nature is ruthless. Bad things can happen to you there if you aren't careful. My cousin and his friends learned that the hard way. Not being able to afford those fancy ski trips with my family anymore is one of the only things I don't hate about being poor.

I shiver and shake away the morbid thoughts. A bunch of teenagers dying in a winter storm is not what I want to be thinking about right now, especially when it seems like we might very well have our own deadly storm to contend with in a few hours.

While I finish cooking the burgers, adding American cheese on top, Cam assigns Roxy to rummage through the kitchen and pantry to find us more food. A few burgers and some musty rye bread won't cut it for a group this big. The options are limited, though. There isn't a lot lying around other than what the guys bought.

When we packed for this trip, our plan had been to survive on alcohol and whatever we could find at bars and house parties. We brought a few snacks with us. Some candy. Peanut butter for late night sandwiches. Fruit and a few veggies for Blake's smoothies. That sort of thing. Roxy grabs some bags of potato chips and works up some dips, mixing onion powder and sour cream into one big bowl and making guacamole in another. We don't have any other ingredients you'd use for guacamole like onions, tomatoes, or cilantro, so it's basically just mashed-up avocado and salt.

Cam gives Nia the easiest task: dessert. Nia is by far the least domestic of us all, unless she's faking it for a post on social media. All smiles, Nia films herself during an Instagram

Live as she pulls out a baking pan and drops the graham crackers, chocolate bars, and marshmallows onto it. She giggles for the camera, pretending like she's having the time of her life making s'mores for July Fourth, but as soon as the camera is off, she spends less than five seconds trying to figure out how to turn the oven on before giving up and shoving the pan at me. Then she accuses Cam of torturing her on purpose because she can't eat s'mores since they have too many calories, and Cam very well knows that.

Sebastian, Jonathan, and Blake return downstairs as I finish with the s'mores. As it turns out, there wasn't enough plywood to protect the whole house. Instead, they had to pick and choose what windows made the most sense to cover based on which side of the house forecasters are predicting will get the most wind in the storm.

With nothing left to do now but wait, we sit down at the long rectangular kitchen table and eat our dinner. As I take my first bite of cheeseburger, I peek through the gap in the plywood covering the patio doors to see how things look outside. The ocean has turned into a wave pool, the tide rushing in and crashing onto the shore. The wind howls and whips palm tree branches back and forth. Debris goes flying through the air. A relentless barrage of rain pounds against the glass while thunder rumbles above us like a freight train, rattling the windows. It's an awe-inspiring display of nature's power and fury.

Suddenly, the lights above us flicker off, casting the house into complete darkness.

"It's just a power surge," Sebastian says and turns on his cell phone flashlight to give a little light around the table. "It'll come back on."

"Maybe. Maybe not," Roxy says. "It could be the first feeder bands arriving."

I gulp down my vodka cranberry drink and remember the newscaster's warning earlier on the TV. Feeder bands are the outermost rainbands of the hurricane. They occur before the main rain shield and are made up of dangerous, dense thunderstorms.

"Should we put out some candles?" Cam asks, her voice tinged with worry. "What about the flashlights?"

"It's fine. Just give it a minute," Sebastian says.

A few more seconds tick by without any power. Jonathan gets up and grabs one of the candles off the kitchen counter and brings it back to the table, lighting it. Though we've been talking about the storm for two days now, this is the first time it's starting to feel real.

"Maybe it's the ghosts having a little fun, eh, Riley?" Blake giggles.

"Shoot!" Cam slaps her knee and snorts. "I forgot to call Ghostbusters."

"Ha ha. Very funny," I say.

Beads of sweat prickle at my forehead, and I wipe them away with a shaky hand.

"Hello, Mr. Ghostman." Blake grins, looking upward at the ceiling. "Can you please turn the lights back on?"

Another crack of thunder answers her. This one is so close, it reverberates throughout my entire body.

"You shouldn't joke about the spirits," Nia says.

"Not in this house, at least," Roxy mumbles under her breath.

Sebastian turns to her. "What do you mean? What's wrong with this house?"

A flash of lightning illuminates her face as she blinks, confused. "Don't you know?"

I sink into my chair. I'm pretty sure I know where this conversation is going, and I don't like it. Not one bit.

"Know what?" he asks.

"This place..." Roxy gulps and wiggles around in her chair, looking uncomfortable. "It's *haunted*."

CHAPTER 11

"**H**AUNTED?**" Nia repeats, sputtering so hard that a few pieces of potato chips—the only thing she's eaten all night—fly across the table. Her over-tweezed, arched eyebrows raise almost to her hairline as she gapes at Roxy. "What do you mean?"

"You seriously haven't heard?" Roxy asks, disbelief flickering across her face. "I can't believe no one's told you about the messed-up shit that's happened here."

Cam coughs next to me. "You're kidding, right?"

"Oh wow. You guys really don't know," Roxy says. "Here, drink," she orders, reaching over and grabbing the bottle of vodka from the middle of the kitchen table. With a heavy hand, she pours more of it into our glasses. "You're going to need plenty of alcohol for this."

My unease grows as I sip my drink, my throat burning as I wait to find out what happened in this house. I guess there's no more hiding from the truth, no matter how much I may want to.

"It all started with the murders..." Roxy takes a big swig straight from the bottle and proceeds to tell us the entire gruesome history of our rental home.

It was almost twenty years ago, on a July Fourth weekend just like this one. The nightmare began with a man named Ed Rawlins appearing out of nowhere, walking off the street and right up to the front door of 21 Seashell Lane. He was a drifter. Someone with no job and no family. He had glasses as thick as a cola bottle and stained crooked teeth, and he wore a dirty yellow raincoat—like the kind fishermen wear.

No one knows why Rawlins chose this home. He didn't know the occupants. They were just a group of six college students from the University of West Florida looking forward to a fun party weekend away from home. They were drinking beer and watching fireworks in the backyard of their holiday rental, living it up, totally clueless about what was about to come for them.

Rawlins' first victim was a sophomore who answered the door and found him on the front porch, holding a gun and a chopping axe. One minute, Cassie Dixon was a well-liked, pretty girl with a fresh summer tan and her whole life in front of her. The next minute, she was dead with a single strike to the carotid artery. Cassie and her friends had just celebrated her twentieth birthday the day before.

After cutting Cassie down, Rawlins dragged her bloody body inside as a warning of what would happen to the rest of the group if they didn't listen to him. He waved his gun around and ordered everybody into the house, locking all the doors so they had nowhere to go.

One by one, he tied them up and ushered them into the basement below. Then he locked the door behind him. What followed was roughly thirty minutes of carnage that brought an end to five more young lives.

When the police found the victims the next day, their bodies were drenched with blood and gore. Each of them had over a dozen stab wounds to the chest and stomach and defensive wounds on their hands and feet. The entire time, he never once used the gun—the axe was far more fun. At some point, hopefully after they were dead, Rawlins decapitated his victims. He separated their heads from their bodies and lined each head up in a row on an empty bookshelf.

Eventually, Rawlins was captured and tried for his horrific crimes. He was sentenced to die by "Old Sparky," the infamous electric chair used in Florida before people protested it as inhumane and the state adopted lethal injection. But he never made it there. Somehow, Rawlins escaped.

"And no one has seen him since," Roxy says, finishing her story. "The authorities say he ran away to Mexico or Canada, but we locals don't buy it. We know what really happened. Rawlins came back here and killed himself underneath this very house so he could stay with his victims' souls. *Forever.*" She swallows hard. "And he doesn't like visitors. His ghost hangs around, haunting this place, terrorizing anyone that dares disturb him."

Beside us, a strong roar of wind rattles the patio doors. It sounds as if someone is picking up the house and shaking it. Another bolt of lightning strikes, and the foundation vibrates beneath my feet. A long, eerie moment of silence follows after.

I knew it.

I knew this house was too good to be true.

"I don't believe you," Nia says with narrowed eyes. "You wouldn't be here if you really thought it was haunted."

"Rawlins doesn't go after locals—just the tourists." Roxy smirks. "Everyone knows that."

Cam pushes her drink to the side and shivers in her seat. "This is so messed up. I can't believe a serial killer was here in this house."

"Well, technically, he was a mass murderer—not a serial killer," Jonathan corrects and reaches across the table for more vodka.

"Didn't know there was a difference," Sebastian says.

He has an amused look on his face I can't help but envy. How can he seem so unbothered by this conversation? I want to run upstairs and hide under the covers and never come out.

"Of course, there's a difference." Jonathan rolls his eyes. "Mass murderers are impatient nut jobs that blow their entire wad in one day. Serial killers are plotters. They're smooth. Calculated. And there's a cooling-off period between kills," he says. "Anyone can be a mass murderer. It takes brains and balls to be a serial killer."

"Can we please change the topic?" I ask. "This conversation is creeping me out."

Uneasiness settles beneath my skin and I get that weird feeling again, like someone is watching me. I peer around the dark room, but nothing in particular catches my eye. I certainly don't see the ghost of a dead killer or anything alarming like that.

"I don't want to be here anymore." Nia pushes both hands against the table and stands up.

"You're being ridiculous." Mason laughs. "It's just a dumbass story."

"I don't care," Nia says. "I want to go home."

Another huge lightning bolt strikes somewhere out back on the beach. The accompanying thunderclap jars the house and shakes the walls. Nia lets out a little scream and grips the back of her chair, her long nails digging into the fabric.

"I told you not to say anything." Blake turns to Roxy with a pinched expression. "I knew they'd freak out."

"Wait—you knew about this?" Cam stiffens.

"Oh relax," Blake says. "Roxy told me when we first met, but I didn't think it was a big deal. I knew you guys would overreact and look—I was right." She gives Cam a smug little smile.

The back of my neck flushes with irritation as I think about the strange sounds I've been hearing since we first arrived at this house. My friends all made me feel like a crazy person when I complained about it, especially Blake, but what if it wasn't the pipes or rats or some other simple explanation?

What if Roxy is right?

What if our house really is haunted?

"Why didn't you say anything when I told you about the noises?" I ask Blake. "You acted like I was making it up. Like I was being dramatic."

"You were being dramatic." Blake reaches over Roxy to grab a s'more from the pan in the middle of the table and takes a big gooey bite. "Mmm. These are divine." She closes her eyes, savoring the treat as melted chocolate drips down her chin. "There's nothing wrong with this house. It's just a silly made-up story."

"It's not made up," Roxy says. "It's the truth."

Sebastian gives Roxy a dubious look. "Bullshit. We all know ghosts aren't real."

"Speak for yourself," Nia says. "Ghosts are very real. As real as we are."

"Not you, too." He groans. "You're joking, right?"

"I never joke about the spirits," she says, shaking her head furiously. "That's what my Grann calls them. She's the one that taught us about Voodoo."

"Voodoo?" Mason asks. "You mean like stabbing dolls with pins?"

"That's just the stupid shit you see on TV," Nia says. "Real Voodoo is a religion. It's this, like, belief system of slaves that got fused with the slave owners' religions. In Voodoo, you honor ancestor spirits, like how Catholics worship saints. According to Grann, you let the spirits enter you."

Mason laughs. "Sorry, but that sounds like straight-up devil worship."

"Voodoo has nothing to do with the devil!" Nia snaps. "It's about healing and protection—just like Catholicism. Only difference is Voodoo sometimes involves blood rituals."

"Seems like a pretty big difference…" Mason says, earning him a dirty look from Nia.

"Keep it up and someone's gonna put a pin in you," she warns.

As we finish eating our dinner and dessert, the weather continues to decline. The wind howls as rain pounds harder against the roof and windows. From what I can see outside the uncovered portion of the sliding glass doors, the sky has turned completely dark. It's pitch black now other than the increasing lightning that illuminates the backyard eerily. Instead of one bolt every few minutes, they now strike one after another every few seconds, in rapid succession.

All of it is another reminder. It's not just ghosts we need to worry about. A dangerous storm is already here and getting worse by the minute. It won't be much longer until things will be so bad we can no longer leave this house. If Val and Tyler don't show up soon, we'll be stranded here all alone at the mercy of Mother Nature. The bridge—along with any last chance we have to evacuate the island—is closing in less than two hours.

"I guess this is the last time we let you pick a rental, huh?" I turn to Cam with a tight-lipped smile, trying to lighten the mood with a joke.

"Me?" she asks. "What are you talking about?"

"You're the one who suggested this place, remember?" I remind her.

"No, I didn't."

"Yes, you did," I insist. "You said it'd be more fun than a hotel."

"Well, yeah, I suggested a rental house because of, well, you know…" She catches my eye with a meaningful glance. "Because Airbnbs are so chic right now, right?"

"Oh, yeah. That's right." I nod along, feeling a pang of gratitude as Cam does me a solid. She doesn't want to embarrass me in front of the guys by letting them know my mom was too cheap to spring for a hotel room.

The funny thing is, as humiliating as that little lie is, it would be a thousand times worse if Cam and the others knew the actual truth. It's not that Mom didn't *want* to pay for a hotel room for me; it's that we're so poor she *couldn't*. None of them would understand what it's like not to have money. Take the twins, for example. Forget a hotel room for the weekend.

They could buy the entire hotel with their trust fund if they wanted to.

"But I didn't pick this house," Cam continues and then points her finger across the table at Nia. "She did."

Nia blinks, looking surprised. "Uh, no, I didn't. I wanted to stay in the hotel, remember?" she asks. "The rooms have way better lighting for photos."

Cam studies Nia. "Are you sure? I could've sworn the link came from you."

"Of course, I'm sure."

Cam turns to Blake.

"Why're you looking at me?" Blake frowns. "Do I look like the kind of person who would spend time searching for rental houses on the internet?"

"Hm. Good point." Cam shrugs. "I guess it must've been Val."

I grab one of the s'mores and chew, ignoring the strange tingling in my chest. I was so sure it had been Cam who had found this place. She's the one who told me about it first. She had all the links and pictures, and she's the one who had the paperwork to sign. She even paid for the place, too, on her dad's Am Ex.

It's hard to imagine Val doing any of the work to book our rental. Like Blake, Val also isn't the kind of person who would spend her precious time researching summer houses online for the group. But if everyone else says it wasn't them, it had to be Val. Right?

I finish my dessert and wash it down with more vodka, drinking the alcohol as fast as I can. A nice, good buzz is just what the doctor ordered to help me relax.

"Look, even if that stupid story is true—and I doubt it— that was years ago." Sebastian gets up from the kitchen table to grab another beer from the fridge. He pops the top off the bottle and takes a long drink before returning to his seat.

"This island is completely safe. They haven't had any murders in Palm Key in decades."

"That we know of," Roxy says.

Mason groans. "Wouldn't we know if people were turning up dead?"

"Not necessarily. Not if their bodies don't show up." Roxy's gaze darts around. "People go missing all the time here, but the police don't do anything. I bet they cover it up. Murder is bad for tourism."

"That's ridiculous," Sebastian says. "If it was so dangerous here, we would've heard about it."

I swallow thickly, remembering the conversation at the police station the other day and all of Grant's strange warnings. Didn't he tell me to be safe that very first night at Beach Club and to keep all our doors and windows locked in this house? Maybe this is what Grant had been hinting at all along. Roxy could be on to something.

"Actually, Grant—the police officer—he did tell us that people go missing here a lot," I say.

"That reminds me of something I read about Palm Key Island when I was booking our trip." Cam looks around the table with spooked eyes. "There was a couple who came here last summer. They rented a boat for the day to sail around the coast and go snorkeling, but then no one ever heard from them again. They just… vanished."

"For real?" Nia asks. "They never found them?"

"Never."

"I'm telling you, it's Ed Rawlins," Roxy insists. "He's still here, haunting this town, taking revenge on anyone unlucky enough to cross his path."

"This is nuts. Dead people don't up and disappear," Sebastian says. "Someone would find the bodies."

Jonathan munches on a few of the remaining potato chips. "Not if they were disposed of properly."

"Oh yeah? Like how?" Mason asks.

"Acid bath. Alligator-filled swamps. Hungry pigs," Jonathan explains with a little shoulder shrug. "There're plenty of ways to get rid of a body."

I stare at him, feeling all sorts of creeped out. "And you know this how?"

He grins. "*Dexter* and *Criminal Minds*, of course."

Sebastian leans back into his seat, stretching his arms overhead. "Sorry, I don't buy it," he says. "No way people are dying around town, and the killer just rides off into the sunset. That only happens in the movies."

"That's not true. People get away with murder all the time," Jonathan says. "Like cops, for example. Did you know the Golden State Killer was in the police department? And don't forget about that patrol officer in Martin County who picked up female hitchhikers. He tied them to trees before killing them." He pauses, scratching at his chin. "Now that I think about it, I bet they use their training to become more efficient killers."

"That's a load of bullshit," Roxy says, slamming her drink on the table. Vodka spills out from the top and sloshes down the sides of her cup. "My uncle's a cop. Police officers protect and serve. They don't kill."

"Eh." Jonathan shrugs. "Plenty of bad cops, just like good cops. Anyone's capable of murder—with the right motivation."

Everyone is quiet for a moment as the wind roars, shaking our makeshift plywood shutters. The foundation makes a low, creaking groan as some sort of debris slams against it. Despite the rather sturdy looking appearance from the outside, the house starts to feel fragile and vulnerable. Breakable. I begin to wonder how bad things might get if the storm actually hits us.

How strong is this house, *really?*

Will it hold up if the hurricane comes on shore?

What if the hurricane is upgraded again, and the winds

become even stronger than predicted? And it's not just the winds we have to worry about. What about the storm surge? Didn't that newscaster earlier say something about waves as high as buildings?

The power suddenly thrums back to life and the lights come back on. I let out a huge sigh of relief.

"Finally!" Blake stands up and walks into the living room, grabbing the remote off the couch where Mason left it. "All this murder talk is bo-ring. Who's ready to shake what their mama gave 'em?"

She turns on the wireless speakers and finds an upbeat playlist on her cell phone. Music starts to blast at full volume throughout the house. Bass reverberates around the room, almost as loud as the thunder. Blake cheers and wiggles her shapely butt in our direction. Britney. Beyoncé. Rihanna. Taylor. All of Blake's favorite ladies, singing their most famous pop anthems. It's the sort of music you can't help but dance to, so we do.

We pour more liquor into our cups, the excess of alcohol a dangerous combination of nerves and boredom. Soon we're done with dancing on the ground and jump up on tables and couches, shaking our asses, our drinks high in the air. Booze sloshes onto our shoes and the furniture, staining it, but we're having so much fun we don't care.

I get lost in the music, forgetting all about Roxy's macabre ghost stories and the murders. Like Sebastian said, none of that is real. Val will show up any minute with that dirtbag Tyler and then we can all celebrate July Fourth together like we planned. Even the weather doesn't worry me anymore. The impending hurricane is going to turn before it hits land, like they always do. Everything is going to be okay.

More than okay.

It's going to be *great*.

CHAPTER 12

The hurricane party kicks into full gear.

Everyone is wasted, twirling and spinning around the living room. We're having the time of our lives. The music pumps and laughter rings through the air, punctuated by the continuous crash of thunder and wind. Despite the bad weather raging outside, the mood is festive and carefree as we all make the most of the unique opportunity to party in the storm.

The boys stand on the dining room table, pouring more shots down each other's throats, while Blake and Roxy make out in the corner. Roxy sways on her feet, clearly wasted. She's having a little difficulty keeping herself upright in Blake's embrace.

Nia puts her arms around Cam and me, and the three of us dance around the living room in a circle. She bumps into my hip, giggling, and snaps a pic of us for her Instagram feed. I laugh as she strikes a sexy pose, sticking her ass out and making kissy faces at the phone camera. We take photo after photo, hamming it up for all the Nia-maniacs out there.

Out of breath, we all fall down to the couch, still laughing as sweat dampens our foreheads and cheeks. Nia edits a few of the best pictures with an app, making her teeth even whiter and her boobs even bigger. She lets out a panicked shriek when she goes to upload them to her socials and realizes the Wi-Fi is no longer working. She promised her manager she'd post at least three more pictures to her socials by midnight.

We're relegated to the dreaded "drafts" folder for now as she darts away in the hopes she can still get service in another part of the house or the covered area of the patio.

Cam and I go back to dancing as Blake sashays over to us. Her lips are purple from Roxy's lipstick and all the kissing. She giggles drunkenly, hugging the tray of s'mores to her chest and licking the mushy remains stuck to the inside of the pan.

"These really are insane," she says and then a sad, faraway look comes over her face. "They were Jordyn's favorite, you know. We used to make them every summer. We'd eat them in her backyard and watch the sunset." She blinks hard. "Do we have peanut butter? Jordyn always said they tasted better with peanut butter…"

"Jordyn? Who's that?" Roxy asks coming up behind us, slurring her words a bit.

Instead of answering, Blake takes off, stumbling down the hallway toward the bathroom. I stare after her as she rushes inside and slams the door shut. Roxy chases after her, and I wonder if I should follow too and make sure Blake is okay. She seemed so sad, and Blake never gets sad. Plus, I've had a lot to drink and think I need to pee.

Except… I'm not sure Blake would open the door for any of us. If she's upset about her friend, she's the kind of person who would prefer space.

"Need another drink?" Sebastian asks, suddenly beside me with that gorgeous smile of his. I forget all about Blake and my need to pee as he gently brushes my elbow to get my attention. Little bolts of electricity shoot up my arm where his fingers graze my skin.

"Sure." I smile. "That'd be—"

"Great!" Cam cuts in front of me. "We'd love a drink. Thanks," she says and gives him a little shove toward the kitchen. She clutches onto my arm, her eyes glassy from drinking, and waits for him to get outside of hearing distance. "I know he's cute and all, but don't forget—he's trouble," she whispers, an angry edge to her voice.

I know she's just being protective of me because she cares, which I appreciate, but the alcohol has made me brave. Hopeful, even. I'm not sure anymore that Sebastian is someone I should worry about. In fact, I'm sort of thinking the exact opposite...

"I don't know, Cammy," I say, staring dreamily after Sebastian, my desire mixing pleasantly with my vodka buzz. "I think things might really be different this time."

"It isn't different, trust me. This is what he always does." The cords in her neck pulse with agitation. "He leads girls on. It's a game to him. He broke Val's heart—and he'll break yours too if you're stupid enough to let him."

Cam still has me in her death grip, her sharp nails digging into my forearm, when Sebastian returns with our drinks. He grins as he holds them out to us. Before I can even say thank you, Cam snatches her cup out of his hands and tries to pull me toward the other side of the living room toward Jonathan.

"Ri Ri," she says. "Why don't we go over there by Jon and—"

"How about a dance?" Sebastian interrupts, holding out his hand to me. His dark green eyes sparkle hypnotically.

I swallow, finding it hard—okay, impossible—to take Cam's advice. Not when the full power of Sebastian's magnetic gaze is turned on me. I know Cam has my best interests at heart, but how am I supposed to resist Sebastian Ramos? He has the power to make me forget all my good senses. When he looks at me like he's looking right now, I'd follow him to the ends of the Earth if he asked me to.

"Sure." I nod.

He closes the gap between us. His hand goes around my waist, and he steers me toward a dark corner in the dining room, far away from a furious-looking Cam. I glance over my shoulder and mouth "sorry" to her even though I'm only sorry she's pissed and not at all sorry to be with Sebastian.

The beat picks up as we sway together to the throbbing music. Our bodies are only inches apart. A little thrill races through me. I can't stop staring at him as he dances. He's amazing, like he's been doing it his whole life. There's something so attractive about a guy who knows how to move his body.

"Quite the vacation, huh?" he asks over the loud music.

I grin. "Definitely not what I expected."

"Yeah, me neither." He reaches out and softly fingers a stray tendril of hair on my cheek. "But I gotta admit, if I have to be stranded on an island in a hurricane, I'm kinda glad it's with you."

An entire family of butterflies explodes inside my stomach. "You are?"

"Of course I am." He laughs. "I mean… in case you haven't noticed, you're completely gorgeous." His dark eyebrows arch mischievously. "And you've seriously got the most kissable lips I've ever seen."

He pauses, his eyes glued to my mouth.

"You can keep going," I say, so coyly, so flirty, I almost don't recognize myself.

It's not just the alcohol, either. I realize I'm starting to relax. Talking with him like this is a lot of fun. It's easy, like it used to be with us. I feel like I can be the real me when I'm with Sebastian.

"You've got a really great smile, too," he says.

I grin wider.

"But it's not just how you look." His expression stills and grows serious. "You're nice. Kind. I can talk to you about stuff no one else gets." My insides warm at the way he looks at me. "And I think it's really cool how smart you are. I remember how you got the highest grade in physics," he says. "Are you still going to Columbia?"

"Uh huh," I say, feeling a little flutter of pride before the overwhelming sense of hopelessness hits me. It's the way I feel every time someone brings up college.

I look away quickly as moisture begins to gather in the corners of my eyes, threatening to kill my buzz. Without a scholarship coming, I'm probably not going to Columbia anymore. I need to stop telling people I am. Everyone's going to find out the truth in a few weeks, anyway.

"What about you?" I ask, changing the subject before he can notice anything is wrong. "I mean, you're going to Princeton. That's amazing!"

"I'm just lucky," he says with a self-effacing laugh as he flips his brown hair adorably to one side. "I definitely wouldn't have gotten in with just my grades. Not like you."

Somehow, he manages to appear humble about going Ivy League on a full athletic scholarship, which is seriously endearing. He's one of the best high school athletes in the South. He'd been heavily recruited all year. His signing with Princeton was such a big deal it made the local news.

"You're kidding, right?" I playfully push at his shoulder. "I only wish I was talented like you. The only sport I've ever been good at was kickball, and that was in elementary school."

"I'm serious," he says, a soft lilt to his voice. "I admire you." His eyes lock on mine and my heart skips. For a moment, I feel like I'm floating.

It's funny. All this time, it turns out Sebastian has been following my life as closely as I've been following his.

Unfortunately, so much of what he knows about me is lies. He knows the carefully crafted illusion of "Riley March" that I've built up all year in order to fit in at Bishop Prep. He knows the wealthy, smart, easygoing, nice girl with the perfect popular friends and an easy life without problems. But that's not the real me; far from it.

If something is going to happen between us, I want it to be

because he knows me—*the real me*, not just who I pretend to be for everyone else.

I should tell him the truth: that I didn't get the scholarship I need. That I won't be going to Columbia after all, and I'll most likely be stuck at Orlando Community College. That my family has no money because my dad's in prison, and even for OCC, I'll have to work nights and weekends at the Mouse Trap just to cover my tuition.

The balls of my feet shuffle against the wood flooring.

"Seb, there's something I—"

"Me first, okay? I've been wanting to tell you this for a while." His hand tightens at my hip. "For the life of me, I can't figure out what happened after Nia's party. I thought we had a pretty great time. And that kiss… I can't stop thinking about it." Slowly and seductively, his gaze slides down to my mouth again. My stomach tingles as I think back to that night and how amazing his lips felt on mine. "But then you disappeared," he says, and a note of hurt enters his voice. "I tried texting, but you never responded, and… well… what the hell happened, March?"

I'm stunned by his words.

"Wait—what?" I blink. "When did you text me?"

"A bunch of times. Right after that night."

"Are you sure? I never got anything."

He takes a step back and regards me quizzically.

"It's okay if you did," he says slowly. "I'm not mad or anything. I just wanted to know why."

A shock runs through me as I study his face. Unlike before, this time I know for sure he's not messing around or trying to make me feel better about what happened between us. He's telling the truth. He seems as confused about our kiss as I am.

"I swear, I didn't get your texts. I would've responded," I say. "I thought *you* were the one ignoring *me*."

His arms encircle me, one hand on the small of my back, as he pulls me in close. "Good, I'm glad," he whispers into my hair. His fingers flutter against my skin as he tucks a few loose strands behind my ear. "Honestly, I sort of figured it was Val. That maybe she told you something about me that made you change your mind. I know how she can be. She'll pull out all the stops to get what she wants."

A strange expression slides across his face and makes me curious to know more about him and Val. They dated so long ago, way before I even knew anyone at Bishop Prep, so I've never heard the full story about why they broke up. There was supposedly some big blowup fight right before sophomore year, but Cam claims she never learned all the details. Before Sebastian Ramos, Val had never been dumped by a guy. She was the one who did the dumping. She didn't take well to the rejection, and so she never wanted to talk about what happened with any of us—not even Cam.

Even now, years later, Val still hasn't gotten over the sting. She's always trying to flirt with Sebastian whenever he's around, always hoping to win him back, but Sebastian avoids her like the plague. Whatever the reason, it wasn't an amicable breakup.

"What happened between you two?" I ask, stirring in his arms. "Why did you break up?"

He stops dancing.

"I ended things because Val's a liar."

"What do you mean?"

His eyes meet mine, an unreadable expression on his face. "She would tell me things when we were dating, and then I'd find out they weren't true."

"Like what sort of things?"

He stares at his flip flops, studying them with a strange intensity. "Like how she only wanted to be with me, but she was actually dating other guys behind my back the whole time."

I gasp. "Val was cheating on you?"

His eyes drill into mine. "Yep."

This is almost impossible to comprehend. Val is a lot of things, but I've never pegged her as a cheater and a liar. Lying means you have to care enough about what others think to hide the truth from them. Like me. I'm a liar because I care too much. Val couldn't care less. Not to mention, Val's held onto this obsession with Sebastian for so long, I can't see her ever risking her relationship with him for anyone else.

"Are you sure?" I ask. "How do you know?"

"Someone told me. Doesn't matter. It was a long time ago," he says. "It really sucked at the time, though." He pauses, biting at his lip. "You think you know someone, and then it turns out you never knew them at all. That's the part that got me. I knew I could never trust her again after that."

His words gnaw at my insides. I start to rethink everything all over again. I don't know if I can ever tell him the truth now that I know all of this. If he feels this strongly about Val's lies, what would he think if he knew about mine? Could he still like me if he knew all the secrets I've been hiding?

"Oh Jonny, *you're so funny!*" Cam squeals several octaves above the music.

I whip around to see Sebastian and I are no longer alone in the dining room. Cam and Jonathan now dance just a few feet away from us. For a second, our eyes meet across the room. I give Cam a little smile, but she frowns at me like she's angry, a cold glare in her eyes. I'm a little taken aback. I get that she's protective of me, but this seems like overkill.

Is she really that mad I didn't listen to her and am dancing with Sebastian?

But then she blinks, and the look is gone. She returns my smile and gives another high-pitched giggle as Jonathan twirls her in the other direction. Her hand is on his shoulder. Her perfect straight bob bounces in the air, shining under the lights.

"Good for him," Sebastian whispers, nodding over at his friend. "I'm glad Jon is getting some female attention." He pulls back and gives me a smirk. "Since, you know, you're not giving him any."

Embarrassment skitters up my back.

"What do you mean?" I ask, playing dumb.

He nudges my chin with his finger and turns my gaze toward Jonathan. Even though he's dancing with Cam, Jonathan's eyes keep flickering back to me.

"Don't tell me you haven't noticed the way he looks at you."

I sigh. "Okay, yeah, I've noticed, but I don't want to be a jerk."

"It doesn't make you a jerk because you don't feel the same way someone else does," he says, his voice going soft. "Nothing to feel bad about. Not unless you're doing something wrong. Cheating. Lying. That kind of stuff." My insides squirm again. I doubt Sebastian would be dancing with me like this if he knew my whole life is one big lie. "Jon's a great guy, but he's not for everyone."

"I think he's really, er, nice." I phrase this as tactfully as possible, worried that we're heading into dangerous territory. I don't want to insult Sebastian's friend, but I can't help that the guy weirds me out. "He's just... um... he's a little different, isn't he?"

Sebastian gives me a rueful smile. "Jon hasn't had the easiest life. You didn't know him before everything happened with Jordyn. It changed him," he says and his eyes cloud over, a troubled expression falling across his face. I can almost feel the waves of sadness roll off him.

It hits me again just how little I know about Jordyn Chang, the girl whose spot I took in the 10-Squad. In the beginning, when I first started hanging out with my friends, I felt like I was filling someone else's shoes. The shadow of Jordyn followed me everywhere those first few weeks of senior year. People would look at me funny when I ate with my new friends in the lunchroom, sitting in the spot Jordyn used to sit in. I'd see the other students whisper to each other in the hallway whenever I walked by. I even had Jordyn's old locker, right in between Blake's and Nia's.

Of course, no one ever dared to say anything out loud. My friends were too powerful for that. No one would ever go up against the 10-Squad or question them about anything they did. But I always knew what the other kids in school were thinking: What made me so special that I was accepted so fast? Why me and not them? And how could I ever think I could replace a girl like Jordyn Chang? Beautiful. Talented. Smart. Adored.

It wasn't just the other students, either. Once Val brought me into the group, Cam and Nia fell in line right away, but Blake took a while to warm up to me. She was so cold and distant at first, I didn't understand. I thought it was personal and there was something about me, specifically, that she didn't like. Now, in hindsight, I know it's because she's the one who was closest to Jordyn. None of the girls ever said it to my face, but Blake must have resented how easily I took Jordyn's place.

I'm still thinking about Jordyn when Jonathan inches up next to Sebastian and me. He stares at me invitingly as he moves his hips back and forth off beat. I glance around the dining room, searching for Cam, but she's suddenly nowhere to be seen.

Shit.

I feel a wave of apprehension as Jonathan keeps looking at me and smiling. I'm pretty sure I know what he's going to ask even before he opens his mouth, and I don't think there's a graceful way out of this.

His hand is hot and clammy as he reaches for me.

"Mind if I cut in?"

CHAPTER 13

Before stepping aside, Sebastian glances over at me first to make sure I'm okay dancing with his friend. I nod back and force a small grin. It's just one dance. What can it hurt? At this point, we're all locked in this house with nowhere to go, at least for a little while longer. It would be far more awkward to make things into a big deal and have Jonathan upset at me for the rest of the trip.

Besides, everyone keeps saying Jonathan's such a nice guy. I don't want to be an asshole.

Sebastian offers to get us waters and disappears into the kitchen, allowing Jonathan to take his place. I let out a sigh as Jonathan smiles from ear to ear and twirls me around the dining room. His hands tighten around my waist as we dance, but I make sure to keep my arms loose around his neck to keep distance. I can't help but notice he's shorter and much skinnier than Sebastian. Already I miss Sebastian's muscles, tight and well-defined from all those hours on the soccer field.

The music switches to a fast, popular song that I recognize right away. It has a familiar, thumping dance beat that's hard to resist. I let the rhythm take over and try to have fun with Jonathan, letting him sway me around to the beat. Perhaps I just need to lighten up. Everyone else seems to love the guy. Cam. Blake. Sebastian.

How bad can he be?

"You smell so good," he says, pressing his nose against my

neck. He takes in a long, shuddering breath, like he's breathing me in. "What's that scent?"

"It's deodorant, Jon."

"Well, it's ah-mazing," he says, sighing against my cheek. "Mmm." His mouth is so close, the smell of alcohol over-powers my senses. It's like he drank an entire liquor store. "I've been wanting to dance with you all night."

"Uh huh," I say, noncommittal.

I close my eyes and shut him out, concentrating on the music. Shake my hips. Spin. Twirl. I lose myself in the song.

I've always liked to dance but never had time for it. Not like Val and Nia did. They were on the cheer and dance squad all four years of high school. Even though I was good enough to join them, I didn't have time for weekly rehearsals or foot-ball games every single weekend. I had to work at the Mouse Trap instead and help Mom pay our bills.

I never stopped loving to dance, though. It's so freeing. You don't have to lie or hide or pretend to be anything or anyone else when you dance. You just *are*.

Jonathan's lips press against mine, shattering the mood.

"Jonathan!" My eyes fly open, and I push him away. *"What are you doing?"*

He freezes in place.

"Whatttsss wrong?" he stammers, complete shock on his face. "I thought you wanted me to kiss you."

"WHAT?" My body stiffens. "Why would you think that?"

"Because we were so close and—"

"It's called dancing!"

He blinks and swallows hard, his face reddening so much the flush spreads all the way to the tips of his ears.

"I'm so sorry, Riley. I really thought that's what you wanted…"

Oh my God. I think he might be about to cry.

"It's fine. Forget it," I snap, flustered. "Let's keep dancing, okay?"

I throw my arms back around his neck and make my feet keep moving to the beat, acting like I'm having a great time with him. It takes everything in me not to make a break for it and flee for the kitchen and throw myself back into Sebastian's arms. But that would just embarrass Jonathan even more. I don't want to kiss the guy, but I don't want to hurt his feelings, either. I know firsthand how bad it hurts to have someone crush your heart. After I thought Sebastian regretted kissing me, I felt awful for weeks. I'd never want to do that to someone else.

"Everything okay over here?" Blake appears, slipping her arm around my waist and pulling me into her side. She must have seen Jonathan try to kiss me.

"I think so?" Jonathan looks over at me uncertainly.

"Oh yeah!" I force a big smile. "We're totally cool."

"Awesome," Blake says and then turns to Jonathan. "Mind if I take over for a bit, Romeo?"

He nods and then, after one more sad glance in my direction, slinks away toward the kitchen.

"My hero," I say as soon as he's out of earshot and throw my arms around her, hugging her. "Thanks for saving me."

She gives me a crooked grin. "That boy has got it bad for you."

"He tried to kiss me." I grimace. "Can you believe that?"

"Aww, he's harmless."

I watch Jonathan in the kitchen with narrowed eyes as he makes himself a drink. I can't be positive from this angle, but I think I see him pull another pill from his pocket and swallow it down, chasing it with vodka. Before he can catch me staring, I turn away. This is the second time this weekend I've caught the guy taking pills with his alcohol. I'm starting to doubt it's something as innocent as Advil.

I wonder if I should say something to Blake but then decide to keep it to myself. No need to cause any more drama with Jonathan tonight. I just have to avoid him for the next few days until we're back home and then everything will be fine.

"Ohhh! Check it out!" Blake whisper-shouts into my ear and points toward the living room where Nia and Mason sit on the couch, taking turns shoving their tongues down each other's throats. "Looks like someone's over Ty," she says with a slow, catty grin. "That was fast."

"Be nice."

"Hey, I'm happy for her. I'm glad she's done with Ty." She keeps a straight face for all of five seconds before bursting into laughter. "I'm just not sure Mason's a big improvement."

A huge lightning bolt strikes so close to the patio doors it momentarily blinds me, and then thunder follows, shaking the entire house from floor to ceiling. The next instant, the music and all the electricity shut off. The house plunges into darkness again.

"What is it? What happened?" Cam asks, bursting out of the hallway bathroom.

We all turn on our phone lights so we can see each other in the dark.

"I think we may have lost the power for good," Sebastian says, reappearing in the living room with Jonathan.

"I bet it's the killer," Jonathan says. "What was his name again?"

"Ed Rawlins," Roxy says, a slight tremble in her voice.

"That's right!" Jonathan snaps his fingers. "Maybe good ol' Eddie wants to join the party. I bet he can really cut it up on the dance floor. Amirite?"

No one laughs.

"Get it?" he asks, making a stabbing motion with his hand. "Cut it up?"

"Knock it off. That isn't funny." Nia huddles even closer to Mason on the couch.

Blake and I hold hands and make our way over to the living room to join the rest of our friends. Just as I get to the couches, a loud, thumping noise that sounds like it's coming from outside the house catches my attention. I twist around and peek out the gap in the plywood covering the sliding glass doors and let out an audible gasp.

Someone is on the patio!

Lightning flashes to reveal an intruder, hunched down and lurking in the dark shadows of the backyard right where the cement meets the sand. He stands silent and unmoving in place, as if observing the surroundings and looking for the best way to break in to our house.

My mouth opens, readying for a scream, but then my eyes adjust further. I realize it's not an intruder at all but broken tree branches that have blown in from the storm.

At this point, the alcohol buzz I was enjoying wears off almost completely. Things no longer seem fun and light anymore as I remember we're about to be trapped in a hurricane—and in a murder house, no less. The only thing worse than that is being trapped in a hurricane, in a murder house, in complete darkness.

"We should put out the rest of the candles," Cam says. "And grab flashlights."

"They're still in the kitchen. I'll get them." Sebastian points his cell phone light toward the kitchen island where we stacked the supplies from earlier. "I'll be right back."

Jonathan groans. "What's wrong with you? Don't you watch scary movies?" he asks. "You never go anywhere alone, especially in a haunted house. Every time anyone goes off solo, they never come back. They wind up dead in some cheesy jump scare in Act Three."

Sebastian chuckles. "Dude, it's like ten feet away."

"Ten feet is all it takes to slice and dice." Dark shadows play over Jonathan's face, exaggerating his sharp cheekbones and chin. The lack of light in the house makes his ordinarily cute features appear almost menacing.

"Those movies are so stupid," Cam says as I sit down on

the couch next to her. Blake and Roxy cram in beside me. We sit thigh to thigh, our legs touching, taking comfort from the closeness and each other's body heat. "Especially the ones where some dumb killer chases slutty girls around in a mask. It makes no sense. Why wouldn't they leave town after the first person dies?"

"What do you mean?" Jonathan takes a seat on the coffee table in front of us, frowning. "They don't leave for all kinds of good reasons. Like the car runs out of gas. Or they're sepa-rated so they don't know someone is killing them off," he says. "Or the killer has them trapped on a spaceship, and they have nowhere else to go."

I snort. "Oh yeah. Very realistic."

"Do not come at *Aliens*." Jonathan smiles at me. "That's one of the greatest movies of all time."

"Hell yeah it is." Blake grins and reaches over to high-five him. "Ripley is a badass."

"Good talk. I'm gonna go grab those candles now," Sebas-tian says and walks toward the kitchen, chuckling over his shoulder as he disappears into the darkness.

Blake stands up from the couch and shines her phone light around the room. "You know, I bet the owners have extra candles around here somewhere, too. The property managers always keep my parents' rentals stocked."

"Houses?" Roxy repeats, her eyes widening. "How many houses do you have?"

Welcome to the Lifestyles of the Rich and Famous Bishop Lake Kids, I think to myself, hiding a grin. But, of course, I don't say this out loud.

"Smart thinking," Cam says to Blake. "You guys check the hall closets. Riley and I will take the pantry."

Cam pulls me off the couch and steers me down the hall, while Blake, Roxy, and Jonathan go in the opposite direction. Nia and Mason go nowhere, unsurprisingly. From the sound of it, I think they may be making out on the couch again.

The door to the walk-in pantry creaks open as Cam and I step inside. I've passed by it a few times since we arrived, but this is the first time I've actually gone in. When we first got here with our own snacks two days ago, we were all so lazy from the drive we just put things out on the kitchen counter.

I hold my cell phone light up and scan the shelves for anything helpful in a storm like more candles or drinking water, but it's practically empty. Not that I thought there would be anything of real value in the pantry like a hidden treasure trove of hurricane supplies, despite what Blake said her rental houses had, but I figured there might be at least something useful. Some old batteries left by prior house guests. Candles. A first aid kit. Some matches, at a minimum. Instead, all I see is a bin filled with cleaning supplies like trash bags, bleach, and disposable gloves, a few rolls of duct tape, and some musty cans of tuna fish.

"So you and Seb seem pretty buddy-buddy all of a sudden," Cam says, leaning in so close she startles me.

"Yeah, I guess so," I say, blushing. "He's being flirty again. It's confusing."

"Not sure what's so confusing. I can't understand why you're still not getting it?" A muscle in her chin twitches. "Seb is doing to you what he does to everyone. He makes girls think he's all into them and then drops them for no reason. Did you already forget how he acted after graduation?"

"No, of course not."

"He blew you off, remember?" She pushes on, relentless. "He doesn't care about you, or he wouldn't have done that, right?"

"That's the thing," I say. "It's so weird. He told me tonight it was all a big misunderstanding. He says he did text me after Nia's party, and—"

"Did you get a text?" she asks, cutting me off.

"Well, no, but—"

"Oh my God. It's called gaslighting, Riley," she says, her

voice thick with exasperation. "Don't be so gullible. You sound like an idiot."

I wince, feeling a small stab of hurt. I know she's had a lot to drink, but it almost seems like Cam is enjoying making me feel badly about myself. Like she's getting some sort of weird, perverse joy out of bringing me down about Sebastian.

Except, no, that can't be right. I shake my head, dispelling the negative thoughts. Cam is my best friend. She cares about me, that's all. She's just a little drunk, so her advice is coming out harsher than usual.

"Look, I'm not trying to be a jerk or hurt your feelings," she continues. "I'm saying this for your own good. You know how badly Seb broke Val's heart. She was so into him, and he just dumped her for no reason at all," she says and grabs my hand, squeezing it. "The guy already screwed over my sister. I won't let him screw over my best friend, too."

I clear my throat. "So that's the other thing," I say. "He told me tonight that Val cheated on him. He said that's why he broke up with her."

"What?" She gasps. "He said that?"

I nod.

"Did he tell you why he thinks that?"

"Just that someone told him." I squint, studying her face in the light of my phone's flash. "Why? Is it true? Do you know who told him that?"

"Of course it's not true," she says. "Val never cheated on him. Either someone lied to him, or he's lying to you. Either way, it isn't true." She stares, intensity flashing in her hard gaze. "Just be careful with him, okay? I'd hate to see you get hurt."

"I know. And I appreciate—"

Without warning, she shoves me to the side so hard I fly into the shelves behind me. I stumble, tripping over my feet in the darkness, and fall on my ass. I cry out from the floor, rubbing at my injured shoulder and watching as Cam reaches into some plastic bins shoved way in the back of the pantry. She pulls out some old birthday candles and a few matches.

"Found 'em," she calls out cheerfully and marches out of the pantry to join the others.

Back in the living room where everyone else is gathered, we survey what we have. It isn't much for a house this big or this many people. Sebastian holds one armful of candles and flashlights, and we have whatever Cam found in the pantry. Still, the birthday candles and matches from the pantry are better than what the others found in the rest of the house, which is a whole lot of nothing.

"Did you guys check the basement?" Cam asks. "Maybe that's their storage area?"

"No way." Roxy shudders. "I wouldn't be caught dead in there. That's where they found the bodies."

Blake reaches for Roxy, rubbing her shoulders. "Let's skip the basement for now," she says. "Unless we get desperate."

We use what we have for now to light up the living room and kitchen as best as we can. Blake suggests we play drinking games to pass the time since we don't have music to dance to anymore. Mason and Jonathan clear off the kitchen table to set it up for Beer Pong, and we break off into two teams. It's guys versus the girls.

We get a few rounds in, and things are not going well for the girls. With the exception of our star athlete Blake—who always slays at these games whether she's sober or drunk— we're getting creamed by the boys.

We try Quarters and then Flip Cup next to redeem ourselves, but we suck at that, too.

By now, I've had so much ping-pong-flavored beer to drink, I'm starting to see double. I get up from the table and grab a glass from the kitchen cabinet, filling it to the top with water from one of the jugs in the fridge. After taking a big drink, I return to my seat and hand my glass to Cam to share.

We need to balance out all the alcohol we've been chugging from our losses.

Finally, uber competitive Blake, who hates to lose at anything, shoves all the red Solo cups off the kitchen table in one fell swoop and demands we play a game the girls can win. I suggest Avalanche because it's a game of luck, not skill. I learned it a few years ago when my dad took us to Mount Sierra to go skiing with our cousins at their cabin. From what I remember, I was pretty good at it, too.

"What're the rules?" Nia asks, her voice slurring a bit.

"First, you fill a glass with beer and then you roll the dice," I say. "You do different things depending on the number. Like if you roll a one, you don't do anything, you just pass the glass to the next person. If it's a two, you add more beer to the glass and pass it again."

"Hmm. I don't think we have any dice," Cam says.

"How'd you forget to pack dice?" Nia asks in a bossy tone, the one she uses with her dad's housekeeper when the poor woman screws up making Nia's favorite morning green juice. "Everyone knows you always bring cards and dice for drinking games."

"I'm not your servant, Nia!" Cam snaps. "You should've packed them yourself if you wanted them."

"Why don't we just check the house?" Roxy asks, grabbing the bowl of onion dip from dinner and pulling it close. The sour cream has already started to curl, but she doesn't seem to care as she scoops out the remainders with some leftover chips. She's a bit of a sloppy drunk and some of the dip dribbles onto the collar of her *Metallica* T-shirt. "I bet they have some games stashed around here somewhere."

I glance down at the display on my cell phone. "It's almost eleven. Has anyone heard from Val or Ty?"

Everyone shakes their heads around the room.

"What's taking them so long?" Cam asks, a note of worry entering her voice.

"I'm sure they're just stuck in the storm," Sebastian says. "They'll be here any minute."

Blake drains her vodka and drops the empty cup down onto the kitchen table. "I'm gonna go look for those games," she says and walks over to the entertainment center in the living room. She bends down under the big screen TV and reaches inside the row of cabinets underneath, quickly dismissing what's inside.

Photo albums. Puzzles. Books.

"Holy shit!" she exclaims an instant later, jumping up and looking back at us with a mischievous grin. "They have a Ouija board. We have to play!"

CHAPTER 14

Blake pulls out the game from the shelves underneath the entertainment center and walks back to us with the rectangular Ouija board in one hand and a white triangular planchette in the other. With a huge grin, she drops them both down onto the kitchen table and takes a seat. Everyone except for Nia hovers around her while Jonathan brings the candles in closer. He rearranges them in a row so we can view the board better.

I stare down at the game with a tightening in my chest. I've never been a fan of these things. When I was younger, back in junior high, I was up late one night and saw a story on one of those weekly news magazine shows, *Dateline* or *20/20* or something, about a group of girls playing with a Ouija board at a sleepover. They claimed they contacted a spirit—a demon—named "Donnie" that wanted them to come outside the house to play. He spelled it all out using the board and said he'd be waiting for them at midnight. The girls all thought it was some kind of joke, that one of them was moving the planchette on purpose, even though they all swore they weren't.

Later that night, after everyone else had fallen asleep, the prankster in the group—Lucy—snuck out of the bedroom window to play a joke on the others. She was planning to make up a creepy story about her night "hanging out" with the devil to freak out her friends, except, to her shock, when she got outside the house there was a tall, skinny man dressed all in black waiting on the corner under a streetlamp. He spotted her right away, turning around and waving, beckoning her over. She told her friends afterward that she couldn't see his face because it was too dark but, as soon as he looked at her, she was filled with an overwhelming sense of impending doom. Immediately, she turned around and ran back inside the house.

One week later, Lucy was dead. She burned to death in a freak house fire that started in her bedroom. They never figured out the cause.

Maybe the girls had made it all up, or maybe it was some wild coincidence that Lucy had used the board before her death and the guy outside had been a complete stranger, but ever since hearing that story, I've never once had the urge to play with a Ouija board.

"What happened to Avalanche?" I ask, wiping my clammy hands against the sides of my shorts. The pointy end of the planchette is pointed right at me, as if mocking me.

"Screw Avalanche." Blake dusts off the board with the back of her hand. "Let's talk to some spirits!"

"No way." Roxy shakes her head, inching away from the table. She gives the game some serious side-eye and throws back another shot of liquor. "I'm not touching that thing. Playing with a Ouija board in a haunted house is a little too on the nose for me."

"Oh, come on. Don't be such a sissy," Blake says and reaches out to pull Roxy in closer. "This'll be fun. I promise."

"I'm not a sissy." Roxy pushes Blake's hand away. "I just think it's childish. It's a game for little kids."

Blake's flirty little smile drops away and, for just a moment, darkness flashes across her face. It makes me wonder if Roxy is a little closer to hitting Blake's usual relationship expiration date than I originally thought.

"I'm with her," Nia says, nodding over in Roxy's direction and walking away from the rest of us. She chooses a spot over by the kitchen island, a safe distance from the Ouija board. "I don't mess with that shit. It's dangerous."

"Aw, don't be like that," Mason says to her, taking a seat at the table and patting at the empty chair next to him. "You can hold on to me if you're scared." He licks his lips at her in a way that I think is supposed to be sexy but comes off as lecherous instead.

"No thanks," she says. "My Grann always told me those things are gateways straight to hell. Once that connection is open, you can't close it."

"Well, *I* think it looks fun," Blake says and picks up the planchette, turning the triangular piece of plastic over, studying it. "And anyone else who's not a complete chickenshit is welcome to join me."

A flicker of hurt flashes across Roxy's face.

"I'm in!" Jonathan says, plopping down next to Mason. "I love Ouija boards."

I stifle a little snort. *Of course he does.*

Sebastian goes to join the others at the table, and I raise a brow in his direction. "Wait—you're playing, too? I thought you didn't believe in this stuff."

He grins back. "I don't."

Cam takes a seat next to Sebastian, scooting her chair in close so she can reach the planchette. Sebastian pulls out the open seat on the other side of him and looks back at me. "Come on, March. I'll keep you safe," he says with a cute little wink.

Playing with the Ouija board isn't something I want to do, but it's hard to resist Sebastian when his full attention is on me. It's pretty obvious he wants to hang with me, so I'm not going to let some random story I heard on TV years ago—no matter how terrifying—mess that up.

Reluctantly, I slide into the seat beside him. He scooches in closer, until our legs are touching, and throws an arm around the back of my chair. The heat from his body sends a dizzying current through me.

I sigh and put my finger on the damn planchette.

Here goes nothing…

Roxy hesitates for a moment and then follows suit, slumping down into the seat on the other side of Blake. She gazes at the board warily but, like me, I guess she's also willing to take her chances with the spirits. True love requires sacrifice, right?

"Last chance." Blake cocks her head in Nia's direction. "Stop being a baby and come play."

"Or at least come sit next to me. You don't even have to do anything," Mason says.

"No thanks." Nia leans up against the island counter with her arms crossed over her chest. "I'm fine right where I am."

Blake rolls her eyes at Nia and turns her attention back to the Ouija board. She flips the game box over a few times, trying to find the directions to figure out how to play, but there's not a lot of writing on it. "Anyone remember how this thing works?" she asks, looking around at the rest of us.

"It's pretty simple," Jonathan says. "You just put your fingers on the planchette and ask questions. It spells out the answers."

There's only enough room on the small plastic indicator for each of us to place one finger on top. My pointer finger brushes up against Sebastian's and a little thrill races through me. I'm so hyperaware of his body, it's crazy. Even just our fingers touching sets me ablaze.

"I'll ask the questions," Blake says.

Nia snickers in the kitchen. "It's your funeral."

Blake ignores her, taking in a deep breath and slowly blowing it out so that it makes a soft whistling noise between her lips. We all huddle closer to the board and stare, waiting for more. Without the music playing or even the familiar hum of electricity in the house, the room is oddly quiet—save for the constant thrashing of the wind and rain outside.

Excitement mixed with apprehension fills the air as Blake waves her free hand overhead in a grand, swirling motion. She's so dramatic, like she's reaching for the heavens themselves.

"Spirits, hear us now," she says in a booming voice, filled with authority. "We come to you with honor and respect. We have important questions we'd like answered. Are you willing to talk to us?" She looks around with a wry grin. "Oh, yeah, and if you're those slaughtered kids, we're totally sorry you're dead. We know your deaths were untimely, and that sucks." Everyone around the table holds their breath, fixated, as we stare at the dimly lit board with anticipation.

A few seconds of nothing and then a full minute passes, while the planchette remains unmoving in the center of the board. Nervous laughter fills the air. We take turns shooting little glances at each other, uncertain what's happening.

"Looks like the spirits are busy tonight." Sebastian chuckles next to me.

"Give it a minute," Blake says. "You can't rush the super-natural."

"This is lame." Mason lets out a big yawn across the table.

"Shut up." Blake glares at him. "You're ruining the vibe."

The minutes continue to drag by while we all wait for something, anything, to happen. Still, the planchette doesn't budge.

"I told you this was a stupid idea," Roxy mumbles.

"Everyone be quiet and keep your hands on the board!" Blake says, her freckled neck dotting with little bursts of angry red. She closes her eyes and her forehead furrows with concentration. "Something is happening…"

Slowly, ever so slowly, the indicator begins to move.

I blink, unbelieving my eyes at first.

Did I drink too much? Is this really happening?

Sebastian stiffens next to me as Cam gasps out loud. That's how I realize it's not just me. Others are seeing it, too.

"See—I knew it would work." Blake grins as the planchette skates across the board in a small circle that rapidly grows bigger and more erratic. It swings wildly between YES and NO before eventually settling on YES. "They're answering us. They're willing to talk."

There's a moment of restless silence as we each sneak little looks at each other, trying to see who of us is scared and who believes. Are we truly communicating with something beyond this world? Or is this just our own subconscious guiding the planchette?

Sebastian reaches his free hand under the table and squeezes my knee. Amusement glints in his gorgeous green eyes as he catches my gaze. "It's Mason's big ass fingers moving it," he says with a chuckle.

"Is not!" Mason says.

"Hush!" Blake gives them both a sharp look and turns back to the board. "Who's there? Who's speaking to us?"

The planchette dances along the board as if in answer.

"There! It's moving again." Blake's eyes shine with excitement. The planchette slides back and forth along the board, landing on different letters, and Blake calls them out. "C... A..."

"Ca?" Jonathan asks, a note of hesitation entering his voice. "The spirit's name is *Ca*? That doesn't make sense."

"Relax. It's still spelling," Blake whispers in a revered hush as the circling continues.

"Wasn't that girl who was killed here named Cassie?" Cam asks, her voice shaky. She glances at Roxy with a nervous look. "Isn't that what you said?"

Roxy's eyes widen in alarm. "That's right! Cassie Dixon!"

My pulse skitters. "No way..."

Is the board seriously spelling out a dead girl's name?

Beneath our fingers, the planchette keeps going as if we aren't even talking about it.

"S!" Blake yells out.

"Oh my God." Jonathan's jaw drops. "It's really her. It's Cassie."

My heart hammers so loudly in my chest, I'm sure the others can hear it, too. It sounds like it's going to beat right out of my body.

"P!" Blake's voice rises as she continues to yell out new letters as they come in. "E! R!"

"Wait—now I'm confused." Cam looks around the table, blinking hard. "Did it just spell out *Casper?*"

Just then, something explodes in the kitchen with an earsplitting crack. We all jump out of our seats, shrieking, as sparks of red, white, and blue shoot across the table followed by a series of loud pops like a machine gun. The jarring sound reverberates around the room as smoke fills the air. My jagged breath bursts in and out as I twist around, scouring the room for the source of the blast.

Right away, I spot Mason. His arms are wrapped around his belly, and he laughs so hard he falls out of his seat. A cigarette lighter falls from his hand, tumbling to the floor. I'm still sucking in air and trying to recover from the shock as he sits there, howling like a hyena and wiping tears from his eyes.

"That isn't funny! You can't set off firecrackers in here, you moron," Cam says with a murderous expression on her face. "If I lose the deposit, you're paying me back."

Sebastian groans. "The cherry bombs were for tomorrow, man," he says to Mason.

"Sorry, I couldn't resist." Mason laughs so hard he starts to hiccup. "Things were getting way too serious."

"Nice one." Jonathan bends down and high-fives Mason who continues to roll around on the kitchen floor. "Casper the Friendly Ghost making an appearance—that's classic."

"You guys are idiots," Blake says to them. "Someone is trying to talk to us, and you're screwing it all up." With a huff, she sinks back down into her chair and scoots it into the table with such force the legs make a loud scraping noise across the wood. Her lower lip trembles angrily while she waits for us to rejoin her.

I know Blake's annoyed with the guys for making the Ouija game into a big joke, but this seems like more than that. It's as if she's disappointed as well, like she was hoping it was all for real and not something people do as a lark. It makes me wonder if there's more going on here. Does this have something to do with Jordyn?

While I find the idea of the supernatural sort of terrifying, if my best friend was dead, maybe it wouldn't be so scary. It might be kind of nice, comforting even, to think you could still communicate with them in the afterlife. That they weren't gone forever.

"This isn't the kind of stuff you joke around with," Nia says, her eyes narrowing in Mason's direction. "The spirits don't like to be taunted."

"Oh, come on," Mason says. "There are no spirits. It's just a silly—"

"Don't say it," Blake hisses. "Either shut your mouth and behave, or you can join Nia in the corner."

I'm not sure what comes over me, but I get this terrible feeling of dread in the pit of my stomach. Something deep inside urges me to stop whatever is about to happen next. Perhaps we just dodged a bullet. Mason is a moron, but the game was getting freaky even before his silly prank. If we stop now, it's all a funny joke. A story we can talk about for years to come. But if we continue?

What if something bad happens? What if we find out this house really is haunted?

I open my mouth to protest, but it's already too late. Everyone has returned to their seats again, and Blake has her finger back on the planchette. "Is there anyone here tonight?" she asks the board, starting the game again.

It takes a moment, but then the planchette swings to YES.

Blake beams. "Thank goodness."

"Well, technically, we're here." Cam shuffles in her seat. "So yeah, someone's here."

"The board knows what I meant," Blake says.

Roxy takes her finger off the planchette and pours fresh drinks for the table. We're all out of vodka and most of the beer now, so she uses the tequila instead.

Blake glances around the kitchen table. "So what should I ask it?"

"Ask it if I'm going to be rich," Roxy says.

"Ask it who I'm going to marry," says Cam.

Mason smirks. "Ask if I'm getting laid tonight."

Blake ignores them all. She licks her lips and grins at the board. "Am I going to live a long and happy life?"

It goes to NO. Everyone but Blake laughs.

"Knock it off, douchebag." Blake turns to Mason with fire in her eyes.

"I swear, I didn't touch it this time," he says.

"Someone did," Cam says. "I felt it swing too fast."

"We'll have to do it over," Blake says.

Nia makes a little clucking sound from across the room. "If you aren't even going to listen to the spirits, Blake, then why are you bothering them?"

There's a long beat, and Blake gets a wicked gleam in her eyes. She clears her throat loudly. "Is Nia going to be rich and famous after she moves to LA?"

Nia bangs her glass down onto the kitchen island. "I told you! I don't want to play."

Blake rolls her eyes. "Oh, relax, Nia. I'm just messing with you."

"Well, don't."

"Okay, okay. You're so sensitive," Blake says, holding her

hands up. "Fine, whatever. I'm done with these stupid questions, anyway. I want to ask it something that matters. Something important." She gulps. "I think we should ask about
Jordyn. I want to know why she did it."

There's an audible gasp around the room.

Cam lurches in her seat. "Blake, no!"

"*Are you crazy?*" Nia screeches. "We can't ask that."

"Why not?" Blake asks. "Don't you care? Don't you want
to know what really happened?"

Mason lets out an obnoxious snort. "We know what
happened. She sliced her wrists in a bathtub."

Across the table, Jonathan makes a strange clicking noise
in his throat as he sucks in air. His hands clutch at the edges of
the table, his knuckles turning white.

"Oh shit. I'm sorry, man." Mason looks over at Jonathan
and winces. "You know what I meant."

"That's it. This is going too far now," Sebastian says,
jerking his hand off the planchette and standing up. He
pushes his chair into the table with a loud thud. "I'm out."

"Is our friend Jordyn with you?" Blake asks the board,
ignoring everyone.

YES.

"Really?" Jonathan's voice cracks with emotion, his fingers
back on the planchette.

YES.

The atmosphere in the room changes. It's subtle at first. A
strange heavy feeling like something—or someone—is sucking
up all the oxygen. Then the temperature drops. Out of
nowhere, it feels at least fifteen or twenty degrees colder.

I shiver in my chair and scan my friends' faces to see if
anyone else notices it. It's such a dramatic difference, I can't
be the only one to sense it. As I'm looking around, a flicker of
a shadow catches my eye. Something is in the kitchen, right
behind Nia.

It looks like a person, at first. The shape is so big and tall, it's the only plausible explanation I can think of. Well, except for the fact that everyone in this house, other than Nia, is at the kitchen table with me.

My fingers start to shake on the planchette. I blink my eyes, and when I open them again, the shadow behind Nia is gone.

"Is Jordyn okay? Is she safe?" Blake asks the board.

NO.

Cam cries out and backs away from the table.

"Whoever is doing this shit, knock it off right now!" Sebastian looks around the room with fury in his eyes.

"Is she still hurting? Is she still in pain?" Blake prods.

YES.

"You have to stop, Blake!" Nia yells from the kitchen. She begins to pace back and forth. "I told you. This is dangerous."

"It isn't real." Jonathan sniffles, shaking his head back and forth. *"It isn't real!"* he repeats to himself, louder, like a mantra, and jerks his fingers off the planchette.

"No! Everyone, keep your hands on!" Blake shouts. She turns back to the board game, pushing onward. "What happened? Why did Jordyn kill herself?"

My pulse thumps wildly as the planchette moves across the board.

"WHY DID SHE DO IT?" Blake screams, her voice filled with emotion.

M... U... R... D... E... R...

K... I... L... L... E... R—

Jonathan rips the planchette from underneath our fingers and throws it across the room just as a huge lightning strike flashes outside the glass patio doors. The house grumbles with thunder strong enough to make the kitchen table shake, and the Ouija board goes crashing to the floor. Some of our drinks and the empty chip dip bowls spill onto the ground.

My heart is still racing as I run for the paper towels on the kitchen counter to clean up the mess before it can stain and ruin anything. Jonathan rushes over and drops onto his hands and knees beside me to help. My fingers shake as I dampen and scrub the ground. What the hell just happened...

Cam bursts into tears.

"You asshole!" Blake glares at Mason with burning, reproachful eyes. "I'm going to kill you."

"Oh, come on." He blinks with bewilderment. "You can't really think that was me?"

I sneak a peek at Mason out of the corner of my eye. He's still hovering next to the kitchen table, pale and unmoving. If I'm being objective, he seems as shaken up as the rest of us. While Mason is a lot of things, a good actor is not one of them.

No, this can't be Mason. Even he's not messed up enough for that.

"Damn, that was screwed up. I need a smoke," Roxy says, pulling a cigarette out from her pocket and placing it between her trembling lips.

"Does no one understand this is a rental house?" Cam bellows in between sobs. Her damp eyes are huge and livid as she glares at Roxy. "I told you—you can't smoke in here!"

"Shit, Cammy. Don't have a heart attack," Blake says. "We'll go outside, okay?"

I stiffen on the floor. "You can't go out there. It's getting really bad."

Sure, Roxy is cute and all, but not cute enough to be outside during a hurricane. Besides, Blake doesn't even like to be around smoke. She's a Division 1 star athlete.

"We'll stay under the awning. It'll be fine." Blake gives me a reassuring nod and puts a hand on the small of Roxy's back, escorting her outside.

"She shouldn't be smoking, anyway. That shit will kill you!" Cam yells at them and then turns to me after they're gone.

"What do you think the spirits meant about Jordyn?" she

asks, wiping her wet cheeks and blowing her nose. "Why did it say all that stuff about murder?"

"Just forget it. It was nothing, okay?" I throw the soaked paper towels in the trash and rush over to give her a hug. "It was someone's idea of a bad joke," I say, patting at her back, ignoring how freaked out I am by everything so I can comfort her instead. As terrifying as that just was, it must be far worse for Cam. I didn't even know Jordyn.

"Yeah, you're right." She nods slowly. "I just drank too much. And Val's not back yet. I'm getting worried and, well, you know it's July Fourth tomorrow. That's the day Jordyn... well—" She glances over at Jonathan still on the floor cleaning and stops herself mid-sentence, suddenly remembering Jordyn's brother is here, only a few feet away. Of everyone in the room, Jonathan is the most entitled to be angry and upset by what just happened with the Ouija board. Jordyn was his little sister.

None of us—not even Blake—can know what it's like to lose a family member the way he did. He could be crying like Cam or screaming and threatening violence against Mason like Blake, and it would all be understandable. No reaction would be out of bounds or too inappropriate.

Instead, he remains silent.

His eyes are glassy and dazed as he continues to clean the floor, as if he's not even here. It's like his mind has escaped off into another world. He keeps scrubbing at the ground, over and over in the same spot, even after the floor is dry and all the spilled liquor is gone.

CHAPTER 15

B lake and Roxy return from the covered patio shortly after
we've got the kitchen floor all cleaned up. I almost gag
on the heavy stench of burned ashtray that clings to Roxy as
she goes by me. They weren't even outside for all that long,
but she smells like she may have smoked the whole damn pack
of cigarettes.

I peer past them to the uncovered part of the sliding glass
doors to the patio outside. The backyard is plunged in the
deepest, darkest night I've ever seen. Rain now comes down in
torrents and sleets, pounding against the rooftop and walls.
Rapid-fire lightning illuminates the latest casualty of the
increasing strength of the storm: Our neighbor's picket fence
now lies broken in two pieces on our patio deck, dozens of feet
from where it should be.

Jonathan remembers then that he grabbed a radio at the
grocery store earlier. He disappears down the hallway and
returns a moment later with a hand crank wind-up radio that
looks like it was made in the early 1900s. It's funny. I don't
think I've ever seen a portable radio before, except in old
movies. It's not something I thought I'd ever need or use, but
with the power out and our cell phones without service now,
it's our only connection to the outside world.

Everyone gathers around the kitchen island, and Jonathan
cranks up the volume as loud as it'll go. A woman's voice rings
out, crackling as the reception goes in and out.

"What'd she say?" I ask, leaning in closer to the radio.

"She says the storm's still strengthening. It'll be another three hours until the eye hits," Jonathan says, his ear right next to the speaker. "That's when things will get worse—once the eyewall comes ashore."

"They think the eyewall is heading *here*?" Roxy asks, her kohl-rimmed eyes widening with alarm. "For real?"

One thing I know about hurricanes, you don't want to be anywhere near the eyewall when it comes on land. This is something Florida kids learn from a young age. The eyewall is where the most severe winds in a hurricane occur. It's the part of the storm where tornados are most likely to form. It's always where you get the worst damage.

"I knew we should've gone to Miami." Mason scowls at all of us.

Jonathan looks at his watch. "It's almost midnight. Bridge is about to close," he says. "Guess Val and Ty aren't showing up after all."

Cam chews on the inside of her lip and glances over at Sebastian. "You still think they're okay, right?"

"Absolutely," he says. "I'm sure we'll hear from them as soon as the power comes back."

"There's still a chance the storm will turn, right? Or lose strength?" I ask, my palms starting to sweat. It's now officially too late for us to leave. Between the power dying, the Ouija board fiasco, and this news about the weather, my alcohol buzz has completely worn off.

"Sure." Sebastian gives me a comforting smile.

"Well, this is just great," Nia says. "What're we supposed to do now? Just sit around and wait for it to hit?"

"We could try to get some sleep," Sebastian says.

"You expect us to sleep in *this*?" Nia asks while we all watch through the glass doors as a full-size trash can blows past the yard, mid-air.

Sebastian shrugs. "It's only going to get worse. Might as well try."

"Come on, let's go," Blake says to Roxy. She grabs her beer and one of the bigger candles off the kitchen table and heads down the hallway to her bedroom. Roxy follows, unsteady on her feet, stumbling and swaying a bit. For a bartender, she's not very good with her own alcohol. Sebastian gets a bottled water from the fridge and jogs after them, calling out Roxy's name.

"I'll crash with Nia," Mason says and pulls Nia out of her bar stool. "This way she won't be all alone."

"And I'm only saying yes because this storm is freaking me out," Nia mumbles, allowing Mason to lead her away toward the other downstairs bedroom. I know Mason well enough to know he's only pretending to be chivalrous when he's just hoping to get in her pants. "You're on the floor, got it?" she says to him, so I think she knows it, too.

Jonathan looks at me with a hopeful glimmer in his eyes. "I can stay with you, Riley, and make sure you're safe?"

"Oh, er—" I stammer.

"I've got it," Sebastian says, returning from delivering the water to Roxy. His gaze meets mine, and I feel a lurch of excitement. "I'll crash with March."

I can't believe it!

Sebastian Ramos wants to sleep in my bed!

My fantasies take over as I imagine us together in the bedroom upstairs. His arms wrapping around me in the darkness, pulling me in close to him. The room silent except for the sound of our breathing and the rain crashing outside the window. The gentle rise and fall of our chests as we gaze longingly into each other's eyes.

Will he try to kiss me again?

What else will he want to do?

"And Cam, too, of course," Sebastian adds. His grin flashes briefly, dazzling, in her direction. "I'll keep an eye on you both."

"That'd be great," Cam says. "I'd really like that."

Oh.

My heart shrivels up and deflates like a week-old balloon.

Sebastian's offer to bunk up isn't about me at all. It's not that he wants to be alone with me in the bedroom like I'd hoped. He's just being a good friend and gentleman and making sure both Cam and I are safe.

"Alrighty then, I guess I'll take one of the couches," Jonathan says, his eyes narrowing in Sebastian's direction. An angry blush creeps over his cheeks. "By myself."

I sort of feel bad for him. It looks like neither one of us is getting what we want tonight.

"See you losers in the morning," Mason says before disappearing into the downstairs bedroom with Nia, and everyone goes their separate ways for the evening.

Once we're upstairs, Sebastian places one of the lit candles from the kitchen onto the cherry wood dresser in the bedroom. The light flickers and casts shadows along the planes of his handsome face as he drops a throw blanket onto the floor and fluffs up some extra pillows he found in the hall closet. Even if he may not be here just for me, I'm still glad for his company. I'm having a difficult time not thinking about the brutal murders that took place within these walls or what happened with the Ouija board earlier. It's hard not to be creeped out, especially in the darkness. Sebastian's presence definitely helps.

After we change into pajamas and brush our teeth, Cam lies down on one side of the bed while I take the other. She watches Sebastian, twisting and turning on the floor, and offers to make room for him in our bed. At first, he tries to be a gentleman and turns her down. I hear him grunt hard on the ground, trying to maneuver into a good spot. The floor must be really uncomfortable, though, because eventually he gives in.

There's a bit of rustling as he climbs into the empty space between Cam and me and slides under the covers. There's not a ton of room with all of us on the bed as the mattress was built to fit two people and Sebastian is a tall, muscular guy. He lies dead center of the bed to start, but after a few moments, his body starts to relax.

He shifts just a tiny bit closer to me. The far side of his arm and leg brush against mine. It's just a slight movement, a few inches toward me and away from Cam, but it happens. Heat radiates from his body, burning my skin. It makes me heady, being this close to him. I let myself melt in closer and wait, gauging his reaction.

Time ticks by slowly at first. I wonder if I made a mistake.

Was I too forward? Am I embarrassing myself?

But then he sets his arm down on me, pulling me to his chest. His hand rests lightly against my stomach. Even though he's taller than me, we line up in all the places you're supposed to. We fit together perfectly.

Slowly, his hand begins to move. Soft, fluttering fingers find a gap of skin on my stomach between the top of my pajamas and waist band. It makes me shiver with excitement.

I can't believe it. I'm in bed with Sebastian Ramos and he's touching me!

His feet find mine under the covers and then they're sliding on one another, our limbs tangled together. I feel his breath on the back of my neck while his hand continues tracing circles on my abdomen. All I want to do is turn around and face him so that maybe he'll kiss me, but then Cam lets out a loud sniffle, and I remember. She's still here with us. We aren't alone in the bed.

"You guys still up?" she whispers.

Sebastian's fingers stop moving.

"What is it? What's wrong?" I ask, trying to keep my voice steady as I straighten myself in the bed.

"I can't stop thinking about her." Cam twists around and grabs the top of the sheets, pulling them up to her trembling chin. Her hands shake. "I can usually ignore the bad thoughts, but this week it's been harder than usual. Pretty soon we'll all be getting ready to go off to college and start our lives, but Jordyn will never get to go anywhere," she says. "It doesn't seem right."

"That's because it isn't right." Sebastian's voice is hard and flinty.

"I know you must think I'm an awful person because we act like she never existed," she says. "I know it's totally messed up, but it just hurts too much to think about her. I miss her so much."

"No one thinks that," I lie.

The way my friends have handled Jordyn's death is, objectively, completely messed up. It's like they've erased the girl from their memory. There are no posts of Jordyn on their social media, except for the old ones from before she died. Nothing to remember her by in their bedrooms, either, like pictures and collages of them and Jordyn. Even my mom has a photo in our living room of my grandmother who passed away and they were estranged for years. The whole thing seems weird.

Not that I personally know a lot about this stuff.

I've never known anyone our age who died. I don't know how I'd react, either. It seems shitty, but maybe it really is just easier for them to not think about Jordyn. Look at Jonathan and his family. They never bounced back from the loss. Jordyn's suicide destroyed them. I guess it's hard to blame my friends for not wanting that to happen to them, too. Perhaps death is just easier to ignore than to deal with.

"For the longest time, it didn't seem real that Jordyn was gone," Cam says and flips over on her side, laying her head atop the pillow. "I kept seeing her everywhere. In class. In the hallways. In my bedroom late at night. Sometimes I'd even hear her calling my name." She sinks deeper into the sheets, like she wants to hide under them. "I couldn't sleep for weeks."

Before I lose my nerve, I ask a question I've always wondered. "Did you know she was going to do it?"

This is the first time Cam has ever wanted to talk about Jordyn, so I've never had the chance to ask her things like this before. I've always been curious how much my friends knew about Jordyn's suicide. It's hard to believe someone like Jordyn —pretty, popular, and rich, someone with so much to live for —would take her own life without any signs.

There must have been signs, right?

"Of course not," Cam says. I hear a few sniffles and know she's crying. "I had no idea."

I reach past Sebastian to squeeze her shoulder. "I'm so sorry, Cammy. It must have been so horrible for you."

"Yeah right..." Sebastian mumbles. In the flicker of candlelight, I can see he's frowning.

Cam stiffens. "What's your problem?"

"Never mind. Forget it," he says.

"No, just say it. Say what you're really thinking," she insists. "I know you want to."

"Okay, fine. I will." He sits up in the bed, cocking his head at her. "If I'm being honest, watching you all pretend you were clueless about Jordyn's death has never sat right with me. Jon knew something was wrong. He knew something bad was happening. He said Jordyn was sad. She would cry in her room every night." His lips push together into a thin, tight line. "Jon was certain it was a fight with one of you—or maybe all of you. Jordyn always said you girls could be ruthless."

"That's not true!" Cam shouts, her cheeks red. "We weren't fighting. She was our best friend."

My breath quickens at her denial. Why is Cam lying?

I may not know much about what went down between my friends and Jordyn before she died, but I know what I saw in the bathroom last spring. The girls were definitely fighting over that video. I'm positive of that. So why is Cam denying it?

"So then, what happened?" Sebastian presses further. "What do you know?"

"It was a suicide, Sebastian! This isn't some bad teen drama on Netflix," Cam says. "What exactly are you implying? That we're somehow responsible for Jordyn's death?"

"I'm just saying it doesn't add up…"

Cam turns away from him and faces the wall, starting to cry. The room is silent except for her soft sobs and the sounds of the storm. I reach over, past Sebastian, and lightly stroke her hair.

"It might help to talk about it," I say. "It's not healthy to keep things all bottled up."

"It wasn't anybody's fault," she whispers. "Even if there was… I don't know… stuff she was upset about, we were all upset about things sometimes. How were we supposed to know how sad she really was? That she was capable of something like *that*." She lets out an agonizing sob. "It's been so hard. I miss her so much."

Her chest heaves up and down as she cries in the bed. My heart clenches almost painfully as I watch her. I hate to see her so upset. It makes me want to cry, too. I don't know what to do or how to make her feel better.

"I'm sorry," Sebastian says, reaching over to give her a hug. "I shouldn't have said all that. It's just… she was a good person. This never should've happened." He sighs. "And I hate what it's done to Jon and his family."

"It's alright. I understand." She sniffles into his chest. "But if it's okay with you both, I don't want to talk about it anymore."

She closes her eyes, exhausted. Sebastian untangles himself from the embrace and rolls back into the middle of the bed.

Sadly, the heat between us from before has now cooled off

due to the heavy conversation. There's no more cuddling or playing footsie under the covers, and definitely no kissing in bed like I had hoped for. The three of us lay there in silence, lost in our own thoughts, until sleep eventually comes.

That's when the nightmare begins.

CHAPTER 16

DAY 4: Sunday—July Fourth

The screaming of the storm yanks me from my bad dreams.

For a few seconds, I'm still caught up in my nightmare. My adrenaline races as I run from the man with the axe, desperate to escape certain death. The same faceless, imaginary killer cloaked in his yellow hooded rain slicker—the same man I've been dreaming of these past few weeks—is trying to kill me and my friends. I smell the musty damp walls of the basement where he keeps us, mixed in with the acrid, pungent odor of fear. The agonizing screams of my friends reverberate in my ears.

Even as my eyes slowly adjust to the four walls of the rental house bedroom, I can still feel him nearby. Stalking. Hunting us. My feet kick at the sheets as sweat pours off my body. It rolls off my skin in waves, dampening the bed sheets. It all seems so real. More like memory than dream.

I'm okay, I tell myself. *It was just a nightmare.*

A horrific, traumatizing nightmare, but a nightmare, nonetheless.

The vision, still so fresh in my head, spurs an alarming question. I wonder how, exactly, Ed Rawlins came upon Cassie Dixon and her friends that fateful July Fourth night. Was it planned? Did he know them?

Or was it just pure bad luck?

I'm not sure which is scarier—the idea that the murders were premeditated or that they were completely random. Probably the latter. At least if the killer had planned it, there'd be warning signs or clues along the way. If you were paying attention, maybe you could stop it. At least then you'd have a chance to outsmart the killer beforehand and escape death. Maybe that's why so many people, like Jonathan, love true crime and horror movies. They think if they can see the patterns and figure out the plans first, they can stop the bad things from happening to them or the people they love. But if it's arbitrary and pure chance—if there's no rhyme or reason to it? There's nothing you can do. All you can hope for is to survive.

"Everything okay?" Sebastian asks from the doorway. "I thought I heard screaming."

He leans against the frame, light from the candle in his hand casting shadows that dance across his worried face. I lift away sticky, matted hair from my neck to cool down. Trying to slow the furious beating of my heart, I exhale in and out, feeling my breath as it fills my nose and expands into my lungs.

"Just a bad dream," I say. "Where'd you go?"

"Downstairs for a bit. I couldn't sleep."

I roll over onto my side and reach for Cam only to realize the bed is empty.

"Cammy's gone," I say, sitting up and looking around. "Was she downstairs with you?"

"Nope." He yawns and stretches his muscular arms overhead. "She's probably in the bathroom."

The wind wails outside, violently shaking the plywood on the windows. The eyewall must be close because the noise has reached a level far more disturbing than I'd ever imagined. People always describe hurricanes as "loud," but a simple adjective doesn't even remotely prepare you for the actual experience. In reality, it's like an enormous freight train roaring past, the sound relentless as it hammers in your head. It feels like it will never stop. Never slow down. Never give up.

"I'll go find her," I say, wiping underneath what I'm certain are raccoon eyes, hoping to catch whatever mascara and eyeliner clotted overnight. I throw the covers off and grab a flashlight from the nightstand.

"You want company?" he asks.

"I'm okay, but thanks."

Of course I want his company, but I also don't want to seem like a wimp who can't walk ten feet down the hall by herself.

As I go past him, the beam of my flashlight shines on his face. Unlike me—a hot mess from all the tossing and turning and sweating—he appears fresh and dewy. Even this early in the morning, he looks amazing.

I inch down the dark hallway alone, taking small, tentative steps, doing my best not to trip and fall on anything. At the very end of the hall, the bathroom door is slightly ajar. The hinges creak and groan as I push it all the way open and walk inside, shining my flashlight around.

I stifle a scream as a horrifying image in the bathroom mirror catches my eye. A hideous ghoul with eyes so big and dilated they're as black as a monster's and a hollowed-out skeletal face stares back at me. I remember the Ouija board and, for an instant, I'm convinced this is one of the evil spirits of the house we communicated with, coming to kill me. It takes another few seconds before I realize, with a rather unpleasant shock, that the terrifying apparition I see is actually just my own reflection and not some evil demon come to life. The harsh beam of the flashlight in the darkness is super unflattering, to say the least.

I scan the rest of the room, my heart still thumping in my chest as I look around, but I see nothing else alarming. The bathroom is empty. No sign of Cam.

That's odd.

This is a big house, but it's not that big. If Cam isn't upstairs, then she must be downstairs somewhere. It's weird that Sebastian didn't see her down there, but maybe she's in one of the bedrooms with Blake or Nia? No way would Cam leave the house, not without telling me first and not with the storm raging like it is.

Right as I close the door to go back down the hall and keep looking for Cam, something flickers in my peripheral vision. It's a slight movement in the corner of the mirror, directly behind my garish reflection. Something lurking just beyond my sight. The rational side of me says it's nothing to worry about. It's only a trick of the light or a glitch in the mirror's surface. But the older, primordial bird-part of my brain returns right back to thoughts of the supernatural and something far more ominous like a malevolent presence.

My spine tingles as I whip around to see who—or what— is with me in the hallway.

"Hello?" I call out to the darkness.

The only reply is another crash of thunder and the screaming of the wind.

Hair prickles along my scalp. I tell myself to relax, that it's only my imagination making me see things. I'm totally fine. I'm not in any danger.

Relax, Riley. There's nothing there.

You're completely, utterly, absolutely fine…

Somewhere nearby, I hear what sounds like the creep of footsteps along the wooden floor.

With a gasp, I turn around, swinging my flashlight toward the opposite end of the hallway. "Who's there?" I call out, my voice shaking. I take a step forward and drift further down the hall, unable to shake the sense I'm being watched. Someone is here with me. I can feel their eyes on me.

Creeeaaak…

I hear it again.

It sounds like it's coming from below. Maybe someone is in the kitchen, after all? Cam? Jonathan?

I keep walking toward the staircase, but as I approach the first stair, the sound becomes more muffled. It sounds as if it's coming from somewhere even further away than the kitchen. The basement, perhaps?

But why would someone be in the basement? How did they even get in there without a key and—

Sebastian grabs my shoulder, spinning me around.

"You okay?"

"Holy shit, Seb!" I yell. "You scared the crap out of me." My pulse pounds so hard in my chest, I think I may be having an actual heart attack.

"Sorry," he says, smiling sheepishly. "You were gone so long I got worried." He squeezes my shoulder. "Everything alright? You look like you just saw a ghost."

I lean against the hallway wall, sagging into it.

"I'm fine," I say, swallowing down my panic. "I just thought I saw someone."

Now that Sebastian is here, I'm already embarrassed for freaking out over nothing. It's just that the macabre history of this house and the creepy seance earlier are getting to me. I guess the bad dreams aren't helping, either.

Damn Val for getting us into this ridiculous situation.

"Did you find Cam?" he asks me.

"No." I shake my head. "She's not in the bathroom. I was about to check downstairs."

He eyes me with a concerned glance. "I think I'd better come with you."

This time I don't disagree.

Sebastian walks in front of me, swinging his flashlight ahead so it illuminates the staircase in front of us. He starts to take a step down the stairs but turns around first to make sure I'm following. My knees are still shaky from the scare, and I can't seem to get my feet to move forward. He grins, reaching back for my hand. His long slender fingers encircle mine and warm my insides as he steers me down the stairs, pulling me along. I use my free hand to grip the wooden banister and steady myself as we descend.

We step into the living room where Jonathan is still fast asleep on the couch, despite the chaos of the storm going on outside. A flannel throw he must've found in the linen closet is pulled up over the bottom half of his body. The blanket rises and falls to the rhythm of his heavy breathing.

Still holding my hand, Sebastian guides me past the living room and into the kitchen. Our flashlights shine toward the fridge and the kitchen island. I expect to see Cam grabbing food or a drink, but the room is empty. There's no sign of her here, either.

"I don't get it," I say, raising my voice to be heard over the raging of the wind as it pounds against the patio doors. "Where is she?"

Now I'm really starting to panic.

"She's got to be around here somewhere," he says.

Sebastian separates from me and takes a few steps down the hall and toward the front door. He aims his flashlight at the side table in the darkened entranceway, illuminating the bowl where Cam and Sebastian tossed their car keys earlier.

"Yep, they're all still there," he says with an assuring glance backward. "Don't worry. We'll find her."

He's saying all the right things. It makes sense Cam must be in the house somewhere, that's what I thought before myself, and yet…

A slow, unsettling feeling washes over me as we continue to search around the first floor. We peek into the dining room, the downstairs bathroom, and even the walk-in pantry. Still no sign of Cam anywhere. I can't shake the notion that something is wrong.

"I'm gonna wake the others. We should check their

rooms," Sebastian says, heading for the bedroom where Nia and Mason are asleep. "She's probably with one of them."

I nod and take off in the opposite direction toward the downstairs bedroom Blake and Roxy share. As I walk by, I notice a rather large puddle of water gathering in front of the sliding glass doors and wander over to examine. At first glance, it looks like someone must have spilled a drink on the ground and forgot to clean it up. It doesn't appear as if any real damage has been done to the wood floor, but I can't believe someone would leave such a mess.

When I bend down to get a better look, I realize with a little shock that the water isn't from a spill at all. It's coming from outside. The uncovered portion of the patio door is cracked open. It's not much, just a few millimeters. It wouldn't even be noticeable if I wasn't so close. Either the power of the storm forced the door open, or someone went outside and forgot to fully shut it behind them. Was it Blake and Roxy? Did they forget to lock the door after their smoke earlier?

I reach around to close the door, my eyes widening as flashes of lightning illuminate the deck. It's like a war zone outside. The once immaculate swimming pool is now an over-flowing sinkhole filled with debris, and not just dirt and sand from the beach and leaves from trees, but all sorts of things like a gorgeous Royal Palm tree that used to be planted right next to the patio. The tree has been uprooted and lies halfway inside the water, as if some rogue superhero lifted it up and tossed it there. I cringe, spotting two of the house's lawn chairs at the bottom of the deep end.

Oh shit.

We should've secured the outdoor furniture, but with so much going on, none of us even thought about it.

Something big and wide floats along the surface of the pool, grabbing my attention. The top half of the object is a fresh, vivid red. It's the color of freshly picked cherries, skim-ming the water like threads of silk from a spider's web. This seems like something I should recognize, but my brain is having trouble identifying and putting a name on it. It doesn't look like any patio furniture or decor I've seen on the deck, and yet there's something so familiar about it...

Battling against the wind, I heave the patio door all the way open and step outside. Harsh wind and stinging rain pelt my body as I head for the pool. The downpour of water soaks through my thin pajamas, causing goosebumps to rise along my arms and legs. I know I should go back inside and at least put a sweatshirt on, grab an umbrella or something, but I can't stop. I have to see what's in the pool. As if in a trance, I keep going until I reach the water's edge.

The glint of a nose ring catches the beam of my flashlight.

Silver angel wing earrings.

A swath of black fabric and raised, embroidered white letters spelling out *Metallica*.

It all comes together at once. My throat goes dry as my brain connects the pieces and finally deciphers what I'm seeing.

It's Roxy!

Roxy's body is floating in the pool!

Leaves and sand whip against my face while I stare, horrified, unable to turn away. An absurd idea flashes in my head. Perhaps Roxy went for a midnight swim and fell asleep? She's simply floating along in the water, peacefully dreaming. That must be what I'm seeing.

Except, that isn't how physics works. People don't float on the surface of the pool. Not unless they're dea—

I don't wait to complete the thought.

Cold, dirty water rushes over my face and chest as I dive headfirst into the pool. I paddle as fast as I can to Roxy's body, the bitter taste of chlorine filling my mouth and nose. As soon as I'm close enough, I hook my arms underneath her armpits and kick us both back to the shallow end. My feet skid across the slippery deck as I try to drag her out of the pool. It isn't easy to haul her up, not with the pounding rain and wind and the added weight of our soaked clothing. My arm muscles scream in agony.

Then Sebastian and Jonathan are beside me. They grab Roxy's body from my arms and carry her away, placing her down underneath the covering of the patio awning. The three of us stand over her stiff, unmoving body, looking down in horror. Her skin is pale and bluish under the light, and her glossed over eyes stare out at nothing. Any sign of life on her face is gone.

"What do we do?" I scream over the howling wind. My teeth chatter as I wrap my arms around my shaking, freezing body. "Are we supposed to try CPR?"

Jonathan bends down to check Roxy's pulse.

"She's dead," he declares, dropping her limp wrist back to the ground. "And from the look of things, she's been dead for quite a while."

My stomach rolls with nausea. I think I'm going to be sick.

"I don't understand. How did she wind up in the pool?" I ask.

"She was pretty drunk," Sebastian says, his mouth tight and grim. "She must've slipped and fallen in somehow."

"But why would she be outside in this weather?" I stare up at the menacing sky. Constant lightning continues to cackle above while punishing rain pelters the backyard.

"I don't know." Sebastian regards Roxy's body quizzically for a moment. "She was drinking so much. Maybe she woke up and got confused? Or she wanted another smoke?"

I can't stop staring at Roxy's face. There's something strangely mesmerizing about it, like what they say about witnessing a terrible car accident. I want to turn away, but I can't. I think I can see fear in her final expression. Or is that shock?

What had Roxy felt in her last moments?

Jonathan pulls down the collar of Roxy's T-shirt. His eyes

narrow as he shines his flashlight down on her, examining her neck and the very top of her chest. He lets out a little gasp and reaches out to touch her skin, then he whips back, and his eyes whirl toward the pool deck and the backyard. He scans the area suspiciously, like he's searching for some kind of clue.

"What is it?" I ask, struggling to stay upright as the wind whips the rain in all directions. "What are you thinking?"

"Anything I say would be pure speculation. I'm not a medical examiner or anything," Jonathan says. "You know, they're the ones who determine this type of thing. They can examine a body and see how much water is in the lungs. They can tell all sorts of things…"

"But?"

"But I don't think Roxy drowned."

"You don't?" My teeth chatter something terrible as the wind whips harder. "You think it's something else? Something… bad?"

A cold knot forms in my stomach.

"Yeah," he says. "I do."

"C'mon, man." Sebastian snorts. "What are you talking about? Of course she drowned. She was a nice girl, and it's really sad, but she had way too much to drink and fell in. Reading a few books and listening to some podcasts doesn't make you a crime scene expert."

My shivers grow worse, and not just from my drenched pajamas and dripping hair, but from whatever Jonathan is implying.

"What if Jon's right?" I ask. "What if it's not an accident? That means somebody intentionally—"

"March, you're freezing. We need to get you inside," Sebastian says, grabbing me by the elbow and pulling me into his chest to shelter me from the wind and rain. He attempts to steer me toward the sliding glass door. "We'll let the professionals handle this after the storm is over."

"Hold on." I dig my heels in. "I want to hear what Jon thinks."

Jonathan exhales loudly, motioning me back over. I break free of Sebastian's embrace and join Jonathan a few inches from Roxy's body. I lean down closer as he pulls back Roxy's T-shirt collar for me so I can see her pale skin underneath. She's got small, blotchy red markings around her neck. They're faint. Only visible at close range if someone knows what to look for.

"See this here," Jonathan says, pointing to the marks at Roxy's neck. "I can't be sure, but it appears something was wrapped around her neck."

"Something? Like what?"

"Could be anything," he says, swallowing. "Maybe she got twisted up in the fallen branches. Maybe she had a tight necklace on, and it fell off in the water."

He turns away, not making eye contact with me anymore.

"But that's not what you think, is it?"

There's a long, brittle silence before Jonathan answers me.

"No, that's not what I think." Fear, stark and vivid, glitters in his dark eyes. "I think someone strangled her and threw her in the pool to make it look like an accident. I think Roxy was murdered."

CHAPTER 17

All the blood rushes to my head as the implication of Jonathan's words hits me.

Jonathan thinks someone killed Roxy.

He begins to cover Roxy's face and body with a beach towel he grabs from inside the house while I stare past him, scouring the backyard. I scan every dark corner of the pool patio, every tree that blows in the wind, every shrub—no matter how small—for signs of danger.

Is the killer outside watching us right now? Is he hiding in the shadows, waiting for a chance to attack again?

Are we next?

I shudder, my whole body shaking with cold and fear as I stand up and back away from Roxy's body. I reach for Sebastian's hand. His squeeze is firm, reassuring. "Alright. Time to go," he orders, pulling me toward the house again.

"Do you think he's still here?" I ask. "Whoever did this to her, I mean?"

Jonathan's expression is grim. "It's a real possibility."

"That's enough, March," Sebastian says, his voice tight. "We need to get you inside and into some warm clothes."

This time I sag into his embrace, letting him steer me away. I'm too wet and scared to argue anymore. I don't want to stay on the patio any longer, anyway. If there's someone out here trying to kill us, inside is better. At least we can lock the doors in the house.

We're almost back inside when I spot something shiny and

black lying on the deck a few feet away from the sliding glass doors. Breaking free from Sebastian's grasp, I walk over and bend down under the patio awning, squinting to get a better look. It's the latest and greatest iPhone model that just came out a few weeks ago. The phone case appears brand new, too. It's all black, and the familiar blue Orlando Magic logo covers the entire backside.

"Hey! That's Ty's!" Sebastian lets out an audible gasp as he comes up next to me. He grabs the phone and, sure enough, a photo of Ty hanging from a basketball net shows up when he taps the screen.

"What's it doing here?" Jonathan asks, inching in between Sebastian and me to get a look.

"I dunno." Sebastian shrugs. "Maybe they came back while we were sleeping, and he dropped it? Or maybe they stopped by the other night when you all were out?"

"You think they came back here and didn't tell anyone? Really?" I ask.

"What other explanation is there?" he asks.

I don't know if I buy his logic, but phones don't just show up randomly on someone else's patio, either. Someone has to put them there. And seeing as Tyler's phone still works and even has half a battery life left, it must have been put on our patio recently. Sebastian's explanation is as good as anything I can think of.

"Or maybe whoever killed Roxy killed Ty, too, and took his phone and dropped it here during the struggle," Jonathan says, his mouth pulled into a sour grin.

"And maybe you should quit playing Sherlock Holmes," Sebastian says and pushes his friend through the patio doors. "Go wake the others, okay? I'm gonna help March dry off."

As Sebastian ushers me up the stairs, we can hear Jonathan waking the others to tell them what's happened. Their shouts echo through the house, bouncing up and down the hallways, each louder and more alarming than the next as he tells them Roxy is dead.

Sebastian waits patiently outside the bedroom while I change out of my wet clothes and into my warmest sweats, and then he helps me dry my soaked hair with a towel from the hallway bathroom. I'm still shivering as he picks up a blanket from the bed and places it over my shoulders, bundling me inside.

When we return to the living room, our friends are a mess. An ashen-faced Nia is huddled next to Mason on one of the couches, so close she's practically in his lap. The two of them take turns drinking straight from the tequila bottle while Blake bawls in Jonathan's arms on the other couch. Her entire body quakes as he pats at her back awkwardly, doing his best to comfort her.

I don't think I've ever seen Blake cry before. Not like this, anyway. Even when she pulled a calf muscle at a track meet this past spring, she barely shed a tear. The injury had been so bad she'd had to sit out of her beloved races for almost three weeks, but she'd taken all of it, even the pain, in stride. It makes me feel awful to see her this distraught. She must have really liked poor Roxy.

Blake turns to me when she spots us, mascara streaking her face. "I don't understand," she says, sniffling. "She said something about swimming before bed, but I thought she was joking..."

"We need to call the police," Nia says. "They'll know what to do." She takes another swig of tequila before handing the bottle back to Mason.

"There's no cell service, remember?" I remind her.

"Just use the Wi-Fi!" she snaps.

It's such a dumb thing to say, I ignore her.

"Has anyone seen Cammy?" I ask, glancing around. Cam is the only one still missing from the living room.

Well... besides Roxy.

"Nope," Jonathan says. "I couldn't find her."

"Shit…" The edges of Sebastian's voice are raised. He doesn't sound panicked, not yet, but like he's getting there.

Well, that makes two of us.

"She's probably just asleep in one of the bedrooms," Nia says. "Go get her, Riley."

"I checked all the rooms," Jonathan says.

"Okay, so?" Nia shrugs. "Then maybe she went out to get something?"

I give her a look. "In a hurricane?"

"I don't know!" She glares at me. "Maybe it was an emergency."

"No," I shake my head. "Cam wouldn't go anywhere without telling me."

"You don't think…" Jonathan hesitates for a beat, swallowing hard before continuing. "Cam didn't have anything to do with Roxy drowning, did she?"

I gasp. "Cam would NEVER!"

"I told you that Ouija board was a mistake. I told you not to play!" Nia stands, shaking the tequila bottle at Blake's face. "But no—you wouldn't listen, would you? You never take anything seriously, Blake. It's always fun and games with you."

"Why're you mad at me?" Blake's lower lip trembles. "This isn't my fault."

"Relax, babe. Everything's gonna be okay." Mason pushes Nia back down onto the couch, prying the bottle away from her trembling hands. "As soon as our phones start working again, I'll get Dad's company jet to fly us out of this shithole." He takes a swig of the tequila and lets out a loud belch.

"It's this house," Blake says. "Roxy tried to warn us. She said it was evil."

Sebastian stiffens next to me. "There's nothing wrong with this house. That girl drank too much and drowned. It's sad, yeah, but it's not supernatural," he says. "And Cam will turn up any minute."

"Oh yeah? Like Val's turned up? Or Ty?" Nia asks, her voice filled with sarcasm.

"So, uh, that's another thing." I give an anxious little cough. "We found Ty's cell outside. Looks like it's been out there for a few hours, too."

Blake stares at Nia, baffled. "I thought Ty was texting you? That's what you said, isn't it?"

"I said that *yesterday*," Nia says. "I haven't heard from that jackass since then."

"You're sure it was yesterday? And it was Ty who messaged you?" Blake asks.

Nia gives her an irritated glare. "Of course I'm sure. Why would I lie about that?"

"It's just interesting, is all." Blake's eyebrows furrow together. "You're the only one who's heard from him, and now his phone is there lying in our backyard…"

"Oh, screw you, Blake!" Nia barks. "I don't even know what you're trying to imply here—that I what? Got pissed at my cheating boyfriend, killed him, killed one of my best friends, and stole his phone to send myself messages?" She snorts. "Get real."

"That's not what I—"

"And Roxy? You think I pushed her in the pool for fun?" Nia asks, throwing back her head and tossing her hair. "I already told you—it's the spirits. You never should've messed with them."

"It's not spirits," Jonathan says. "Spirits don't leave ligature marks."

"Huh? What's that supposed to mean?" Blake asks.

"Jon thinks someone strangled Roxy," I explain. "She's got these strange marks around her neck."

"Holy shit… You think this is Ed Rawlins?" Blake whispers, extricating herself from Jonathan's arms. She wipes away the wetness on her cheeks with the back of her hand and tilts her head up to face him. "You think the killer from Roxy's story is back?"

A sudden, heavy knocking sound from behind interrupts us. It's so loud and unexpected that I let out a half chirp, half shriek, and huddle in closer to Sebastian. My knees shake as we all stare at each other with confused expressions on our faces. It sounds like someone is outside the house, trying to get in.

As the knocking grows more persistent, it becomes clear it's coming from outside the glass patio doors. Sebastian flashes his light toward them and lets out a loud groan. He stomps over and slides open the doors to reveal Officer Grant Topper, still in full police uniform, all alone and standing on our back deck.

I laugh nervously as Grant walks inside the house. I feel silly for losing my cool over someone knocking on the patio door. It's just that a lot of scary things are happening so fast. The lack of electricity and darkness also doesn't help. It makes everything seem so much more frightening, more ominous somehow.

"Thank God you're here, Officer Topper," I say, rushing over to him.

"What is it? What's wrong, Riley?" Grant asks, his deep voice filled with worry. He reaches out a hand in my direction, but Sebastian steps in front, blocking me, as though I need to be protected from a cop. It's a little alpha-male and very unnecessary, but I guess we're all on edge.

"What's going on, Officer?" Sebastian asks, eyeing Grant with a narrowed, glinting glance. "And what, exactly, are you doing in our backyard?"

Grant's gaze shifts from me to Sebastian. "I rang the front doorbell a few times, but I don't think it's working," he says. "Must be the power outages."

"Uh huh. Is that right?" Sebastian asks, continuing to look skeptical.

Sebastian shines his flashlight up and down Grant's body,

examining him, and I'm able to take in Grant's disheveled appearance more closely. His police uniform is soaked through and caked in mud. With the sleeves of his work shirt rolled up to the elbows, I notice for the first time the intricate tattoos that cover his arms. Skulls and crosses and even some bloody daggers. Not what you'd expect on a cop. Clenched in his left hand is a yellow hooded raincoat.

I stiffen.

"Wait a minute—were you here Thursday night, by any chance?" I ask, my pulse quickening as I fixate on his jacket. My mind flashes back to the intruder on our pool deck two nights ago who wore an almost identical coat.

"Huh?" He blinks, confused.

"Like, were you on patrol or something out back?" I clarify. "On our patio?"

"No, why?"

I shake my head, ignoring the little nagging feeling in the back of my mind. He looks so innocent, so completely clueless, I know the raincoat thing must be a coincidence. It's like Blake said the other night at the Beach Club. There must be tons of people running around in yellow rain jackets with this storm going on.

"Uh… never mind," I say.

He kneels next to me and unties the laces of his soaked leather boots. One by one, he takes them off and places them down by the patio doors to dry out.

"I'm so glad you're still here," he says, standing back up. "My car hydroplaned while I was out patrolling. It's stuck in a ditch. I've been walking around forever, knocking on every door, but you're the first to answer."

"Doesn't your little walkie talkie thing work?" Sebastian eyes the two-way radio attached to Grant's utility belt.

"'Fraid not." Grant sighs. "Damn thing died on me."

"Don't you have a partner working with you then? What about his?"

"Relax, Seb." I groan. "What's with the third degree? Leave the poor guy alone."

"It's okay." Grant laughs. "It's a small department, and we're kind of tapped out right now with the hurricane and all." His mouth twitches with amusement as he stares back at Sebastian. "Any other questions?"

"No!" I give Sebastian a warning look. "Actually, we're glad you're here, too. We need your help, Officer." I gulp. "Something terrible has happened…"

Sebastian and I take Grant outside to show him Roxy's dead body under the patio awning. He lets out an involuntary gasp, and his eyes water for just a moment. I remember then our first night out at Beach Club and that Grant knew Roxy. I think they were even friends.

It's obvious he's upset seeing her like this, but he quickly recovers and becomes the picture of professionalism. Immediately, he instructs us to cover her body back up to preserve evidence and reassures us everything is fine and we're perfectly safe. We also share Jonathan's crazy murder theories, which Grant agrees are a little far-fetched.

After the three of us are back inside the house, we all move to the kitchen table. Everyone wants to know what Grant thinks we should do, but he says there's nothing more to be done until the phone lines and electricity are working again. He can't even call for backup. We just have to sit tight, with a dead body in our backyard, and wait the storm out.

"Have you guys eaten anything yet? What about water?" Grant asks. "It'll help you relax."

Mason holds up what's left of the tequila. "Shots?"

"Not exactly what I was thinking." Grant smirks. "You're all underage."

"I'll make us some coffee," Blake says, getting up and pushing her chair into the table. She uses her cell phone light to guide her way over to the stove and turns one of the burners on.

"You can make coffee without electricity?" Nia's lashes fly up.

"Seriously, Nia? I'm using the gas," Blake says. "Duh."

Blake strikes a match underneath the burner and begins playing with the dials to turn on the gas and ignite the stove top. She places a small pot of water on top, and we all wait for it to heat up. Seconds later, little flames leap up and the water whistles as it reaches a boil. After she mixes in the coffee grounds, she fills a few mugs and places them on the kitchen table for us to share. Of course, Mason grabs one of the mugs first.

"Shit! This is terrible," he sputters, making a disgusted face. "I think you burned the pot."

"It's called cheap coffee." Blake rolls her eyes. "All Cam's good stuff is gone. I had to use an old bag I found in the cabinets. The last renters must have left it."

"It's fine. Thanks Blake," I say, giving her a grateful smile and gulping my own drink down. Unlike spoiled Mason Larper, I've had more than my share of bad coffee. I find it easy to ignore the slightly bitter taste if it will calm my nerves.

I can't believe what a nightmare this trip has turned into.

This was supposed to be the party weekend of our lives. Our last big blowout with all our high school friends before going our separate ways to college in a few weeks. I was expecting some dancing. A few drunk, debaucherous nights. If I was lucky, perhaps a hot make-out session—or two—with Sebastian.

Instead, we're trapped on an island in the middle of a hurricane with no way out for hours, at least. Three of our best friends are missing and someone is dead. Either we're having the worst luck ever, or Jonathan may actually be right. Maybe a killer really is on the loose—real or super-natural.

Fear takes hold of me. My stomach twists as the hodge-podge dinner from earlier and all the drinks I've had start coming back up. Worried I might throw up right there on the kitchen table, I bolt for the bathroom down the hall.

I make it inside just in time to slam the door shut behind me and empty the entire contents of my stomach not once, not twice, but three times into the toilet. After it's all over and there's nothing left inside my body but stomach acid and air, I dry-heave for a few minutes longer. Tears prick my eyes as I lean weakly against the toilet, wiping bile away from my lips and chin.

"March? You okay?" Sebastian asks from the other side of the door. "Need any help?"

"I'm fine," I shout back, embarrassed. "I'll be out in a minute."

"I can come in if you need me?"

"No!"

"I don't mind. You sure?"

I shine my flashlight into the mirror and stare at myself. My eyes are red and bloodshot, and my skin is blotchy and gross. I look like absolute shit. I am one-hundred percent certain I don't want Sebastian to see me like this.

"Uh huh," I say. "I'm sure."

I hear a loud thump and realize he's decided to sit on the other side of the bathroom door to wait for me and make sure I'm okay. Warmth rushes up the back of my neck. It's strangely flattering. I can't help but think if everything wasn't so twisted on this trip, I'd be over the moon with all his sudden attention.

It takes a few more minutes until I feel strong enough to attempt to leave the bathroom. After splashing some cold water on my face, I search for toothpaste to wash the sour taste from my mouth. Sitting on the bathroom counter is Blake's cardinal red cosmetic bag with the Stanford logo on the front, but there's only one empty travel-sized container of toothpaste inside. Next to her bag is a black nylon pouch, bigger and masculine looking. There's no toothpaste in there, either. Instead, I find two amber-colored medical prescription bottles prescribed to Jonathan.

I know I shouldn't snoop, but I can't stop myself from taking a peek at the labels.

Clozapine and Risperidone.

I'm not sure what kind of drugs these are, but they sure don't seem like the sort of things a normal guy would have in his weekender bag. Not like Tylenol or Advil. So why does Jonathan have them? Is this what he's been taking all weekend when I've seen him sneaking pills?

With a shaky hand, I tuck the bottles back inside the bottom of the pouch and find an old tube of toothpaste under the sink. I squeeze the gel out and run it between my teeth, wishing my cell phone reception worked so I could Google the drug names.

Sebastian knocks on the bathroom door.

"You still alive, March?"

"Coming!" I yell.

I shine my light around the bathroom, searching for a towel to dry my face. Right above the toilet is a storage cabinet. Standing on my tippy toes, I reach inside to grab a towel and something shiny and shimmering goes clattering to the floor. The warmth drains from my body as I realize what it is. Val's diamond tennis bracelet—her most prized possession, the one thing she never, ever, leaves home without—is lying on the dirty bathroom floor.

CHAPTER 18

Everyone looks up from the table as Sebastian and I return from the bathroom together. His hand is on my elbow, steadying me, as he walks me back into the kitchen. I'm grateful for the support. My knees are still a little wobbly from my upset stomach and all the vomit, not to mention the shock over the discovery of Val's most treasured bracelet hidden away in the bathroom cabinets.

Sebastian pours me a glass of water to help settle my stomach. I sip from it gratefully, trying to keep it down, as he takes the seat next to me. My stomach gurgles uncomfortably as I finish the drink. I'm not sure if the water is helping things or just giving my body something new to regurgitate.

"You look like crap," Nia says to me. Sebastian gives her a dirty look, but she only shrugs her shoulders. "Well, she does."

"You okay?" Grant asks.

I nod even as my belly continues to make strange sounds, indicating I'm anything but okay. Val's diamond tennis bracelet is heavy in my hand. I clench and unclench it in my palm, feeling it cool against my skin. I think I'd better tell the others about it now, just in case I'm forced back into the bathroom for another round of vomiting.

"I found this in the downstairs bathroom," I say, dropping the bracelet onto the kitchen table where they can all see it.

"What is it?" Grant squints and shines his flashlight on it. The diamonds catch light under the bright beam, sparkling and shimmering in the darkness.

"That's Val's!" Nia's eyes widen. "What's it doing here?"

Mason yawns beside her. "Who cares?"

"You don't get it," Nia says, shaking her head. "Val never takes that bracelet off."

"Exactly," I say. "So how the hell did it get here?"

I look around the room, making eye contact with each one of them. I'm not sure who to trust right now. Roxy is dead. Cam is missing. I'm really starting to wonder about Val and Ty now, too. Finding Ty's cell phone abandoned in the backyard and Val's bracelet hidden away inside a bathroom storage cabinet isn't making me feel better about the fact no one has seen either of them in two full days. I may not know what's going on here, but I can no longer ignore the fact that something is very, very wrong.

If Val wore that bracelet at Beach Club on Thursday night, like I remember, that means it could have only gotten in the bathroom if someone who had access to our rental house put it there. Except for the Tennessee boys who are no longer even in Florida anymore, the list of who's been inside our rental is pretty small. Basically, it's the people sitting right in front of me.

"Hold up," Mason says, dropping Nia's hand and frowning in my direction. "Why does your voice sound like that?"

"Like what?" I ask.

"You know—all accusing," he says. "Like you think one of us had something to do with it."

"Well, did you?"

"Hell no, I didn't!" Mason says. "Why would you even ask that?"

"You slept down here. You've been using that bathroom," I say.

"So what?" Nia asks. "I've used it, too. So did Jon. So did Blake and Roxy. We all slept down here. Not to mention, anyone can come downstairs and use it whenever they want."

"Yeah, that's right. How do we know you didn't leave the bracelet there yourself?" Mason smiles snidely at me. "And you're the one who found the bartender bopping around the pool like a cheap float, aren't you?" He waggles his finger at me. "Honestly, I gotta give you credit. It's not a bad plan. No one would ever suspect quiet, boring, nice-girl Riley March to be a vicious killer, would they?"

"Oh, please," I scoff. "That's ridiculous."

I can't believe he just said that.

"Lay off her, man," Sebastian says, giving Mason a sharp glare.

"Yeah, Riley would never hurt anyone," Jonathan says.

"Hey, she started it!" Mason's cheeks puff out with indignation. "She's the one saying I murdered my best friend and his girlfriend—or ex-girlfriend, or whatever the hell she is these days." He lets out an ironic laugh. "Be serious, would you? Murder takes way too much effort. All that cleanup? I don't even clean my own room. That's what maids are for."

"That's true," Sebastian says with a tiny nod. "I can attest that he's the laziest person I know."

"Thanks, man." Mason grins back and then adds, "I think?"

"Even so, Mason's still a far more likely suspect than Riley," Jonathan says, his hands steepled against his chin. He seems deep in thought.

"Oh yeah?" Mason sneers. "Why's that, smart guy?"

"Simple—women aren't serial killers," Jonathan says.

"Oh my God." Blake groans. "That's so sexist. Killers can easily be female."

"That's right," I say, nodding. Even if Jonathan is defending me, I'm not going to let that kind of misogynistic talk slide. "We can do anything guys can do, usually better."

"Respectfully, I must disagree," Jonathan says. "Sure, there are your odd ducks like Lizzy Borden and Aileen Wuornos, but the fact remains that women account for less than twelve percent of all serial killer cases."

"He's got a point. We learned that in the Academy." Grant finishes up his coffee and pushes his mug away. "Serial killers, mass murderers, terrorist attacks—we always look for male perps."

"Plus, Roxy was strangled. When women kill, it's quiet, like poison or smothering," Jonathan says, scratching at his temple. "You'd need a helluva lot of upper arm strength to choke someone to death. It takes a man to do a job like that."

Sebastian lets out an annoyed sigh. "I keep telling you— that girl drowned."

Another wave of nausea surges through my body.

"But Val's bracelet—"

"Means nothing," Sebastian says. "You're still in shock, March. Paranoia is a natural reaction, but that doesn't mean anyone's guilty of anything." He bends down to examine the bracelet closer, his eyes widening as he fingers at the clasp. "Look—see? The clasp is broken. Maybe she took the bracelet off so she wouldn't lose it? Or maybe it didn't go with her outfit? Who knows? There's a million reasons Val might've left it behind."

If I close my eyes, I can still see the flash of diamonds in the Beach Club bathroom as Val applied Blake's red lipstick. The image is so clear, she might as well be standing in front of me right now.

"But I saw her," I insist. "She was wearing it that night."

"Okay, so what if she came home after the club and took it off? Isn't that possible?" he asks.

I'll admit, what he's suggesting sounds reasonable.

If Val and Tyler had rekindled their relationship and she was about to run off and shack up with him somewhere else for the rest of the weekend, it makes sense she might have come back to our rental house first to get some things. And I did hear those noises while I was lying alone in bed. Maybe someone was in the house with me that night after all? Maybe it was Val and Tyler trying to be quiet and get in and out before anyone spotted them.

But if Val came back, why didn't she take her cell phone with her? Why weren't any of her things missing the next morning?

Her makeup? Toiletries? Clothes? Why is it all still in the upstairs master bedroom, waiting for her to return? It's hard to imagine that Val, who loves her makeup and clothes collection more than almost anything else in the world, wouldn't take at least some of it with her on her little rendezvous with Tyler.

And even if Val did come back with Tyler on Thursday night... Even if she decided not to take her cell phone or her makeup or any of her clothes... Even if she left her bracelet in the bathroom because the clasp broke. That still doesn't explain what I saw that night.

Who the hell was running around in that damn yellow slicker, and what were they dragging across the deck?

So many things don't add up. Even if I want to believe Sebastian, even if it feels safe and nice and wonderful to agree with him, I can't do it. Something deep down inside me, the primal part of me that's like a sixth sense, tasked solely with survival and keeping me alive, knows the truth. It won't allow me to pretend anymore. Something terrible has happened to Val and Tyler and probably Cam, too. I'm sure of it.

A deafening sound booms from somewhere on the other side of the house.

"What was that?" Nia asks as we all jolt out of our seats. Her eyes dart left and right, like an animal detecting a predator. "It sounds like someone's banging on the roof."

"Relax, babe." Mason reaches out to grab Nia's hand. "It's just the storm."

A moment later, another loud rumbling sound reverberates throughout the house.

"There it is again!" She jumps away from Mason and turns in the other direction, pointing toward the staircase. "It's coming from the basement. That's where Roxy said the bodies were!"

"Oh, for Christ's sakes, there's nothing in the basement." Sebastian looks upward. "It's just the wind."

"Actually, it sounds like the garage." Grant gets up from the kitchen table and aims his flashlight down the hallway. He cocks his head to the side, listening carefully, but the noise has stopped. Taking a step toward the garage, he puts a hand on his gun holster, bracing it. "I'm gonna go check it out."

"I'll go with you," Sebastian says.

"Me too," says Jonathan.

Grant puts a hand up, stopping them. "No, everyone stay here. It could be dangerous."

"I think you'd better let us come with you, Officer," Jonathan says. "Police are usually the first to bite it in horror movies. Haven't you seen *Halloween?*"

Grant shakes his head.

"*Nightmare on Elm Street?*" Jonathan asks.

"'Fraid not," Grant says.

"Well, if you had seen them, you'd know the cops are always getting killed in pretty messed up ways. They're never the hero—that's our 'Final Girl'," Jonathan explains. "She's the one who gets to slay the 'Big Bad', otherwise it wouldn't be a true slasher movie, and—"

"Okay, okay. You can come." Grant sighs impatiently. "Just be careful."

The three of them disappear down the hall and into the garage.

Less than five minutes later, they rush back into the kitchen, their shoes squishing and leaving water trails all along the hardwood floor. Their clothes are soaked through, which makes no sense at first since they've been indoors, but then they explain that a tree has somehow crashed through the garage door. There's a huge hole, and it's flooding the house with water. They need to fix it right now before things get worse.

They throw open the doors to the linen closet and grab all the towels left to help plug things up and soak up the water streaming into the garage. The three of them hold stacks going up to their chests.

"Are you sure this is safe?" I ask Grant. "Aren't you the one who warned us about people getting hurt during cleanup?"

"Yeah, I did," he says. "But if the garage door goes, well… It won't be good."

Sebastian turns to me with a comforting smile. "Don't worry. We got this."

"God speed," Mason says, mock saluting the guys, not even bothering to get up and help. He really is worthless.

"You go on ahead. I'll meet you there," Grant says, giving his towels to Sebastian and Jonathan and waving them toward the garage. "I've got extra cables in my car I need to grab. They'll help."

I gape. "You're going outside?"

"I'll be fine," he says. "The eye is over us right now. I just have to be fast and get back before the eyewall arrives."

"But I thought you said your car was stuck miles away?" I ask.

Some emotion I can't quite place flickers across his face. "I did?"

"Yes." My body tenses as I replay the earlier conversation in my head. "When you showed up at our back patio. You said you'd been walking forever."

"No, I didn't," he says. "My car's only a few blocks away."

"Yeah, you did," I insist.

I don't understand. Why is he lying?

A subtle unease washes over me, like a slight prickling sensation that travels along the back of my neck. It's such a strange thing to lie about. I can only think of one reason someone would claim their car broke down when it didn't—to play victim and get us to let our guard down. To be invited inside our house.

"Oh, wait. Now I remember." He scratches at his chin and stares at me oddly, as if he can't understand why I'm getting so upset about something so trivial. "I see why you're confused. I said it *felt* like I'd been walking forever. I was exaggerating." He pauses and then grins. "Can I go now? Or you want to keep drilling me about semantics when there's a tree literally in the middle of your garage?"

I study his face, looking for more red flags. I guess it seems like a simple enough explanation. On the surface, there's nothing sinister about his story, but it doesn't help things when he reaches for that damn yellow raincoat and puts it on before disappearing outside.

My apprehension grows, wedged like a big piece of food stuck in my throat. A slight twist of phrase, some menacing tattoos, and an overly common rain jacket. It's not much to go on, but I still can't help feeling that something may be off with Officer Topper. I don't care how attractive he is…

After he's gone, and I'm alone with Blake, Nia, and Mason again, I remember the other thing I found in the bathroom that worried me besides Val's bracelet. I realize it's not a great look to talk about someone's history of mental illness, but people are dying here. Even if I feel yucky disclosing it, my friends should know about the prescription drugs Jonathan has stashed away in his nylon toiletry kit. We need to get all the facts out in the open. If it's true that Jonathan snapped last summer after his sister died, then he may be capable of snapping again.

What if he's having another breakdown?

What if he's the one responsible for Roxy and our missing friends?

Hesitantly, I turn to face the others. Nia will want to know about this, but I'm not so sure how Mason or Blake will react to the information. Blake especially likes Jonathan, so she's going to be the hardest to talk to about it. I take in a deep breath and just go for it.

"Jon has a bunch of drugs," I blurt out. "I saw them in the bathroom."

"Drugs?" Nia straightens in her seat. "What kind of drugs?"

"Clozapine and Resperteral."

"You mean Risperidone?" Blake asks, correcting me.

"Yeah, that's it. You've heard of it?"

"Sure." She nods at me. "It's used to treat mental disorders."

Nia sucks in a surprised breath. "How do you know that?"

"Jon told me, okay?" Blake turns back to me with a distinct hardening in her cool blue eyes. "Why were you snooping through his stuff?"

"I wasn't snooping. I was looking for toothpaste," I say, crossing my arms. "But you have to admit it's kind of suspicious, right? I know you said he's doing okay, but what if he never got better? He's clearly still on drugs for whatever mental thing he's got, and now some really messed up shit is happening."

"So what if he's got drugs?" Mason shrugs. "Lots of people have drugs."

"Not to mention, taking care of your mental health is considered the responsible thing to do these days," Blake says with a disgusted frown that makes me feel like crap.

I sigh and slump back into my chair with a heaviness in my chest. I almost regret opening my big mouth in the first place, but now is not the time to tread lightly. Not when a killer may be on the loose.

"Now wait a sec. Riley has a point." Nia chews at her lower lip. "My friend Jamel—he's, like, this big time influencer with over a million followers—anyway, he just posted about a guy who said his pet snake told him to kill his neighbors. And get this, the guy totally did it, and then he ate them! What a freak show." She snorts. "So really, if we're being honest, nut jobs and killing do kinda go hand in hand."

"You can't say stuff like that, Nia." Blake groans. "It's not PC."

Nia juts her chin out. "I'm just saying, we barely know Jon."

"I know him," Blake says. "He's a good guy."

Mason nods along. "I agree," he says. "Plus, he's a total pussy. Dude couldn't hurt a fly."

"But he's older than us, too," I say. "It's not like any of us have spent much time with him this past year. Who knows what he's been up to?"

Blake snorts. "We know what he's been up to—college."

"Allegedly," I say. "None of us go to Central Florida." An icy chill taps up my spine. "What if... I don't know... What if he's been in an institution or something this whole time? What if he just escaped?"

Nia nods along. "It's not, like, a total shot in the dark to imagine Jon as some crazed-type killer."

Blake stands and slams her chair into the kitchen table with a loud banging sound. "You guys are real assholes, you know that?" Her nostrils flare as she glares at us. "Okay, so Jon's a little weird. So he takes drugs. So what? His little sister killed herself—*and he's the one who found her!*" She throws her hands up in the air. "Of course, he's messed up. It doesn't mean he's some kind of psycho."

"Doesn't mean he's not," I mumble.

"I want to go home." Nia puts a hand to her forehead as if feeling faint. "I hate this house. I wish we'd never come here."

The nausea from earlier returns, hitting me full blast. It rolls over me, even stronger than before, in waves of heat that go all the way from my toes to the very top of my head. My stomach grumbles in a sick, super uncomfortable way that has me eyeing the bathroom again. I think all the stress and shock from tonight is really getting to me.

"You okay?" Blake asks me.

"I'm not sure. My stomach is killing me."

Mason smirks. "That's just Blake's shitty coffee." He puts a hand dramatically to his belly. "I think my delicate digestive system is traumatized."

"Well, geez. Sorry the service wasn't to your liking," Blake says sarcastically. "When the hurricane is over, feel free to drive your ass over to Starbucks."

"Your coffee was great—it's not that." I smile at Blake to make up for Mason being such a dick. "I don't know what's wrong with me. Maybe I ate something bad?"

I try to stand and am overcome by another onslaught of sickness. The cramping is so bad, I begin to wonder if this is more than just stress or even food. Did I somehow come down with a nasty stomach bug on top of everything else?

"Now that you mention it. I don't feel so good, either," Nia says, her face turning ashen. "I thought it was all that skinny tea I've been drinking, but now I'm not so sure." She attempts to get up from the kitchen table and loses her balance, falling back down into her chair.

"I feel great. It's just your fragile female nerves." Mason stretches his arms overhead and yawns. "You all need to relax. How about a group massage?" He gives us a big, sleazy wink.

Nia burps loudly and then covers her mouth, as if shocked by her own bodily functions. Looking panicked, like she might throw up on herself, she makes a run for the bathroom. She doesn't even get halfway down the hallway before collapsing into a heap on the floor.

"Nia!" Blake rushes to her side.

My intestines recoil again, and I throw a hand in front of my mouth. Vomit seeps out between my fingers.

What the hell is happening to us?

I try to get to the bathroom, but my body has turned to

cement. Everything becomes heavy and sluggish. My movements are too slow. Too uncoordinated. I tumble forward to my knees, no longer able to control my legs or arms. Fingers are all I can move now.

The room recedes as I fight to stay awake. It becomes a struggle to keep my eyelids open. Things become foggy and blurry around the edges, as if I'm caught in some kind of dream-like state. The ceiling above my head swirls like a crazy abstract painting until my eyes roll back into the sockets. Slowly, the world begins to fall away, and I slide toward the darkness.

With my last thought, I realize what's going on. This definitely isn't stress, or food, or even the stomach flu.

We've been drugged...

CHAPTER 19

"**R** *iley!* Open your eyes!"
"I really think she's dead…"
"Oh, shut up, Mason!"

The darkness fades away as I blink myself back into reality.

I don't immediately recognize my surroundings. Wherever I am, it's a big open space. Dark and damp. Windowless. It's like I'm underground somewhere. The air is thick and musty, like a damp sponge that's been left in a dark corner for far too long. The sickly, stagnant smell of something gone bad mixes in and wafts toward me.

At my feet, large round red pillar candles have been placed onto the dusty cement flooring. Wax drips off the sides and onto the ground, gathering there like little pools of blood. Light from the flames casts shadows around and reveals unfinished walls and a low ceiling filled with small cracks and gaps.

I turn to my right and Nia's blurry face comes into view. An intense desire to vomit again and an overwhelming sense of dizziness takes over my body. I shut my eyes, taking deep, ragged breaths in and out, praying I won't pass out for a second time.

"No! Don't go back to sleep!" Nia yells, her voice floating toward me.

"Shake her," Mason says. "Keep her eyes open."

"Fabulous idea, Mason. If I could reach her, which I can't,

because we're tied to these damn chairs like lambs to the slaughter!" she shrieks at him. "You're closer, you try."

"Your arms are longer."

"You really are worthless, you know that?" She groans. "I can't believe I let you kiss me."

Somewhere next to me, I hear the sharp scraping of chair legs moving against the floor. Nia lets out a painful cry and curses out loud. "Dammit. I can't move," she says. "Hell, maybe we should let her sleep. I wish I was still asleep."

"No one sleeps!" Mason's voice thunders so loudly, my eyes snap back open. "We gotta get out of here!"

As the fog in my brain lifts, I notice my arms and legs are aching something terrible. I try to stretch them out to get relief and realize, with panicked shock, that my hands and feet are bound to the chair. I twist and try to turn my wrists, but some kind of rope digs into my skin, chafing me. It prevents me from moving more than a few inches left or right.

What in the…

I'm wide awake now, my vision and my brain both returning to full capacity. I realize with a burst of fear that it's not just me. Nia and Mason are also tied to the chairs next to me. Someone clearly drugged us and dragged us here—wherever *here* is—in order to trap us with no chance of escape. Whatever they want from us, it can't be good.

I grunt hard and try again, pulling against the ropes until I feel a sharp sting and the wetness of blood trickles down my wrists.

"Forget it. It's hopeless." Nia sighs. Her eyes are rimmed with red, like she's been crying.

"What's going on? Where are we?" I ask, my stomach lurching again, a bad combination of whatever we've been drugged with and the terror of being captured by someone—or something—terrible. This isn't some ramshackle sort of half-ass job, either. Whoever tied us up isn't playing games. It looks like they have experience with this sort of thing.

"I thought you were supposed to be smart." Mason snorts. "Isn't it obvious? We're in the basement."

Now that he says it, I realize, in fact, it is obvious.

I stare closer and see that the chairs we're tied to are the same chairs from the kitchen table. If I listen hard, I can even hear the thunder and rain from upstairs, though it's muffled now, since we're down here.

Okay, so we're clearly still in the rental house, but then where are the others? Why are there only three of us shackled up and trapped in the basement? Are the guys still in the garage fixing the door, unaware of what's happened to us? And where are Blake and Cam?

"Where's everyone else?" I ask. "Are they okay?"

"How the hell would we know? We woke up here, same as you," Mason says.

"Whatever you do, don't look in the corner," Nia warns in a low voice and then starts to gag.

"Why not?" I ask, and then do the very thing she advised against.

Moments later, after I've finished dry heaving, I wish I had listened to her. No longer do I need to wonder what happened to Val and Tyler. Their bodies lie motionless on the concrete floor, discarded like bags of trash. In the flickering candlelight, their flesh appears bloated and discolored, their skin mottled with patches of blue and green. Dried blood clumps around their slashed necks, pooling onto their chests and staining the floor. It turns out the red candle wax at my feet wasn't wax after all...

I gasp, tears catching in my throat. The weight of the atmosphere presses down on me, as though the very walls are closing in. This can't be happening. I can't truly be seeing this.

Am I dreaming? Is this another one of my crazy nightmares?

I blink again, but the horrific image doesn't go away.

Next to their dead bodies is a stockpile of gruesome weapons, stacked together as if put on display to elicit some kind of reaction from us. At the front of the heap is an axe. Beside it lies a hacksaw. A machete. A scalpel. There's even a trio of kitchen knives with blades as long as my arm.

"Could this be some kind of bad practical joke? Like a hologram or something?" I ask, desperate for anything that might explain what I see. As absurd as those ideas sound, they're still far easier to believe than our friends being murdered.

"Ty and Val don't have the imagination to think this up." Mason smiles without humor. I notice blood dripping down the side of his face, falling from his temple onto the collar of his shirt. He must've hit his head. It looks like it hurts.

"Oh my God, are you okay?" I ask.

He glances over at our dead friends. "Better than they are."

"It's the Ouija board," Nia says, a tremble in her voice. "I told you all that dark energy attracts bad shit."

"Stop being ridiculous. A person did this—not some stupid board game," Mason says. "And when I find the sick son of a bitch, he's toast."

"Oh yeah, tough guy?" Nia sneers. "And how're you gonna do that tied up?"

"'Cause I'm gonna get out of this damn chair," Mason says. "And when I do, I'm gonna make that psychotic rent-a-cop pay for this." He rocks himself back and forth, putting all his body weight into the motion. Then he kicks his legs against the wooden chair with all his strength.

"Wait—you think the cop did this?" Nia asks.

"Hell yeah, I do." Mason huffs from exertion, but no matter how hard he tries to break free, the chair remains intact.

"You can't be serious," I say. "Grant's a police officer."

"Or maybe he was just pretending to be one," Mason says, still breathing hard from all his efforts. "How do we know he's who he says he is? He could be lying about being a cop."

I stare at him. "I saw him at the station. I really don't think he's faking it."

"Okay, so then he's a police officer. So what?" Mason shrugs. "You heard what Jon said—cops make great killers. It's so obvious it's him. That's why he's not here hog-tied to a chair like we are."

I open my mouth to defend Grant again but then shut it. True, Grant has only ever been anything but nice to me, but… well… I only met the guy a few days ago. He's basically a stranger.

The more I think about it, I can't help but recall all the little red flags I've noticed. For one thing, his "stranded car story" still doesn't sit well with me. Did I really hear him wrong about that? And how did he show up at our house in the first place? Was he truly going door-to-door warning citizens to leave and just stumbled upon our house?' There must be hundreds of houses on this island. What are the chances?

And most troubling of all, what about the yellow slicker? I still can't seem to get my mind off it. Is it just a coincidence he has the exact same jacket as whoever was lurking on our patio that very first night?

"Okay, so maybe it's not a completely crazy idea," I say. "But what would his motive be? We never even met him until this weekend."

"Why does he need a motive?" Mason asks. "Doesn't sound like that Ed Rawlins guy had one."

"Okay, that's fair, but I still think Jon's the most likely suspect," I say. "I mean, where is he?" I look around the basement. "And he clearly isn't back to normal like he's been pretending. What if the 1-year anniversary of his sister's death made him snap?"

Plus, Jonathan had access to the downstairs bathroom where I found Val's bracelet. He was also in the living room when I discovered Roxy's dead body. Not to mention he was outside with us when we found Tyler's cell phone. And Grant's not the only one with a yellow slicker. Jonathan also has one, too.

"I vote for Jon too," Nia says. "Do you see the books he reads? And his clothes? He dresses like a poor person even though his family is loaded." She wrinkles her nose. "If that's not a psychopath, I don't know what is."

"No way. Did you see what that asshole did to them?" Mason gestures toward Val and Tyler's butchered bodies lying in the corner. "Jon's way too much of a pussy for that."

"Yeah, but Jon has drugs in his bag and everything—"

"Yeah, *prescribed* drugs," Mason says, cutting me off.

"I bet he volunteered to help fix the garage right after he poisoned us," I say, barreling on. "That gave him enough time to disappear and throw suspicion off himself. Then once we all passed out, he came back here, dragged us down into the basement, and tied us up."

"And Seb?" Mason looks unconvinced. "You're forgetting Seb's not here, either. He's gotta be with Jon somewhere. You can't possibly be saying Seb's in on it, too?"

Damn, he's right.

Sebastian's presence and proximity to Jonathan—both physically and emotionally—is a big wrench in my theory. As much as I think Jonathan is guilty, I don't want to see Sebastian as a killer, too.

Not that I should care about any of this right now. What matters is escaping this damn basement alive, not whether the guy I've been crushing on for a year is a crazed lunatic killer. Except, well, I've spent hours and hours with him. We've *kissed*. I don't want to believe he could be involved. And yet… Nothing is off the table at this point. How well do I actually know Sebastian?

How well do we know anyone?

"Just because Jon did it, doesn't mean Seb's in on it," Nia says matter-of-factly. "For all we know, Jon killed Seb, too."

I frown in her direction. "Not helpful."

Nia looks over at Val and Tyler's bodies and shivers, a horrified expression on her face. She resumes struggling against her ropes, trying to get free. "Listen, I don't give a shit who did it or why. The police can figure all that out later," she says. "The only thing we need to do is get out of here."

We all get to work on our bindings again, trying to loosen the ropes and moving around as much as possible in the hopes it will somehow help things. My fingers claw at the fibers as I try to undo the rigid knots, picking and pulling until my wrists start to bleed. Twisting and turning, I strain against my restraints and fight against the feeling of hopelessness that threatens to overwhelm me. Unable to stop myself, my eyes flicker back to the stack of weapons in the corner next to our dead friends.

I gulp. "Why do you think he put the weapons on display like that?"

Mason pulls harder at his ropes. "Because he's a sick bastard."

Gooseflesh breaks out along my bare legs and arms the longer I stare. From the looks of Val and Tyler's bodies, whoever killed them has no problem with death, but I think there's more than just murder going on here. There's something purposeful about this setup. It feels too planned out. Too strategic.

"But why go to all the trouble of bringing us down here and tying us up?" I ask. "Why not kill us after we passed out? Sure seems a lot easier." I lean forward in my chair to get a better look at things. "No, this feels personal. It's like he's sending us a message."

"Stop babbling and keep working on your ropes, Riley," Nia pants as she strains harder against her bonds. "This isn't some exam at school, for God's sake."

Something new occurs to me then.

"Wait—take a closer look. Don't you see it?" I ask. "They're all things you use to cut with. If it was just about killing us, why not use a gun? Or, hell, stick with the poison and simply up the dosage." I shake my head. "No, whoever is doing this is going to a lot of effort. He wants something else from us."

"I don't give a shit what he wants!" Nia says.

I glare at the ceiling, frustrated with myself because I don't know the answer to this riddle. The clues are all here. I should be able to figure this out, but murder is so far out of my comfort range. What do I know about how killers think?

"I've almost got it!" Mason shouts, yanking harder at his ropes. His muscles strain in the candlelight as he tries to rub the rope against the edge of the chair, creating friction. "If I can just get to one of those knives…" He grunts and uses his legs, pushing his chair against the wall with all his force.

Footsteps thump loudly right above us. Someone is heading down the stairs.

"He's coming!" Nia's face goes slack with fear.

I freeze, every muscle in my body tightening with dread.

"We have to think! There's gotta be a reason he wants to hurt us!" I say to them. "Maybe if we can figure it out, we can convince him to leave us alone."

"Why're you looking at me?" Nia snaps. "I didn't do anything to cause this!"

Frantically, I pull again at the bonds securing my hands and pray I can loosen things up enough to get free before the killer gets in the basement. Rope fibers rip and shred my already bloody wrists, cutting my skin even deeper. Daggers of pain rush up my arms and I cry out in pain. Everything is knotted together so tightly, it feels like I'll never be able to get loose.

The footsteps inch closer. It sounds like he's right outside the basement door.

"He's almost here!" Nia rocks in her chair so fast I worry she's going to fall over and hit her head on the ground and knock herself out. Or worse.

"Holy shit!" Mason shouts, his face red and puffy from strain. "I did it!" He breaks his rope into two pieces with a loud snapping sound and jumps to his feet. With a triumphant scream, his bonds fall away to the ground.

"Oh my God—you're free!" Nia's voice floods with relief. The legs of her chair squeak against the basement floor as she scoots toward him. "Come on, untie me next!"

Mason doesn't seem to hear her. His eyes are locked on the basement door a few feet away from us. Tentatively, as if testing something, he takes one step toward the exit.

"Mason?" Nia asks, her brow beginning to furrow. "What are you doing?"

He takes another few steps away from us.

My heart sinks as I realize what he's doing.

"Mason, please," I beg. "Don't do this."

"I don't know what you all did to wind up here, but this has nothing to do with me," he says, now almost to the door. He doesn't even have the balls to look back as he speaks to us.

"What are you doing?" Nia asks.

"Sorry, babe," he says with a small shrug. "But it's like Riley said. This seems personal, and if I untie you, he's just gonna get mad and come after me again."

Nia figures it out a few moments after me.

"You bastard!" she yells. "You can't leave me here. You can't do this to me!"

"I'll get help, I promise." He reaches for the doorknob, pausing. "I mean, if I can…"

Suddenly, the basement door swings open on its own. Something silver and shiny catches the corner of my eye and then sharp steel arcs through the air, nailing Mason right in the chest. He squeals in pain and crumples to the floor with a horrifying thud. The next instant, a figure in a yellow rain slicker strides through the doorway.

Between the hood and the darkness, I'm unable to see his face as he stands over Mason and plants one foot on Mason's groin, steadying himself. He pulls the sharp object out of Mason's body with a sickening wet sound. Mason lets out one final death cry before his body stops twitching and convulsing, and no more sounds come.

I gasp, panting in terror, as the killer holds the weapon high above his head. He shakes it like a victory trophy, the bloodied blade catching the glint of candlelight. Finally, I can see what it is, though some part of me suspected it all along.

It's an axe.

The killer steps over Mason's dead body and turns until he's staring right at us. Using one hand, the hood falls down, and I gasp as his—*HER*—face is revealed.

"Perfect aim as usual," Blake says, kissing the bicep of her trophy-winning-discus-throwing arm. "I've been dying to do that since the first day I met that asshole."

CHAPTER 20

B lake giggles as she wipes the axe blade clean on the back of Mason's sweatpants. His blood spreads across the floor of the basement, seeping into tiny cracks and crevices in the cement. I stare, horrified, as it creeps toward my bare feet. There's so much of it. I never understood how much blood was inside the human body until now.

Fear and shock knot inside my chest as Blake stalks toward us. Closer and closer she comes, until she's standing right in front of our chairs. She cocks her head sideways and starts to grin.

"Now, what to do with the two of you?" she asks.

"You killed him!" Nia cries, her breath rattling in her throat. She stares at Blake with wide, terror-stricken eyes. "Why... why would you do that?"

"Oh, come on, Nia. You still haven't figured it out?" Blake lowers her axe to the ground, her lips puckered with annoyance. "Even you're not this dumb, are you?"

"It's you!" I gasp, putting it all together in a flash, as if unlocking something buried deep down in my brain that's known this all along. It was never a stupid haunted house, or ghosts, or Grant, or even Jonathan. It's been Blake this entire time. "You're the one who brought us down here."

"Ding ding ding." Blake grins. "Poor Jon, huh? The guy is practically in love with you, and you cast him as some crazy psycho killer," she says, making little tsking noises at me.

"I don't understand," I mumble, my mind reeling with

confusion. "I was so sure. Jon even has a yellow raincoat and everything—"

"Oh, you mean this raincoat?" She pops the collar on the hood of her slicker. "He lent it to me at Beach Club that first night when I left early. He's such a sweetheart," she says. "Bad luck you catching me on the patio when I was getting Ty and Val squared away in the basement, huh?" She winks. "You really should've stayed at the bar with Officer Hottie like I told you."

"You tricked me," I whisper.

"Hey, I'm the one who kept telling you Jon was innocent, remember?" Her mouth turns downward. "But, okay, yeah, it didn't hurt for you to be suspicious of him. Or the cop. Or a returning serial killer. Hell, even a haunted house. Just so long as you didn't suspect me."

My cheeks heat with shame. I can't believe how easily I fell into the whole mental-illness-stigma-trap. I never should've suspected Jonathan when he was only ever kind to me. Weird, yes, but being weird isn't a crime.

"I haven't even gotten to the good part yet." Blake rubs her hands together eagerly. "I've got a little surprise for you. You're gonna love this!"

She uses the flashlight on her cell phone to guide her way to the other side of the basement. There's a door there that looks like it leads to a closet or some kind of storage area, and she steps inside. I hear mumbling and a loud slap, followed by an agonized moan. The next instant, she pulls someone out through the doorway.

It's Cam!

My body fills with relief at seeing my best friend alive, even if she looks like she's close to dying. Her usually polished, shiny bob is gnarled at the back of her head in a bloody mess that drips down onto her flannel pajama top. A checkered bandana is fixed in her mouth like a gag, her hands tied behind her back.

Blake drags Cam by her hair, and she shoves her down into Mason's old chair so hard that she cries out in pain. With a loud tearing sound, Blake rips out Cam's bandanna and then ties her up. As Blake secures the knots, I notice Cam's pajama bottoms are wet in front. She must have soiled them.

The shocked, almost cartoonish expression on Cam's face as she takes in all the dead bodies would almost be comical if it wasn't so horrifying. First Mason. And Tyler. Then her eyes land on her dead twin.

"OH MY GOD! Val! No!" Cam lets out a heartbreaking wail, her body slumping in despair as she stares at her dead sister's remains. She starts to weep aloud, rocking back and forth in her chair. *"You bitch!"* she screams at Blake with burning, hateful eyes. "What have you done to her?"

Blake raises her weapon in front of Cam's face, shaking it. "In case you haven't noticed, Cammy, I'm the one with the axe. That means I ask the questions—not you," she says. "And now that the gang's all here, you're going to tell me who sent that damn video to Jordyn's parents."

"Video? What video?" Nia blinks, bewildered.

"The video of me and Jordyn kissing behind the bleachers, you imbecile!" Blake says.

"It wasn't me." Cam tears her gaze from her twin's body. Tears of anguish fill her eyes as she lifts her chin and meets Blake's glare. "I loved Jordyn. I'd never do anything to hurt her."

I'm caught off guard when Blake turns, the full power of her fury now fixed on me.

"You… you can't be serious," I stutter. "I didn't even know her."

Blake points the axe at Nia next.

"Well, I certainly didn't do it!" Nia says.

"Someone did," Blake says. "It didn't just appear out of thin air."

"It was Val then—she must've done it," Nia says quickly. "She always was a real bitch."

A vein throbs in Cam's forehead. "Don't talk about her like that."

"She's dead. What does it matter?" Nia asks. "It had to be Val."

"No. I don't think so…" Blake strolls over to the pile of weapons in the corner and trades in her axe for one of the knives. It's a butcher knife with a long, sharp blade. "Did you know this is the type of knife Jordyn used? You'd never imagine something you can find in your kitchen could do so much damage, would you?"

She walks back to us and runs a fingertip along the blade's edge, testing it. She pricks herself, either on accident or on purpose, and one little drop of blood drips from her finger to the floor.

"I thought it was Val too, at first," she continues. "I kept hoping she'd come clean. Stupid, I know. Val never did have much of a conscience." She chuckles to herself. "When she didn't, I came up with the perfect plan. I found this rental in a Reddit thread about haunted houses. I thought the serial killer story was a nice touch. The timing was perfect. July Fourth— the anniversary of Jordyn's death. I even made sure Jon came along to witness justice. Poetic, huh?"

"What did you do to my sister?" Cam snarls, fighting against her ropes.

"I only wanted to scare her," Blake says. "I was going to make her think the house was haunted, and that Jordyn was back for revenge. I just wanted her to confess, but that imbecile Ty wouldn't leave her side." She glances over at Nia, almost apologetic. "Sorry sweetie, I know you liked him, but he really was a dog.

"I used the same stuff I put in your coffee—a tiny bit of Jon's benzos," Blake continues, glancing in my direction. "You were right about that part, Ri Ri. It's just that I was the one drugging people," she says. "But then Ty woke up before I could get them into the basement. Guess I didn't use a high enough dose. He went berserk and ruined everything."

"But Val didn't do anything," Cam says. "She didn't send the video."

"Well, yeah, I know this *now*." Blake almost looks rueful. "See, when I was carving into her, Val swore she was innocent. Her story never changed, and, trust me, I was very persuasive right up until the end."

"You're a monster!" Cam sobs.

"The Ouija board? That was you, too?" I ask.

Blake scowls. "Well, it wasn't Nia's silly evil spirits," she says. "I was hoping that little game might scare a confession out of one of you, but that didn't work, either."

"You're insane." Nia gasps. "You've gone completely nuts."

"And Roxy's murder? Was that just to scare us, too?" I ask, still trying to understand what's happening here. Killing her crush as part of her plan seems extreme, even after all I've seen tonight, but at this point I can't put anything past Blake.

"Don't be ridiculous," Blake says. "Roxy was just collateral damage. While the rest of you were sleeping, Cam confronted me. She found Ty's phone in my backpack. She was going nuts, saying I had something to do with him and Val disappearing—"

"And I was right!" Cam yells, her voice filled with rage. She bucks in her chair, as if trying to jump out of it and get to Blake. "I *knew* you were—"

Blake waves her knife at Cam, silencing her. "Cammy wouldn't let it go. You know how annoying she can be, always thinking she's right," she continues. "I shoved her a little too hard, and she hit her head. Roxy saw the whole thing. She grabbed Ty's phone and ran out the back door. I had no choice."

"But I thought you liked Roxy?" I ask.

Blake shrugs. "Sometimes you gotta break a few eggs to make an omelet."

I can't believe how cold Blake is being. It's horrifying. Roxy was a person, not a breakfast item.

"Oh, don't look at me like that, Riley—all judgy and stuff." Blake frowns at me. "No one here is innocent, believe me. Ty was a dog who couldn't keep it in his pants. Val—a narcissistic bitch. We all know Mason was just a few bad dates away from becoming a full-blown rapist. And Roxy, well, she was too damn nosy for her own good."

"What about Seb and Jon? And Grant?" I ask. "What did they ever do?"

"What about them?" She laughs. "I didn't hurt them. They're passed out in the garage. They'll be my alibi and rescue me after I'm done with the rest of you."

There's a moment of brittle silence as the full impact of Blake's confession hits me.

"Well, it seems like you've thought of everything," I say, my stomach churning with dread. "So what are you going to do with us?" I ask even though I'm pretty sure I already know the answer. Blake may be crazy, but she's no idiot. She wouldn't be admitting all this if she planned to let us escape.

"You killed Jordyn," she says. "Obviously, you have to die."

"Blake, please. You're not making any sense," I say. "None of this makes sense."

"Jordyn committed suicide, you psycho!" Nia cries at Blake. "No one killed her."

"That isn't true." Angry red dots burst across Blake's cheeks. "She killed herself because of that damn video. She begged you to delete it, and you *laughed* at her!" Blake yells. "Remember that summer in seventh grade when Jordyn came back all screwed up? That was because her parents sent her to conversion therapy camp! You know, where they brainwash gay kids into becoming straight? She told me all the messed-up shit they did. Shock therapy. Drugs. They left her outside in the freezing cold without food or water for days," she says. "She told me she'd rather die than go back there."

"But it was just a stupid video of you kissing? So what?" Nia lowers her gaze in confusion. "You kiss everyone. It didn't mean anything."

"It meant EVERYTHING!"

The anguished look on Blake's face says it all. In that moment, the rest of the pieces of the puzzle come together.

I finally understand why Blake is always jumping from fling-to-fling without ever making a real connection. Why she never talks about relationships or love. Why she never lets anyone get too close. I think about the way she is with Jonathan, surprisingly sweet to him when she's not all that sweet to anyone else. She's always had such a soft spot for him.

I even see that fight in the Bishop Prep bathroom last spring in a whole new light. Blake was the only one defending Jordyn that day, which isn't a very Blake-like thing to do, in hindsight. Blake is the one who makes jokes, having fun and doing her best to avoid confrontation. When Blake rushed out of the bathroom and no one knew why, it was right after Jordyn said their kiss meant nothing. After Jordyn said it would never happen again.

"Oh my God." I gulp. "You were in love with her."

A single tear escapes Blake's eye. "She was so scared," she says. "We kept it a secret, but somehow her parents found out. After that damn camp, she had to promise she was 'cured.' We were always in hiding.

"After her dad saw that video of us, he beat Jordyn so badly she couldn't sit for days." Blake wipes her runny nose with one hand, clenching and unclenching the knife in her other hand. "She knew they were going to send her back to that hellhole and things would be even worse the second time. I told her we could run away together, but she said there was no running from what she was." She closes her eyes, her face the picture of pure agony. "I'll never love anyone the way I loved her."

I can't help but feel a small twinge of sympathy watching Blake break down in front of us. Regardless of all the horrific things she's done, despite being a crazed murderer, I can almost see how losing the love of your life so tragically could break a person and drive them to the depths of insanity. A part of me almost understands why she might snap and want to hurt anyone she thinks responsible for Jordyn's death.

But that doesn't mean I want to die.

"We didn't know any of that," Nia says. "We're your friends. Let us help you heal—"

"Oh, save it, Nia!" Blake's eyes flash. "Friends don't bully each other the way you bullied Jordyn. And then, after she died, none of you even gave a shit. You've all been so happy. Going to your little football games, and your stupid parties, and out on your silly dates. Homecoming. Prom. Graduation. Never once thinking about what you did." Spittle drips from her lips. "We were never friends. We're just a group of mean girls that hung out together because it made us more popular."

"That's not true." Cam's voice breaks. "We didn't forget about Jordyn."

"That's right." Nia nods along. "It's just that, uh, it hurt too much to talk about," she says with such fake sincerity even I cringe. It sounds like a line from a bad *Lifetime* movie.

"Would you give it up already?" Blake shouts at Nia. "You're an Instagram influencer, not an actress." She brings the knife down, caressing the blade against Nia's long swan-like throat. "Honestly, I'm doing you a favor, Nia. You were never gonna be famous. Better to die now, while you still have clout."

Nia looks nauseous. "You're insane—just like that psychopath Ed Rawlins."

"No, he was a mass murderer!" Blake snaps, taking a step

back. "I'm a serial killer. They're the ones with strategy and brains, like Jon said. God, Nia—do you ever pay attention?" she asks. "No wonder your parents had to bribe the headmaster to let you graduate."

"That's not true," Nia protests. "I passed those classes all on my own."

Blake groans. "Even seconds from death, you still can't be real, can you?" she asks. "Enough of this. I'm running out of patience. I think I'll just start hacking body parts until someone spills the beans. Who wants to go first?" She raises the knife, pointing the tip at each of our heads. "Eeny. Meeny. Miny." The knife stops on me. "Mo."

I tremble as she strides toward me. She brings the blade so close to my neck, I can practically feel the razor edge cool against my bare skin. "Don't let her do this!" I scream to the others, blood roaring in my ears. "Tell her what she wants to know!"

"Sorry, Ri Ri. Better you than us," Nia says. "Survival of the fittest, babe."

A suffocating sensation tightens at my throat.

"I'm sorry about what happened to your friend, I really am," I say to Blake. "But I didn't even know Jordyn. I don't understand why I'm even here."

Blake's eyes narrow. "Ah, yes. Riley March—the mysterious new girl who walked straight into Bishop Prep senior year, with no friends, no connections, and somehow got in with the coolest clique at school. Now how does that happen, I wonder?"

"I… I didn't do anything wrong," I whisper.

"Are you sure?" She gives me a cold, hard smile. "You certainly had no issues taking advantage of the situation. Couldn't steal her spot fast enough, could you?"

"That isn't… that's not what happened," I say, heat running up the back of my neck. "*Val* approached *me*. I heard you all arguing in the bathroom about the video last year. I was hiding in one of the stalls right before summer break. Val asked me not to say anything and I agreed—but that's it, I swear."

My words are the truth but, also, not the entire truth. Even though I didn't purposely try to harm anyone, deep down, I always knew something was wrong. Val didn't do favors for people. If Val was willing to exchange her friendship for my silence, my words meant a lot. Maybe I didn't actively do anything to hurt Jordyn, but I kept silent about the truth when I knew I shouldn't have.

"Hm." Blake hesitates. "In that case, it really is a shame you got yourself wrapped up in all this. But you know what they say—you should be careful who your friends are."

I cry out in pain as she starts to press the blade against my neck. Maybe Nia is a lost cause, but Cam... she's my very best friend. Surely, she won't let me die like this.

"Cammy please!"

But Cam remains silent, looking away. The floor, the ceiling, her bare feet; Cam stares anywhere else but at me. My bladder loosens and warm urine trickles down my leg. I know I'm going to die.

Without warning, something big and heavy, like a tree or some other hurricane debris, slams upstairs against the roof. Distracted, Blake turns so fast her knife slips, narrowly missing my throat and finding Cam's left thigh instead. Cam lets out an agonized scream as the blade lodges itself half in her leg, half in the chair.

I look over and gag. A chunk of Cam's flesh is now missing. I think I can see bone.

"What did you do to me?" Cam asks, her eyes going wide with shock.

"Whoopsies," Blake says with a little giggle. "My bad."

Cam starts to gag and convulse. She seems to be on the verge of passing out. "I don't feel so good," she whimpers. "I need to go to the hospital. Please Blake, I need—"

"Shut up," Blake says. "No one is going anywhere."

Blake jerks the handle back and forth, trying to pull the blade from Cam's leg. She huffs out air, her face red with effort. With a string of curses and one more powerful yank, she finally gets the knife free. Blood gushes from Cam's wound like a small geyser and soaks her pajama bottoms and the floor. There's so much of it, I start to feel woozy.

"Blake, please," I plead. "She needs a doctor—"

"I SAID SHUT UP!"

Blake kicks the foot of my chair so hard that I go flying to the ground. The back of the chair, along with my entire back-side, shatters against the floor with a loud cracking sound. The wind is knocked out of me, and pain reverberates throughout my body as I lay there, stunned and helpless, still tied to the chair. Tears fill my eyes as my wrist throbs in agony. It feels badly hurt, maybe sprained or even broken.

"That was my last warning," Blake says. "This is not a negotiation. I am going to find out what really happened to Jordyn, and if you all have to bleed a little first, *I don't give a damn!*"

"We never meant for this to happen," Nia wails, tears rolling down her face. "Maybe we shouldn't have filmed you guys, but Jordyn was being so terrible. She knew how much I wanted cheer captain. She knew what it meant to me, and she didn't even care. She always had to be the best at everything!" Nia's eyes cloud over, and her chin jerks in Cam's direction. "It was Cam. She's the one who suggested we blackmail Jordyn. She said we could make her do whatever we wanted."

"You're a liar, Nia! I told you to delete it!" Cam says.

Blake's knife wavers back and forth between Cam and Nia, as if she's unsure who to listen to. That's when I remember Blake left the bathroom early last spring. She never heard Nia and Cam talking afterward. I'm the only other person here that knows what Cam said about Jordyn that day.

Dark and heavy understanding settles over me as I lie on

the ground, tied to my chair with no hope of escape. It's clear to me that Blake has no intention of letting us out of here alive. We're going to die. The only question is how soon and how much it's going to hurt.

If this is the end, I don't want to stay silent anymore. I'm done with letting my friends push me around and bully me into keeping quiet. I'm over doing anything and everything they tell me to. I'm sick of saying yes. Of always hiding who I am. Of lying.

If this is it, I'm going out knowing that I told the truth.

"Cam's the liar," I say, lifting my chin and meeting Blake's eyes. "I heard them in the bathroom. She said Jordyn deserved it. She said the video would bring her down a peg."

"Shut up, Riley…" Cam's voice trails off. She's losing a ridiculous amount of blood. I'm surprised she's still conscious.

"Well, this just got interesting," Blake says, the corners of her lips turning upward. "Look who grew a spine."

"She's lying. They're all lying," Cam mutters.

"Are they?" Blake draws a deep breath and examines Cam thoughtfully before turning back to me. "I bet she never told you she's in love with Seb," she says, almost looking sorry for me. "She's been obsessed with him since middle school. Thought she was gonna lose her mind when he started dating Val. Good thing that ended. Some nasty little cheating rumor, I heard. Right, Cammy?" She chuckles. "She wasn't too happy about you either, Riley. Fed you some bullshit that he was a player. Deleted his texts from your phone."

My mouth goes dry. "No… She wouldn't…"

"Sorry, sweetie," Blake says. "Cammy doesn't let anyone stand in the way of what she wants. The question is—did Jordyn have something Cammy wanted?" Blake pushes the knife against Cam's neck until Cam shrieks and cries out. "I'll count to five and if you don't tell me the truth this time, I'm going to cut out your lying tongue first very, very slowly *before* I kill you."

Blake leans closer to pry Cam's lips open. Cam tries to resist, but she's far too weak from losing so much blood to put up much of a fight. Blake gets her hand inside Cam's mouth, holding it open and reaching for her tongue. She begins to count down.

"I... I..." Cam sputters. Blake releases her tongue. "It was me. I did it."

Cam hangs her head in despair.

"Cam, no..." I whisper. "Why?"

"You didn't know her!" she cries. "Jordyn was insufferable. Always trying to outdo us. Always having to be number one. She was after my valedictorian spot, even when she knew how hard I'd worked for it," she says. "She was after Seb, too. She wanted to prove to her parents she wasn't gay. She didn't even like him—not like I did. I couldn't let her keep stealing!" Cam's leg starts to spasm. More of her blood splatters onto the ground. "I didn't want her to die. I only wanted her parents to take her out of Bishop Prep; I just wanted her gone."

Tears well up in my eyes as I stare at Cam. She always pretended to be so proper and pure, to be a good person, but it's all one big act. She was going to let Blake torture me to death—her best friend—and Nia, too. Even Val—*her own sister*—died for her lies.

I shudder on the ground, feeling waves of emotion I've never felt before, never even knew existed. Shock. Anger. Hate.

Blake was right. None of these girls were ever my friends.

All year, I've been lying about myself. About who I really am. I've been pretending to be something I'm not, so caught up in wanting to be popular and liked by these people who couldn't have cared less about me. All of it—for what?

For this?

"You were going to let her kill me," I say to Cam. "How could you?"

She begins to cough, the spasm lasting a full minute. There is very little life left in her anymore. She knows it, too. Now that she's confessed, she's as good as dead.

"Sorry," she says. "It wasn't personal."

Blake places the blade at Cam's throat, her eyes dark with hate.

"Just one last thing, Cammy dear," she says. "I'd like to believe you when you say you didn't want Jordyn to die, but she told me she'd kill herself if that video ever got out." Blake pauses, the knife shaking in her hand. "I bet she told you that, too, huh?"

"She didn't even try." Cam sniffles. "She never even worked for it. It wasn't fair."

"Good girl." Blake nods. "At least you can be honest before you die."

"Go to hell."

"You first," Blake says and then slices the blade across Cam's neck in one smooth motion.

CHAPTER 21

I'm paralyzed on the floor.

I can't move. Can't speak. I can barely even breathe.

All I can do is stare at Cam's dead body while my heart speeds in my chest with unexplainable terror. I know this is the end. Blake has all her answers. There's nothing left to wait for. I'm only eighteen years old, I haven't even lived yet, and I am going to die.

Cam's blood drips down the blade's edge and onto the front of Blake's silky pajama top. Blake doesn't even bother to wipe it away. She just drops the butcher knife at her feet, and walks back to the weapons in the corner for something else to use. She pauses for a moment and then reaches for a machete.

My blood runs cold as I stare at the gigantic blade. I can't take my eyes off of it. It's the size of my entire arm, from elbow to wrist. So sharp, it looks like it could chop a person in half with very little effort.

Blake picks it up with one hand and returns to Nia and me in our chairs. She grins at us and takes a few practice swings with the machete, slicing it through the air with a sickening crisp swishing sound. Nia starts to wheeze and blubber next to me, begging for her life. She still doesn't get it. Nothing we say is going to save us. Blake has made up her mind.

"I've always wanted to see if these things work in real life like they do in the movies," she says. "Any last words?"

I let out a resigned sigh, sick of all the cat and mouse

games. "If you're going to kill us, stop screwing around and get it over with already."

A flicker of admiration flashes across Blake's face.

"Brave words."

With nothing left to do and no hope for escape, I close my eyes and pray my death is at least quick. I hear a whoosh of air as Blake raises the machete and then—

"What the hell is going on?"

I glance up to see Jonathan plowing inside the basement. He's soaking wet and muddy, eyes bulging from his head as he takes in the sight of all our dead friends. Shock siphons all the blood from his face.

"Jon, thank God!" I yell to him as our eyes meet. I've never been so happy to see anyone before in my entire life. "Help us!"

"I don't understand," he sputters in a daze. "What is this?"

"It's Blake—she's the killer! She murdered them all!" Nia struggles against her bindings.

"And I'd do it again," Blake says, her machete still trained on Nia and me. "They deserved to die for what they did. You all do!"

"What are you talking about? What did they do?" Jonathan asks as Blake raises the blade again above Nia's head with a murderous look on her face. "Holy shit, Blake!" He gasps and reaches for something behind his back. "STOP!"

But Blake is not stopping.

Her hand makes a smooth arc high above Nia's head and swings downward. Nia's screams reverberate around the room, bouncing off the walls and the ceiling. Just as the blade is about to reach her, gunshots ring out across the basement.

Blake freezes in place, bewildered, and almost drops her machete. Intense astonishment touches her face as she searches the room for the source. A small black handgun has somehow appeared in Jonathan's right hand. The barrel is still smoking as it points upward toward two tiny bullet holes now in the ceiling.

"Jesus, Jonny!" she says. "Where the hell did you get that?"

"I took it from the cop." Jonathan's hands shake as he attempts to bring the gun back to level. "I thought I might need it. Turns out I was right."

He steadies the gun's sights, training them on the center of Blake's chest. Her eyes narrow at the barrel as she begins to retreat from her position. Relief floods my body as she takes a few little steps further away from me.

With Blake distracted and focused on Jonathan, I seize a new opportunity to get myself free. Though my wrist still hurts something terrible, it turns out the fall had some advantages. For starters, though my hands are still tied together behind my back, I'm able to get them loose from behind the cracked and broken backside of my chair. I'm also now on the ground, which allows me to crawl toward the butcher knife Blake discarded on the floor without anyone noticing. I pivot my body around until my hands are facing the same direction as the knife and then slowly, ever so slowly, I reach for it.

Shit!

I groan inaudibly. My arms aren't long enough.

If I could just get a little closer…

"You don't understand, Jonny. They killed your sister," Blake says.

"Jordyn killed herself." Jonathan's lower lip trembles. "She was depressed."

"No. They're the ones responsible," Blake insists, pointing her machete in my direction.

I freeze in place. Quiet as a mouse, I hold my breath and hope she doesn't notice I've moved or how close I now am to the knife she dropped earlier.

"Don't listen to her. She's crazy!" Nia says, shaking her head. "Please, Jon. You have to untie us!"

Jonathan takes a step toward us.

"No! Stop!" Blake commands, her voice full of authority as she tightens her grip on the machete. "I need you to trust me. I'm telling you the truth."

Jonathan's eyes ping-pong back and forth between Blake, Nia, and me. He opens his mouth like he wants to say something before abruptly shutting it again.

The seconds tick by as I wait for him to make the right decision and save us, but when he doesn't do this right away, my skin begins to prickle with dread. A terrifying new thought occurs to me: What if Jonathan is like Blake? What if he also wants revenge for Jordyn's death?

Days ago, I never would've thought anyone I knew could be capable of murder, but now? Now, I realize I don't know what anyone is truly capable of. I'd thought Cam, Nia, and Blake were my closest friends, but I was so wrong about all of them. I was wrong about so many things. If they could do what I'd seen them do today, why not Jonathan too?

"What are you waiting for?" Nia screeches at Jonathan. "Get me out of here!"

"*Quiet!*" A muscle twitches in his jaw as he turns back to Blake, his gaze fixating on her. "Who hurt Jordyn? What did they do to my sister?"

"They found out she was gay. They were blackmailing her," she says. "It was Val, Cam, and Nia. They had a video of Jordyn kissing a girl." She looks down at the ground, her eyes darkening with pain. "Kissing *me...*"

"You and Jordyn?" he whispers. "I didn't know..."

"They knew how scared she was of your parents, so they used it to bully her," Blake continues, her voice rising again with anger. "They threatened her. Made her do things. And then, even after she promised to go along with everything they asked, Cam still sent the video to your parents. That's why Jordyn killed herself."

Jonathan stands there, blank-faced and horrified.

"I knew something was going on, like a fight or whatever,

but this? I don't believe it…" he says. "They were her best friends. Girls can be mean, I know that, but—"

"Oh, wake up! This was more than just mean girl shit!" Blake yells at him. "They knew exactly what they were doing, and they didn't give a shit. They killed the only person I'll ever love." Her face is a glowering mask of rage. "They killed your sister!"

I watch with growing fear as Jonathan seems to contemplate Blake's words far longer than it seems necessary. I tell myself that reason and good sense will outweigh any anger he might still have about the death of his sister, but then, ever so slowly, he shifts positions. The gun barrel moves from Blake's chest to Nia's.

"Hey—what are you doing?" Nia stutters, her head flinching back in shock.

"Did you do it? Did you blackmail my sister?" he asks, his voice quivering.

My blood turns cold. All hope I had of Jonathan rescuing us from Blake vanishes. I have no idea how this is going to go down, but it doesn't look so good for Nia and me anymore.

With a renewed burst of energy, knowing this might be my best and last chance, I stretch out as far as I can to grab the knife again. Somehow, my fingers almost reach the tip of the handle this time. Just a little bit further…

I grunt, giving it everything I've got, and… *There!*
I've got it! I've got the knife!

"I only made the video," Nia says. "I didn't know what Cam was going to do. I swear!"

While all eyes are locked on Nia, I go to work on my ropes with the knife. I start with my hands first and pray no one sees what I'm doing.

"All this time, I thought it was something I missed. I thought I was responsible somehow." Jonathan shuffles toward Nia, his eyes clouding over, like he's in a dream. "I lost my sister. My dad. My mother. I have nothing. I have no one…"

The rope silently falls away from my wrists.

I did it! I'm free!

My heart pounds as I glance up anxiously to see if anyone else has noticed what I've done, but they're all still laser-focused on Nia. I go to work on freeing my feet next, keeping my eyes trained on Blake the entire time. If she sees what I'm doing, it's all over.

"Please don't do this," Nia pleads as Jonathan inches closer to her. He places his pointer finger on the trigger and cocks the gun. "We can figure this out together. Let me help you."

"Help me?" Jonathan laughs, the sound sad and hollow. "What could you possibly do to put my life together after the mess it's become?"

"I can help you by being your friend," Nia says.

His hand wavers and the gun drops to his side. For just a moment, I allow myself to hope that this horrible night is about to end with the rest of us walking out of here alive. But then Jonathan raises the gun again, pointing the barrel straight at Nia. His finger trembles on the trigger.

"Oh yeah? Like you were a friend to my sister?" He sneers. "With friends like that, who needs enemies?" he asks and then he fires the gun.

Nia lets out a sharp cry of pain as the bullet penetrates her body and ricochets off the back wall, landing on the other side of the room. The shot goes straight clear through her left arm. Blood spurts from a hole in her bicep and drips down, drenching the floor. Her eyes widen with shock, and she starts to gag.

Still, it could've been so much worse for her. I saw Jonathan's face when he pulled that trigger. He was aiming for her head. The only reason Nia is still alive is because Blake lunged at Jonathan at the last minute, diverting the shot.

"No—not that way! That's too easy," Blake cries out as she

struggles with Jonathan on the ground, battling for control of the gun. "She needs to feel pain like Jordyn did!"

I know I don't have much time left. While the two of them are busy fighting with each other, I grit my teeth and work fast to free my legs. My muscles scream in pain as I stretch down as far as possible and saw at the rope at my feet. Under the sharp edge of the knife, the cord starts to give way. An instant later, it snaps free, just as Jonathan manages to wrestle the gun away from Blake.

Realizing what I've done, Blake comes for me then, the machete swinging at her side. My heart thumps in my chest, and my adrenaline surges. I get into a fighting stance and raise the kitchen knife to defend myself. It's not much of a weapon in comparison, but it's all I've got.

But before Blake can strike, Jonathan pile-drives her like a row of dummies at football practice. She goes crashing to the floor, screaming out as her head cracks against the ground with an ear-splitting screeching sound. The machete clatters to the ground, and Jonathan gets on top of her. He puts her arms behind her back, pinning her down and holding her in place.

"Get off me! We have to kill them!" Blake thrashes and bucks underneath him. "For Jordyn!"

"Not her—not Riley!" Jonathan grunts back. "She didn't do anything!"

"But they all have to pay!"

A second later, Jonathan lets out an agonizing groan and slumps to the ground. To my horror, the machete now juts out of his back. A sliver of blood falls from his mouth as he croaks out my name, reaching for me. Then he goes still.

"Jonny? *Oh shit...*" Blake bends down, feeling for a pulse. Her eyes water as she pulls the machete from his body. The blade shakes in her hand, and his blood gets all over her face and pajama top. "I'm so sorry. I didn't mean to do that," she whispers to his dead body. "You were supposed to be safe in the garage with the others."

For the first time, she seems genuinely distraught at someone's death. She sniffles, nose running, as she steps away from him. Holding the machete above her head again, she turns back. A look of pure hatred is etched across her face as she glares at Nia. "This is all your fault!" she cries.

With Blake distracted again, I inch toward the basement door. Blake doesn't even seem to notice me anymore. She may want to kill me too, but it appears Nia is number one on her hit list right now. If Nia and the need for revenge can distract Blake long enough to bide me a few minutes, maybe I can escape.

"Ri Ri, please!" Nia screams to me. "Don't let her hurt me!"

The desperation in her voice almost makes me pause for a moment. I'm not a bad person. I don't want anyone to die, but what can I do to stop it?

My eyes dart around the room, my brain working at warp speed, analyzing any possibilities. The axe and some other serious-looking weapons are still in the basement corner, but that's pretty far away from where I stand. All I've got nearby is the knife in my hand, which is no match for a machete—much less Grant's gun that Blake now holds as well.

I'm not fast, athletic, or strong like Blake is. It's doubtful I could even get to Nia in time. Blake's way too close to her already. It's far more likely I'd just piss Blake off even more by trying to interfere, and it would cost me my own life instead. This may be my only shot to get out alive.

But more important than the logistics of it all and whether I could do anything helpful if I tried, is whether I should even try at all. If things were reversed, would Nia risk her life for me?

NO. FUCKING. WAY.

"Sorry, Nia," I say. "Survival of the fittest. You remember, right, *babe?*"

Nia's screams follow me all the way up the staircase as I race away as fast as I can. I'm pretty sure I should feel some-thing—guilt, shame, sorrow. Yet the truth is, I don't feel much of anything at all. I just feel numb.

Once I get to the foyer, I realize, with a shock, how many hours must have passed since we were drugged. Sunlight now streams through the uncovered portion of the patio doors in the living room. There are no more signs of lightning or thunder or hurricane-level winds. Even the rain has stopped. The storm has finally passed.

My first thought after I grab the keys from the side table is to get into the twin's SUV and drive away to safety. I'm seconds away from escaping Blake, this house, this whole horrible night, and leaving it all behind me. But then, instead of racing out the front door like anyone with a half a brain would, I do the absolute stupidest thing possible. I run for the garage.

Leaving Nia behind was one thing. She was a selfish, self-absorbed, narcissistic bitch who was all too eager to sacrifice anyone else if it helped further her own needs. Sebastian and Grant aren't like that. They're innocent, good people. I can't leave them here. Who knows what Blake will do to them once she finishes with Nia and gets out of the basement?

I squint into the darkened garage, my vision aided some-what by the sunlight now trickling in from the gaping hole caused by the fallen tree. Sebastian and Grant lie unconscious on the floor, surrounded by puddles of water and twigs and leaves. The cables from Grant's car and extra towels are sprawled between their bodies. They must have passed out right in the middle of trying to patch up the garage door. Unsure how bad off they are, I crouch down to examine them. Grant's fingers twitch at his sides, his eyes moving back and forth rapidly beneath lids.

Okay, good. That's good.

Those little movements mean he isn't dead.

Next to him, Sebastian coughs weakly. One green eye and then the other roll up to gaze at me. Relief explodes through my body at the realization he's alive, too.

"You were right," he whispers. "Something bad is going on. I think someone tried to poison us." He presses a fist to his lips, gagging as he clutches his stomach and writhes in pain.

He's far too weak to get up on his own, so I dig my hands underneath his armpits, attempting to hoist him upward. It doesn't work. He's too heavy and big, and I can't get a proper grip on him. Each time I try, he falls, crashing back to the ground.

"You need to get out of here. Now!" he orders.

"No way. I'm not leaving you."

"Please, March. I can't feel my legs." His eyes plead with mine. "You have to go before they come back. I don't know what they'll do next…"

I know I should listen to him, that every second I sit here is just bringing my own death closer, but so many people have died already because of Blake. I can't let Sebastian die, too.

"Seb, no…"

He swallows hard. "Please, before you go, I just want you to know how much I—"

"Oh my God, Seb. Just shut up," I say. "I'm not letting you die here."

A burst of adrenaline like I've never felt before erupts through my body. I let out a roar—a scream that is both primal and terrifying even to my own ears—and then grab Sebastian underneath his arms again one more time. Using strength I didn't know I even had, I'm somehow able to get him onto his feet.

"I'll get his legs," Grant says, suddenly at my side. "We can carry him out of here."

I nod and yank Sebastian's arms around my neck. My eyes

widen as I take in the huge knot and all the blood caked along the back of his head. He must've taken a hard fall.

Together, the two of us get Sebastian up on his feet and out of the garage. We make it to the front of the house and throw open the door, just as the pounding of footsteps comes up from the basement staircase. Blake must have finished whatever she was doing to Nia and is coming for us. We don't have much time.

My pulse explodes in my chest as Grant and I break into a run, pulling Sebastian toward the SUV. Grant throws open the back door, sliding Sebastian inside, and we jump into the front seats. I turn the engine on and hit reverse, slamming my foot on the gas pedal.

We're almost to the little white picket fence when Blake bursts out the front door. Her long blonde hair catches the wind and lifts around her, making her look like some kind of deadly avenging angel. She runs toward us, axe in one hand, Grant's gun in the other.

For just an instant, I wonder what happened to Nia. Is she still alive in that basement or is she now dead, too? I'm guessing the latter. If so, I hope it was quick, though I don't think so judging by how long we had to get out of the house.

Thankfully, I have little time to ponder all the gruesome implications. We reach the road, and I whip the car around to face oncoming traffic. My foot presses the pedal all the way down as we speed away toward the hospital and help. Without another thought, I leave Blake and the summer rental in my rear-view window, right where they belong.

EPILOGUE

Two Months Later—Labor Day Weekend

Black is definitely Sebastian's color.

The dark polo shirt he wears to dinner sets off his tan and makes the deep emerald green of his eyes pop even more than usual. All the attention in the dining room is focused on our table. The women of Bishop Lake Country Club can't stop staring. Not that I can blame them. He's gorgeous. Who wouldn't be looking?

Then again, it could also be the fact that we're now famous.

Even though it's been two months, the murders at Palm Key Island are still the only thing anyone around town can talk about. The story went nationwide, even making international headlines. Just last week, *Time Magazine* ran its front-page feature "The Palm Key Three" about us—the only survivors from the ghastly murder spree of the most gruesome serial killer in recent history, who also happened to be a beautiful young woman.

People are obsessed with our case. Before Blake Sampson, the rare "female serial killer" category was mostly comprised of quiet murderers like nurses who injected their patients with lethal doses of drugs or wives poisoning unfaithful husbands. They didn't hack apart multiple people with axes and machetes like a villain in a bad slasher movie.

Entire podcasts have been dedicated to Blake. She's

currently the most Googled person on the internet. There was even that controversial *Maxim* article naming her one of the "Hot 100 LGBTQ+ Women of the Year." Everyone wants to know what caused a rich, pretty, popular girl to kill her friends. Some say she was inspired by horror movies, even though Blake herself never cared for them. Others heard about us playing with the Ouija board and say Blake was possessed by the devil. With Blake still missing and very few answers, Sebastian, Grant, and I have all become famous by association.

Everyone wants the inside scoop, but I won't give interviews. It doesn't feel right with so many people dead. Even if some of them weren't the friends I thought they were—even if, as it turns out, they weren't even particularly good or nice people—they didn't deserve to die. Not to mention Roxy and Jonathan were completely innocent. They were just in the wrong place at the wrong time. I wouldn't even be alive today if it wasn't for Jonathan helping to save me.

"Are you packed for Monday?" Sebastian asks, as the waiter arrives with our drinks and takes down Sebastian's club member number.

I take a sip of my iced tea and grin. "I still can't believe I'm going to Columbia—and you'll be so close at Princeton."

"Just an hour train ride," he says, his eyes catching and holding mine. Even after all these weeks of being with him, I still get butterflies when he looks at me like this. "I can be there anytime you want."

I'm still amazed I'll be going to my dream school in just a few days. When the news broke about our story, the truth about me and my family's money scandals also came out. Instead of being upset about it like I always thought I would, I was relieved to be done with all the lying. After all, secrets are what caused everything to go down the way they did.

Well... secrets and bullying and having one completely unhinged psychopath in our midst.

Besides, I know now that being popular is just smoke and

mirrors. It's not what counts. No one should have to hide who they are from their friends. Real friends shouldn't bully you or make you feel bad about yourself; they should love and accept you just as you are. Blake may be a seriously deranged individual, but she was right about that.

Something else good also happened when the truth about me got out. Someone started a GoFundMe campaign to help me pay for college since I was the only female survivor of the murders—the 'Final Girl', as Jonathan called it. Not only do I now have enough money to cover all four years of tuition, I no longer have to worry about food or boarding, either. I don't know for sure who started the account, but I have a sneaking suspicion.

"So... I just paid for my first semester," I say, grabbing a roll and some butter from the breadbasket. I smirk and take a bite. "You sure you don't know who started that fundraiser page?"

He laughs, his adorable dimples showing. "I plead the Fifth," he says even though we both know he's the one responsible. "You sure you still want to go all the way to New York? You wouldn't rather spend your time down south with someone else? A certain cop in Palm Key Island, maybe?"

I hide a little smile. "Grant and I are just friends."

I can't believe it. Not only is Sebastian Ramos into me, he's jealous.

"Sure you are," he says. "Because I drive six hours all the time just to see my 'friends'."

"I told you. He's here for training."

Sebastian's overreaction is cute, even more so because Grant is far too honorable to try something with someone my age. He may be handsome and funny and ridiculously nice, but he's made it clear it's platonic, and that's okay with me. I enjoy having him in my life—as a friend. I could tell Sebastian all of this and reassure him, but it's way more fun to let him sweat.

The surrounding chatter in the country club grows louder. Patrons whisper and point, heads angling at their tables to get a better view as Grant strolls through the entrance just then. He's especially handsome tonight dressed in crisp khaki pants and a white button-down shirt, but it's not his good looks alone that's got people riled up. To see all the *Palm Key Three* in one place—that's a big deal.

Grant gives me a chaste kiss on the cheek and tosses a nod in Sebastian's direction before he takes a seat next to me. Despite his teasing seconds ago, Sebastian's welcoming smile is wide and genuine. The three of us, for better or worse, are forever bonded together by shared tragedy.

"Any news on Blake?" I ask Grant after we've made the requisite small talk. I've got serious things on my mind now that he's arrived.

"Afraid not," he says. "Not even with the entire force patrolling and the FBI involved."

Finding Blake and putting her behind bars has become a personal mission for the local authorities. Blake Sampson has single-handedly turned their posh, upscale vacation town into a side-show circus where newscasters and horror fans alike have been flocking to for weeks now.

The police have searched the swamps. The beaches. Neighboring counties. The FBI even sent scouts to Northern Florida and the Panhandle after rumors arose that someone matching her description was spotted in Jacksonville. But so far, all the leads have turned up nothing.

"I don't understand," Sebastian says with a deep frown that goes all the way to his eyes. "People don't just up and vanish like ghosts. No one has any information?"

"Oh, we get dozens of calls into the station every day, but every time we check, it never pans out," Grant says. "Wherever Blake is, she's hiding herself good."

A little shiver runs through me. I'm not surprised Blake hasn't been found. She's as smart as she is crazy and has plenty of money and the resources to stay hidden for a long time. For all we know, she's already in Mexico or Canada.

I know I shouldn't ask the next question. The answer will only haunt me, and yet it lingers on my lips, begging to be spoken.

"Do you think she'll ever come back here?"

"Not a chance," Grant says quickly. We've talked about this before on so many late-night calls. He knows exactly what I'm afraid of. "You're safe, Riley. Don't even think like that."

"But how can you be sure?" I prod. "I thought once a serial killer starts, they don't stop unless they're killed or caught."

"That's not always true," he says. "Jack the Ripper stopped on his own—he was never caught. Same for the Zodiac Killer. No one knows why, but sometimes they just fade away."

I try to swallow down the lump forming in my throat, but it won't go away.

Logically, I know Blake shouldn't still wish me harm. She even said she didn't believe I had any actual involvement in Jordyn's death; yet that hadn't stopped her from trying to kill me that weekend.

Thoughts of Blake continue to terrify me. I saw something dark in her that night. Just look at what she did to Roxy, and she claimed to like her. As for the people she didn't like…

Poor Nia was found in pieces. Her head was decapitated, arms and legs separated from her body. Her precious cell phone was on, videotaping the entire thing. It was so brutal, so gory, people speculated Blake must have had help. They didn't believe a teenage girl could inflict wounds like that all by herself. This led to a popular fan theory that Ed Rawlins was still alive and had teamed up with Blake to kill everyone.

But I know better.

Blake didn't need Rawlins to do what she did. The capacity women have for destruction is infinite. The harm we can inflict on others—and even ourselves—is boundless. We don't need a man for any of that.

"You're gonna be okay. I promise," Grant says, reaching out to give my hand a reassuring squeeze under the table. "Blake Sampson is gone, and she's not coming back."

Though Grant is the picture of confidence, I notice that Sebastian can't bring himself to make eye contact with me. Grant doesn't know Blake like we do. Sebastian would never want to worry me or say it out loud, but I get the sense he's not so sure Blake has moved on, either. Wherever she is, I'm pretty sure Blake isn't just sitting around, doing nothing. She's patiently biding her time, like she did this past year.

Plotting.

Planning.

Waiting for that perfect moment.

Whether she's thinking of me or Sebastian or even Grant and how we all got away, or if there are other injustices she believes need to be righted, I have no idea. There's only one thing I'm certain of. Blake Sampson is not the kind of girl to just fade away.

But then again, neither am I.

Not anymore.

CONNECT MORE WITH
REKTOK

I hope you loved *Summer Rental*, and if so, I would be very grateful if you could write a review. I'd love to hear what you think, and reviews online make such a big difference in helping new readers discover one of my books for the very first time.

If you'd like to keep up to date with me and be the first to know about any new releases, bookish news, and giveaways, please sign up at the link below. I'll never share your email address, and you can unsubscribe at any time.

Sign up here >>> www.RektokRoss.com

Please know I also adore hearing from readers. You can contact me anytime at my email at RektokRoss@gmail.com or through any of my social media channels (@RektokRoss, everywhere). You can also find and follow me on Amazon and BookBub. And if you like readalongs and talking all things bookish, you can join my Facebook group *The Book Nook by Rektok Ross* or check out my website at *www.RektokRoss.com.*

Thanks so much for all your support, and I hope to hear from you soon!

Rektok Ross

AUTHOR'S NOTE TO THE READER

Dear Reader,

First and foremost, I want to thank you for reading *Summer Rental*. I know there is no shortage of books for you to choose from and that your time is valuable. Please know how grateful I am that you picked up mine and chose to spend some of your precious time with me and my characters.

My goal as a storyteller is always to entertain first, but it's also important to me to explore dynamics and themes I feel passionately about. In my first thriller, *Ski Weekend,* I examined harmful stereotypes and judgments; in *Summer Rental,* I wanted to bring to light another topic that is very personal to me—bullying and toxic female friendships. I'll never forget my own hurtful experiences as a teen dealing with bullying and being excluded & ostracized (often by "friends"). This behavior doesn't end after school, either; I don't know if we ever grow out of it or if any women escape unscathed. This truly hit home for me when I watched, helplessly, as my own step-daughters became victims to it.

I don't confess to know why or how we fall into this "mean girl" behavior; what I do know is that it is a terrible, unnecessarily cruel cycle that is unlikely to end unless we, as women, start an open dialogue and try to do better for ourselves and future generations. We don't all have to be friends, but we can respect one another and treat each other decently. We can choose kindness. This is the heart of *Summer Rental*, and I hope this novel encourages deep conversation and, hopefully, change.

Now for the plot. It has always been my dream to introduce "The Slasher" to others, especially those readers that think they don't like "horror." I believe these stories are universal and can—and should—be enjoyed by all. I will always have an undying love for the great teen slasher films of the ’90s like *I Know What You Did Last Summer, Urban Legend, Halloween H20, New Nightmare* and, of course, *Scream* as well as novels from some of my favorites: Christopher Pike, R.L. Stine, Lois Duncan, L. J. Smith, Dean Koontz, and Stephen King. This is my homage to them and all those that came before.

Finally, for those of you who continue to bully and be cruel to others without thinking of the harm or consequence —BEWARE! There’s a new villain in town, and she doesn’t take lightly to mean girls. Remember, being nice isn’t just the right thing to do. It just might save your life! 😉

All my best,

Rektok Ross

WHAT TO DO IF YOU ARE A VICTIM OF BULLYING

First, know that you are not alone. Almost everyone in this world has been bullied in some way, shape, or form. Bullies can take the form of anyone, from trusted family & friends, to employers or coworkers, to classmates, to complete strangers on the internet. While it can be hurtful, scary, sad, and confusing—please know how strong you are, that you can survive this, and that things will get better! Below are some tips and resources on how to cope with bullying (and toxic relationships) gathered from resources like StopBullying.gov and Mental Health America. Additionally, as a trial attorney for over a decade, I am also including some steps to take if the bullying becomes dangerous or even criminal:

- Stay calm and don't let hurtful words get you down. Remember, bullies are usually in pain, and their bullying is never a reflection of you but a symptom of their own struggles with themselves.
- Talk to a trusted friend, family member, mentor, or therapist. Don't keep this to yourself or be embarrassed to tell others what's happening. Always reach out for help and advice!
- Spend time with family and friends that make you happy and strongly consider taking up a new hobby or skill to focus on something positive instead of the negative.
- If the bullying occurs online, take screen shots to keep as evidence in case you wish to take action. Be careful what, if anything, you write back. (The internet is forever and your words are permanent.) Then get off social media until the bullying subsides.

- If you feel your rights have been violated or you are in danger, talk to your employer or schools who may be legally obligated to help and protect you. Also consider talking to an attorney and/or the police and authorities. There are a variety of federal, state, and cyberbullying internet laws in place to help you.
- If you are feeling very sad, ALWAYS find help. If you do not know who to talk to and feel like you might hurt yourself or others, please call the National Suicide Prevention Lifeline: 800-273-8255.

Don't miss **SKI WEEKEND,**
the bestselling, award-winning
thriller from Rektok Ross!
Available now!

EXCERPT FROM SKI WEEKEND

CHAPTER 1
December 20 • 8:45 p.m. • 6,005 feet
Northern California, 10 miles south of the Mount Sierra Pass

We're almost to the foothills when the trouble begins. Flashes of red and blue light up the stormy night sky as police cars hurry along the side of the snowy mountain highway. My heart does this flip-floppy, somersaulty thing in my chest as I watch them line up, blocking the path ahead. I just know this is something bad.

The surrounding cars slow, but my brother is too busy messing around with the stupid car radio again to notice. He's got the volume turned up so high it takes all five of us yelling over his throbbing techno music to get his attention. Finally, he looks up and then slams on the brakes so hard the SUV's tires buck and squeal beneath us. We skid clear across the left lane, heading straight for the massive semi-trailer truck in front of us.

I let out a scream, my overactive imagination going straight to that place where I like to envision worst-case scenarios. This time it's our car plummeting straight off Highway 90 and exploding into a fiery ball of teenager parts and ski gear.

Somehow tire tread miraculously connects with concrete, stopping us mere inches from the truck's bumper. For a moment, we just stare at each other in shock. My best friend, Lily, does this deep-breathing meditation exercise she learned in ACT boot camp, pinching her nose and blowing out air slowly, while Champion jumps up from the floor, attempting to scramble all ninety pounds of animal muscle and fur onto my lap. I wince as sharp claws dig into my jeans and his wet nose burrows against my chest, hiding there. Gavin's dog is on the verge of a full-scale panic attack, and he's not the only one.

"*Cāo, Stuey!*" Lily yells next to me, breaking the silence.

I roughly translate this into the f-bomb. Lily curses in Mandarin when she's upset, a habit she picked up hanging out with her dad in the kitchen of their family-owned Chinese restaurant. Some words I know by heart now.

"My bad." Stuart turns around in the driver's seat, giving his girlfriend an apologetic half smile. "Sorry, Lils. I didn't know anyone was braking."

"Jesus, Stu! You need to pay attention!" I say, finding my own voice. *"We could've died!"*

He groans loudly. "Alright, now you're just being dramatic, Sam. We're fine, aren't we?" Eyes the same shade as mine twinkle back with laughter. Sometimes I'm convinced our bluish-green seafoam-colored eyes and pale skin that never tans are the only things my little brother and I have in common.

"Barely," I mutter, my pulse still racing from our near miss. I pull out a few peanut butter treats from my pocket and coax the trembling dog back to the floor.

"Just be more careful, okay, babe?" Lily is already grinning at Stuart, letting him off the hook. They've only been dating a few months and are still in that yucky honeymoon phase.

"And *this* is why they don't let sophomores on Ski Weekend," Britney says in the middle row in front of me, making the sign of the cross like she's thanking God we're still alive. "Who invited you on this trip anyway, Stu Poo?"

"Watch it, Miller," I warn. Stuart got his horrible nickname after an unfortunate accident freshman year. It was after his back surgery and the doctors overprescribed his pain meds and … well … it wasn't pretty.

Most people don't have the nerve to call him that in front

of me, but not Britney Miller—Seaside High's queen of everything. Most popular. Head cheerleader. She's even president of our school's prayer group, which is ironic because Britney and her friends are the biggest assholes in school.

"Oh, relax. He knows what I mean." She grins at me, tossing her golden blond hair over one shoulder. "Everyone knows Ski Weekend is seniors only."

Stuart throws the gear into park as car horns blare around us.

"What's going on? Why isn't anyone moving?" Lily asks, adjusting her eyeglasses and tucking a strand of long black hair behind one ear. She cranes her neck above the middle row's headrest, but we're too far back in the SUV to see much.

Gavin's brand-new GMC truck is an extended-cab affair with two seats up front followed by two full row benches and a cargo area in back that we filled to the brim with our luggage, ski gear, my dad's cooler, and a twenty-four-pack of bottled waters for the weekend. It would be considered spacious with plenty of room for six people under normal circumstances, but not when you're crammed in between a dog the size of a small pony, Lily, and every school supply she owns.

When we chose our seats earlier, Lily climbed into the last row of Gavin's SUV thinking it would be the quietest spot for reading. Naturally, I took the seat beside her. That left Gavin's football buddy Hunter in the front passenger seat playing navigator to Stuart's terrible driving and Britney and Gavin in the middle row so they could flirt with each other.

"It's probably chain control," Britney says, applying another coat of pink sparkly lip gloss. I cringe as she pushes her lips together with a loud smacking sound. I still don't understand why Gavin offered her a ride with us.

Oh, wait. Yes, I do. Britney Miller may be terrible, but she's also gorgeous.

"Chain control?" Stuart asks. "What's that?"

Britney snickers. "It's when they stop the dumbasses with crappy little cars that can't make it up the mountain."

For the millionth time today, I find myself wishing I was home snuggled in bed with a good book and my favorite TV show, Pit Bulls and Parolees, on repeat instead of stuck in this SUV. I only agreed to come along on this stupid trip to make sure Gavin doesn't convince my brother to do something crazy. The last time those two were alone without supervision, Stuart came home with his arm broken in three places.

Stuart is only a sophomore and technically shouldn't be coming along this weekend—that's one of the reasons we're staying at Gavin's family cabin instead of the ski lodge with the other seniors. The other reason is that Gavin doesn't go to our school anymore. His parents made him transfer last year to some snobby boarding school in Boston.

"Just tell me when we're there," Lily says, cracking open her AP psychology textbook and turning on her book light. As she rustles through the pages, Hunter flips around in the front passenger seat to gawk at her.

"You're studyin'?" he asks in a thick Texas drawl, scratching at his goatee and looking shocked.

I hide a smile. Supposedly, Hunter Jackson's parents are super wealthy cattle ranchers with farms all over the South, but I've always thought his accent—and that southern good ole boy routine—was purely for show. Hunter grew up in sunny California like the rest of us.

"Obviously," Lily says, not bothering to glance up.

"But why?" he asks.

"Because some of us want to graduate," she says, snickering at her own joke before sliding on her noise-canceling headphones. Hunter and half the senior football players are on academic probation after they got caught cheating on last week's math final.

"Ugh! We're going to be so late." Britney switches from lip

gloss to mascara, fluffing at her lashes using short, angry strokes.

"I bet it's that blizzard they mentioned on the radio," Stuart says.

"That's not supposed to hit until Monday," I correct him, rather glum about the fact. I've been getting weather alerts on my phone all week, hoping for an excuse to call the trip off. A nasty winter storm is supposed to roll across the Pacific Northwest next week, but we'll be home long before that happens.

"Good," Stuart says. "'Cause this weekend is gonna be epic."

"I'm getting laid for sure." Hunter flashes the grin of someone who is super attractive and knows it. With his rich, blemish-free dark skin and gorgeous brown eyes, he looks like a young Will Smith—maybe better—and has no problem getting girls at school, even with his rodeo cowboy schtick.

"You're so gross, Hunt!" Britney wrinkles her nose prettily. "Our bodies are a gift from God. We're supposed to save sex for someone special."

He winks at her. "They're all special, trust me."

I turn to my brother, ignoring them. "Just take it easy on the slopes, Stu. Remember what Mom said."

"Yeah, yeah." He waves a dismissive hand at me, annoyance creeping into his voice.

Using the sleeve of my sweatshirt, I wipe away the condensation forming on the car window beside me to inspect what's going on outside. It was barely raining when we left home hours ago, but now thick snow coats the sides of the glass and piles up alongside the highway. I blink, dumbfounded, as a burly, bearded man in camo exits his eighteen-wheeler truck and walks along the shoulder, heading for the police barricade. *Holy crap.* Probably both.

Soon others follow his lead. They look like little ants, scurrying beneath the snow-covered mountains that rise and tower above us like some predatory, prehistoric monster. A shudder skitters down my spine. The Sierra Nevada mountains are so much bigger than I thought they'd be.

"See anything interesting?" Gavin asks me, his voice low.

I turn, and my gaze locks with those cool blue eyes framed by impossibly long black lashes. It's been so long, I almost forgot how good-looking Gavin is. Model-high cheekbones. Thick, full lips. Even the inch-long scar above his eyebrow only makes him more attractive. It really is a shame he's such a jerk.

Besides a brief "hello" at my house earlier, this is his first real attempt at conversation with me since he left for boarding school last year. He never even bothered returning any of my texts or e-mails. It sucked at first, but I'm over it now.

At least that's what I tell myself…

The Breakfast Club meets *Lord of the Flies* in this gripping tale of survival, impossible choices, and the harrowing balance between life and death that #1 *New York Times* best-selling author Lauren Kate praises as "a pacey thriller with moments of great tenderness—and spine-chilling horror." Anyone who loves *The Hunger Games* and *One of Us is Lying* won't be able to put this book down!

GET SKI WEEKEND NOW!

ACKNOWLEDGEMENTS

Wow! I can't believe my second thriller is out in the world! Thank you first and foremost to all my readers. From the bottom of my heart, thanks for every bit of kindness and support. I am so appreciative of every single one of you— every kind word, social media post, book review, DM, email. I can't thank you enough!

As always, I owe a great debt to my publishing team: Amy Tipton, my amazing long-time editor and dear friend; the incredible Stephanie Elliot for her strong editorial hand and friendship; and Crystal Blanton and Tandy Boese for editing help. Thank you to my wonderful publicist Paul Christensen. I appreciate all your hard work (especially fielding my frantic calls from Sundance, LOL). Thank you also Doris Brandford for all your assistance. Thanks to my cover designers Dane Low & team and my interior designer Leila Pullen.

Thanks to all my friends in the writing community who have provided me with expertise and support. I know I've mentioned many of you before so new thanks goes out to: Dominique Richardson, Kendare Blake, Sara B. Larson, Krysti Meyer, J. Elle, Jessica Goodman, Jennifer Bardsley, Kristin Cast, Naz Katub, Julie Cantrell, Diana Orgain, Kristine Carlson, Brian Cuban, and Meaghan B. Murphy. Thank you to my "Fab 5": Meg Nocero, Suzanne Simonetti, Leslie Rasmussen, and Diana Kupershmit.

Thank you to my industry friends helping me navigate the adaptation world as well. Thanks especially to my producing partners, Oren Koules and Miles Koules. I can't wait to see what we bring to the screen! Thank you Michael Marshall, Yvette Ostolaza, Heidi Dillon, Zack Andrews, Jason Avalos, Danny Jordan, Jonathan Lang, Tanya Vidal, and Rishi Bajaj for all your sage advice and support.

Thank you to all the incredible booksellers, librarians, educators, and media who have championed my books. It means the world to me. Special thanks to all who hosted my launch events: Books of Wonder, The King's English, Orinda Books, Diesel Books, the Library Foundation of Los Angeles's Young Literati, Interabang Books, Veritas Wine Room & the Anderson Family, Books and Books, Georgina A. Agnones & The University of Miami (go Canes!), Maity Interiano, Linden Tree Books, Blue Willow Bookshop, and Lauren Silva and Second Star to the Right Books. Thanks to Elizabeth Aspbury, Kell Austin, Susan Reckers, Estrellita Sibila, Robin Homonoff, Louie B. Free, Shelby Stivale, Perri Nemiroff & the *Collider* team, Kelly Hager, Ann Binney & Mattie Schaffer at the *L.A. Times*, Gordon Jack, Margaret B. Stohl & Melissa de la Cruz & everyone at Yallwest, the good folks at J. Frank Dobie High School library, Anushka Dakshit & the *Independent Florida Alligator* (go Gators!), Olivia Horton & *Live! in the Bay*, Megan Waldrep, Kalie Barnes-Young, Scarlet V. Rose, Andrea Pruden, Michael Boccardo, and Chance Forshee.

Thank you to all my social media friends, especially the book bloggers, bookstagrammers, booktokers, and "booknookers" in my Facebook group The Book Nook. Special shout-out to: Parisa Mirza-Khan, Aurora Dominguez, Kelly Lyco, Dee Jaye Jackson, Debby Stone, Meredith Mara, Macie Dierking, Sandra Brower, Lisa Alvey, Shaley Moreira, Samantha Andrews, Natasha Gordon, Kristy Woodson Harvey & Annissa Joy Armstrong at Friends and Fiction, the amazing community at Books of Horror, and Phoebe Siegel/A Mighty Blaze. Thanks also to Haadiya Wahab & Turn the Page Tours and Berit Lohn & Let's Talk Books and everyone who joined their tours.

Thanks to my street team and friends—you're the absolute best! I've mentioned many in prior books so new shout-outs go to: David, Sarah, Lavell, Conrad, Anne Claire & Judy, Tanya, Mila, Hope & Mike, Lindsey, Kiley, Bre, Mercy, Jill, Mariam,

Anne & Pedro, the Smiths, Bob, and E.J. Weppler & my friends at Weil Gotshal.

Finally, a huge thanks, as always, goes to my family for putting up with my "Authorzilla" ways. Mom, Dad, L, Lance, and Scarlett—thank you for always supporting me. The entire DeCesare and Howard clan (especially Hilary, Inge, and Tim —whose pep talks I dearly miss). Derek, Dani, and Ro: I sure hit the step kid lottery with you three. To my wonderful husband, Michael, none of this would ever be possible without you. And to the best reading and writing buddies—Falkor and Blair (and Crosbie, too.)

ABOUT THE AUTHOR

Author photo © Agency Moanalani Jeffrey

Liani Kotcher (writing as Rektok Ross) is a trial attorney turned award-winning and bestselling author, screenwriter, and producer. An avid reader since childhood, Liani writes exactly the kind of books she loves to escape into herself: exciting thrillers with strong female leads, swoonworthy love interests, and life-changing moments. She graduated from the University of Florida School of Journalism and obtained her juris doctorate at the University of Miami School of Law. Originally from South Florida, she currently splits her time between San Francisco, Los Angeles, and Las Vegas with her husband, step kids, and her dogs. She is the recipient of several awards, including the American Fiction Awards, IAN Book of the Year Awards, Readers' Favorite Book Awards, the Chanticleer Dante Rossetti Book Awards, and Women Writing the West. You can find her online just about anywhere at @RektokRoss, as well as on her website, www.Rektok Ross.com, where she blogs about books and writing. Sign up for her newsletter and stay up on all the latest Rektok Ross book news here: www.RektokRoss.com

Facebook: @TheRektokRoss
Instagram: @RektokRoss
TikTok: @RektokRoss
BookBub: @RektokRoss
Twitter: @RektokRoss